## "How are [...] marriage be[...]een us if we never touch?"

Carefully he moved the wrist he held so that it rested against her own body, near her hip. Then he released her, his fingers unclenching slowly and then closing in upon themselves as his hand retreated.

In a measured tone, his desire now well concealed, he replied, "I shall fulfill the king's wishes on the matter of the Scots. And I will see to your estates as if they were my own, so long as I remain here."

"But we are not to cohabit as man and wife, is that what you are saying?"

He nodded once, his hands gripping the chair so tightly, his knuckles turned white. "You wish me to be blunt? Very well, I shall be. You made a bad move wedding a man who wants no wife...!"

Dear Reader,

Spring is in full bloom and marriage is on the minds of many. That's why we're celebrating marriage in each of our four outstanding Historicals romances this month!

There is a most *unusual* arranged marriage in *My Lady's Choice,* a new medieval tale by the immensely talented Lyn Stone. This is the story of Sir Richard Strode, King Edward's best knight, although some of you might remember him as a toddler in *The Knight's Bride.* When Lady Sara of Fernstowe miraculously saves Richard's life, the king grants her a boon. She demands the fierce knight's hand in marriage.... You won't want to miss what happens *after* Richard wakes fully to find that he's now bound to a—beautiful?—stranger!

Award-winning author Cheryl Reavis brings us an emotional and fulfilling story about a second chance at love and marriage in *The Captive Heart,* when a British officer's wife is imprisoned by her own husband, but rescued by a Native American frontiersman. *Tanner Stakes His Claim,* book two of Carolyn Davidson's EDGEWOOD, TEXAS miniseries, features a marriage of convenience between a squeaky-clean Texas sheriff and the amnesiac—and pregnant—saloon singer he can't stop thinking about. Don't miss this wonderful story!

Rounding out the month is *The Bride of Spring,* book two of Catherine Archer's terrific SEASONS' BRIDES miniseries. Here, a noblewoman desperate to marry to protect her young brother orchestrates her own wedding, unaware that the man she has chosen will be her true love.

Enjoy! And come back again next month for four more choices of the best in historical romance.

Sincerely,

Tracy Farrell,
Senior Editor

# MY LADY'S CHOICE

## LYN STONE

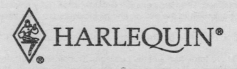

HARLEQUIN®

TORONTO • NEW YORK • LONDON
AMSTERDAM • PARIS • SYDNEY • HAMBURG
STOCKHOLM • ATHENS • TOKYO • MILAN • MADRID
PRAGUE • WARSAW • BUDAPEST • AUCKLAND

ISBN 0-373-29111-6

MY LADY'S CHOICE

Copyright © 2000 by Lynda Stone

Visit us at www.eHarlequin.com

Printed in U.S.A.

Please address questions and book requests to:
Harlequin Reader Service
U.S.: 3010 Walden Ave., P.O. Box 1325, Buffalo, NY 14269
Canadian: P.O. Box 609, Fort Erie, Ont. L2A 5X3

To my daughter,
Pamela Stone Clair,
with love.
Thank you for all your encouragement,
ideas, inspiration and, most of all,
for just being my Pam.

# Chapter One

*Northumberland, 1339*

"Our thanks for making his death more comfortable, Lady Sara," King Edward said softly, his blue eyes already misted with grief. "He looks to be at peace."

Sara of Fernstowe smiled as she rounded the sickbed with the basin containing the bloody rags and arrowhead.

"Your knight is not dead, sire," she assured him as she handed off the container to a maidservant and faced her king. "Nor will he die if I can bring him through the fever sure to take hold."

The handsome blond giant who ruled England abandoned his regal pose beside the bed and leaned over, his ear to the knight's lips, his large hand upon the uninjured shoulder. "'Tis true, he breathes! How is it that my physician declared this man beyond hope, and you have saved his life?"

Sara liked the king. When denied a thing—such as having his knight's life spared—however, she imagined Edward III could be as fierce as his grandfather, the famous Longshanks.

She preceded her conjecture with a small laugh. "Mayhap your healer feared your wrath if he did not succeed in his efforts, my liege. You should not blame him. As you must know, few men do survive such a wound."

She continued, unafraid to state the truth. "There is a chance I, too, shall fail, but I think not. He weathered the cutting out of the point with hardly a grunt of protest. Here is a strong fellow who bears a hurt well. I would say he has borne others in your service, judging by his scars."

The king straightened. "Ah, you do not know the half, my lady. Twice now Sir Richard has thrown himself betwixt me and disaster. The first time we were lads—I, but a fledgling king, and Richard, only a squire."

He continued, pride in his knight visible in the rapt expression he wore. It was as though he could see it all again, there in his mind. "Three assassins attacked me in our camp, intent upon my death. When Richard's overlord fell in the attempt to save me, this one took up the old earl's sword and slew the two remaining. Nearly died then from a sword cut to his thigh."

"Ah, a brave deed for a youth. So you took him into your own service then?"

"Fortunately, or I might lie here this very day and you would be tending me in his stead. Richard must have spied that archer poised to shoot and took the arrow meant for me. Then, wounded as he was, he chased the scoundrel down and cut him in half. What think you of that for strength and valor?"

Sara studied the figure lying on her bed. He nigh matched the mattress in length. Had he stood upright, she knew he would rival the king's great height. If his chest had not that wealth of muscle, the arrow that struck him might have proved fatal, indeed. Aye, he was strong as he was brave.

And handsome. She noted the dark chestnut hair with its faint gleam of red in the candles' glow. His skin looked smooth and lightly browned by sun. His sensuous lips, slightly opened, revealed white, even teeth and his nose appeared straight and unbroken.

If only she could see his eyes, perhaps she could judge the kind of man he was. Sara found she really wanted to know, and so she asked, "What manner of man is he to withstand such hurts? Fierce? Gruff?"

The king sighed loud and long. "Nay, not Richard. Unless provoked, he tends toward gentleness and good humor. He is honorable to a fault. Son to a good father. Father to a fine son. A husband fiercely loyal to his poor, dead wife. Friend to me and mine. A knight who scorns rewards for his valiant doings." Sara noticed tears had formed in the king's eyes.

"Faith, my liege, but that does sound much like a eulogy! Have hope he will survive, for I do!"

That brought a smile, as she had thought it would. He brushed a hand over his eyes and then regarded her with a curiously amused expression. "And you, my lady, do you scorn rewards for good deeds?"

"I? Not for an instant, sire! Do you offer one?" Sara said, more in jest than serious question.

The king tilted his head and considered her for a moment, his arms folded across his mighty chest. "One of the matters I intended to resolve whilst in the North was to see you wed. With your father gone, you know you must marry to hold Fernstowe. Two men have petitioned me for your hand. I would give you a choice of husbands. How does that suit?"

Sara held off answering. She took advantage of the informality of the setting and paced for a few moments, tapping her lips with one finger.

She knew that Aelwyn of Berthold wanted her lands. They bordered his own and he had made no secret of his wish to gain hers, as well. He had been after her since she was a child of twelve. Failing to obtain her father's approval while he lived, and her own since then, Aelwyn must have written to the king.

"Lord Aelwyn of Berthold and who else, sire?" she asked, wondering if it could be Lord Bankwell, a distant neighbor here in Northumberland who had once asked for her. Bankwell was old, enough so that he'd courted her mother before her parents had wed. Likely it was not him. Once he'd met her, he had appeared disinterested and content with her father's refusal of his suit.

"Lord Clivedon of Kent. Do you know him?"

"Nay, I do not." And she did not want to. "You say I have the choice of husband?" She smiled up at the king, watched him nod his assent, and then cast her gaze toward the man on the bed. Did she dare? Why not be bold, since she had nothing to lose?

"By your grace, my liege, I choose this one," she announced, pointing toward the knight in her care.

If she had expected to shock King Edward with her demand, she saw she had not. He settled an assessing look upon her, then glanced at Sir Richard, his eyes narrowing with a certain craftiness. Sara prayed he would say yes.

After several tense moments of consideration, he smiled winningly. "Save him, Lady Sara, and you may have him, will he nill he! My word upon it."

"Good as done! Now I pray you will enjoy my humble hospitality, sire, and that you shall stay for the wedding."

King Edward frowned at that. "I regret I cannot, for I must be in York three days hence for a meeting. Richard is hardly likely to recover by the morrow when I must depart."

"Then, by your leave, may we wed this night?" she asked hopefully.

"How can you do so? The man is insensate," he argued. "'Twould not be legally done if he cannot say his vows."

"Never worry, we could rouse him enough to say aye when asked. May we use your priest, sire? Mine is two months dead and I've not yet replaced him."

Though the king still looked doubtful about the wisdom of rushing the match, he shrugged and agreed. He must realize how this knight of his would rail against this. But, obviously, he had also decided the union would serve England's needs by placing a trusted protector this far north.

Only when he left the sickroom to go below and drink with his men, did Sara abandon her wide smile and expel a huge breath of relief.

She could not have devised a better plan. That a solution to her problems had fallen directly at her feet—well, upon her property, anyway—seemed an excellent omen.

For the past few months, Sara had feared another confrontation with that noxious hound, Lord Aelwyn. This marriage would eliminate that hazard for certain.

And there were the Scots, of course. Always the Scots. They had murdered her father, and since that foul deed, had been harrying Fernstowe, thieving her cattle and killing her people in the outlying settlements. Other estates along the border suffered also.

Sara strongly suspected that threat from the North had lent weight to the king's decision to grant her Sir Richard as husband. He surely had not done so to please her personally, no matter that he called it her reward. Someone needed to take matters in hand hereabout. King Edward needed the border secure as surely as did Sara and the other landholders.

That Lord Clivedon from Kent who had offered for her might have done well enough, but with lands to the south, he would not be present the year round. Sara had no desire to spend half her time in the south of England for the rest of her days.

God only knows what might happen to Fernstowe with

her prolonged absence. The king would definitely benefit by placing a favored and loyal knight in charge here as Lord of Fernstowe. She had merely brought it to his attention by way of requesting this favor.

She glanced toward the injured knight. Here lay her hope. If only she could keep him alive, he would serve her needs quite well. King Edward, well-known for his honesty and values, would never heap such praise on a man undeserving.

Sara knew Sir Richard would recover. All because of her. He would probably hate her then for arranging this marriage while he lay helpless and had no say in it. But his honor would bind him to her, regardless of his personal feelings on the matter.

He would be obliged to defend Fernstowe against all enemies, especially the fierce Scots who raided time and again. And wedding him would disabuse Lord Aelwyn of the notion that he could take by might what was not his by right.

The whole arrangement made good sense to her, and the king appeared to agree. Hopefully, Sir Richard would be compliant.

Sara brushed absently at the dreary brown gunna she wore over her chemise. She grimaced at the stains it bore, the knight's blood, the dirt around the hem where she had knelt over him when they had lowered his stretcher to the bailey. She should change before the ceremony. But what did it matter? The king had already seen her so. And in his fog of pain, Sir Richard would never notice or care.

Even did the sight of her register in his fevered brain, her manner of dress would not make much difference. Ugly and ungainly as she was, even the cleanest and richest of clothing could hardly conceal her frightful looks.

Once her new husband grew hale enough for the task, she might have to drug him to consummate their union.

The thought stung, but Sara accepted it. She was as she was, and he must deal with her appearance as she had always done.

At least he was tall enough to look her eye to eye, which was more than most men she met could ever do. The scar from brow to chin might put him off as it did many, but there was naught she could do about that.

Sara caressed his sleeping face with a longing gaze. Oh, to be as perfect as that man, to draw sighs and tender looks from a lover, to be desired as he surely was. To be loved by him as he must have loved that poor, dead wife the king had mentioned.

'Twas not a fate she could ever look forward to, Sara thought wryly. But for a tower of a woman with a damaged face and no hopes in that direction, she had done right well for herself. The king had seemed pleased to grant her this man. And she *had* earned him. If not for her care, Richard of Strode would now be dead.

She dismissed the childish wish for a love match and rummaged in her herb basket for the extract that might revive Sir Richard enough to agree to the vows.

"Do it and have done!" the king whispered angrily to the priest.

The holy man, called Father Clement, argued. "But Sir Richard has no wish to wed, sire. I beg you wait until he can tell you this himself. He holds constant to the memory of that perfect Lady Evaline, has done for some three long years now! Why, in his confession—"

"Do not dare repeat a word you hold in holy confidence! Not even to me!" King Edward appeared ready to do bodily harm to the cleric.

Sara held her breath.

"Never, sire! But Sir Richard—"

The king drew himself up to full height, which was considerable, rested his fists on his hips and glared. "—will wed this woman! Marry them now or get you from my sight! Permanently!"

The portly cleric jerked open his prayer book and quickly shuffled to the side of the bed. The king grasped Sara by one arm and dragged her to stand betwixt him and the priest.

So there they stood, three in a row, so close they were touching, as they peered down at the knight, who shifted beneath his sheets and groaned with pain.

Sara reached out and took one of the clenched fists in her hands, trying to soothe him. She barely heard the drone of the priest's voice until he stopped for a response.

The king leaned forward a little and commanded, "Sir Richard, say you aye or nay."

The knight grunted harshly as though trying to fight his way out of the fog, "I—"

"There. You have an *aye*, Father. Continue."

The priest chewed his upper lip, apparently decided not to anger the king by refusing, and rattled on.

He paused for Sara to answer his query and then snapped the book shut. "You are man and wife together." Another short spate of unintelligible Latin followed. "Amen."

She and the king responded in unison, "Amen."

Sara watched King Edward lay a parchment on top of Sir Richard's body, then place a quill pen in the knight's hand and guide it to mark. He handed the feather to her and pointed. She quickly signed where he indicated.

When he removed the paraphernalia and stepped away from the bed, Sara bent over and planted a brief kiss of peace on Richard's lips. "Rest now, husband," she whispered. "'Tis done, and all will be well."

King Edward went to the small table near the window and beckoned the two of his retinue whom he had selected to attend the ceremony. They joined him and the priest to sign as witnesses of the marriage.

When the royal party and the priest left to sup in her hall, Sara remained secluded with Richard in the master chamber. He was her husband now. Her place was by his side. Heaven grant he would see the truth of that once he regained his senses.

Richard's eyes protested when he tried to hold them open, but he finally succeeded long enough to determine that he had survived. For certain, this place was not heaven. Nor was it hell, for he felt frozen.

The soft bed beneath him reminded him of the one he had left in Gloucestershire. The hangings appeared rich, though likely older than he was. He sniffed the strong odor of camphor. His body ached right down to the marrow of his bones and his head seemed certain to split should he move it.

He sensed someone nearby. Someone humming. A woman.

"The king—?" he rasped, unable to complete the query.

A hand brushed over his brow, but he could not see the owner of it for she stood near the head of the bed, out of his line of sight. "Your king lives because of you, sir. He is well, and off to York these four days past."

"Aah, good," he said. "My throat…"

"Sore from ranting, no doubt. The fever held you longer even than I feared it would. You should drink all you can manage of this. I know 'tis not tasty, but you must."

Richard's eyes closed of their own accord as he accepted the cup she put to his lips. A foul brew she offered for one who sounded so sweet, he thought. Her low, honeyed voice drifted through and soothed his aching head like a balm.

Once she lowered the cup from his mouth, he asked,

"Where is John of Brabent, my squire?" By all rights, that young man should be performing this task for him.

"Gone to York with the king, sir. It seems his father would attend there and the lad wished to see him. I did promise him I would see to your care in his stead."

"Ah, well, then...since no one stayed to cart my body home, I suppose I shall be obliged to live."

"Aye, you will mend, though you did give us quite a fright for a time."

"I think I can move my arm," he mumbled, more to himself than to her. He raised it a little and grunted. "Though it hurts like hell."

She ran a soft damp cloth over his brow and jaw, cooling him. "It will be fine eventually. I wager you will be up and about in a fortnight. Back to your full strength in twice that time."

"Thanks be to God," he growled, "and to you, I should imagine."

He sensed she leaned near now and wished to see the face of this angel who had tended him. With all his remaining strength, he forced open his eyes again.

Richard had thought her wellborn by the words she had spoken. She had used the Norman French employed by nobles to converse one with another. Her appearance belied that station.

She wore a rough-spun gown of dark color and no head covering at all. Unbound midnight hair, a long curly mass of it, floated round her shoulders like a dark, shifting cloud.

Though he could not feature young John leaving him to be tended by a lower maidservant or some drab, this woman certainly dressed as one of those. Her manner and features seemed rather refined, however, not those of a peasant.

Her mouth was wide and mobile, would be an ever-changing gauge to the bent of her temper, he decided.

Kissable, if he were inclined to indulge himself. He was not, of course. One never dallied with the servants. Hadn't that particular lesson drummed itself home!

Her nose appeared a trifle haughty with its slight tilt, and that chin proclaimed outright stubbornness.

But the eyes were what arrested his breath. Amber with dark flecks of brown. Of a sudden, their beautiful lashes closed off his study of them.

She gave her head a small shake as though uncomfortable under his stare. The movement shifted her hair from the left side of her face, which she then presented in an almost deliberate way.

Richard sucked in a sharp breath. A thin, white scar reached from the tip of one beautifully shaped eyebrow, down the outside curve of her cheek to the edge of her challenging chin.

He stared at it, wildly furious at whoever had marred such perfection. A shallow knife wound, he determined from the evenness of the cut, not deep enough for stitching. Not accidentally done, either, for the depth would have varied over the prominent cheekbone. Some cruel hand had taken a blade and set out to mark her.

A brutal master? He would challenge the man to the death! Or was it a husband? He would kill the knave outright without a hearing!

Only when she turned straight on to face him again did he realize he must have hurt her himself with his foolish gaping.

In truth, the line of the scar did not look awful at all. But that someone had disfigured her apurpose horrified him. Richard swallowed hard and lowered his eyes to her graceful, expressive hands, which were twisting nervously about the drinking cup.

"Who are you?" he asked gently.

One corner of that malleable mouth kicked up as did

both dark eyebrows. "Well, sir, I might as well tell you now whilst you lie there unable to throttle me for it." After a deep, fortifying breath she announced quietly, "I am Sara of Fernstowe, your wife."

Richard closed his eyes again. He might as well shut them, he thought, since he was still asleep and possessed by feverish visions. Just like a disordered mind seeking comfort to conjure up a wife the total opposite of his first.

Evaline was, after all, his worst nightmare.

The memory of her petite, ethereal figure and angelic face flitted behind his eyelids and dissolved into the skeletal corpse she was when last he saw her.

Feelings ripped through him, far less welcome than more arrows; anguish at the untimely death of one so young, sorrow for his son who grieved despite hardly knowing his mother, and most shameful of all, his own relief. Try as he might, Richard could not banish that despised reaction and it near killed him.

He groaned and shuddered violently, welcoming the pain it caused him. Glad of that or any other thing that would distract him from his dark guilt about Evaline's demise.

"Good sir, hateful as it must seem to you, I swear I speak the truth," declared the velvety voice of the woman. "We are wed."

Richard decided to rejoin the object of this disturbing illusion and play it out, though his mind had begun dancing again like a leaf caught in a swirling current.

At least dwelling on this nonsense would remove Evaline from his thoughts before he slept again. Or was he sleeping still? Of course, he must be.

"Wed? The devil you say."

She smiled apologetically and glanced away from his sleepy regard. "Aye. The king approved and witnessed the event before he left."

Richard chuckled lazily. This made no sense, but often dreams were like that.

Then she ducked her head, appearing somewhat shy. "I promise you'll not regret it, sir. No more than you obviously do now. Aside from my ugliness, I have all good wifely attributes."

"Mmm-hmm," he muttered, "Attibutes." She'd given him something in that drink....

"Aye. My housekeeping skills are excellent, as you will soon see. I read, I write, and most consider me a healer of some talent. I healed you when the physician gave you up."

"And modest," he suggested ruefully.

She laughed at herself, a low-pitched and soothing sound. "Oh, 'tis my most laudable trait, that one!"

His cursed chest throbbed dully but incessantly, and Richard tired of this dream. He wanted only to sink back into the nothingness of deeper sleep and escape the discomfort.

"Leave me now," he grumbled, and closed his eyes.

"Of course, husband. But when you wake again, you must try to eat a little."

"A little what?" he asked with a dry half laugh, imagining some small animal squirming on a trencher. His mind floated pleasantly, only a corner of it noting the pulsing pain in his chest.

"I shall have gruel for you. And egg pudding with nutmeg, if you like."

"Nutmeg," he whispered. "A rich fantasy...indeed."

Her silken laughter trailed out of his hearing and he thought he heard the shutting of a door.

For an unknown space of time, he slept again, but awareness returned eventually and Richard woke anew. *She* was here again.

The woman he remembered sat nearby in a large padded chair, stitching something on a small hooped frame.

Through lowered lashes, Richard watched her poke the needle in and out, curse under her breath as the thread knotted, and then put it aside on the floor.

How terribly sad she looked, too morose for tears. She leaned forward, her elbows on her knees and her beautiful, long-fingered hands clasped beneath her chin.

"Please," she whispered, "Please do not let him hate me. I will do anything—"

"Come here," he ordered, curtly interrupting her prayer.

Perfectly lucid now, his dream did not seem a dream at all. He said a quick prayer himself that their former conversation *had* been a daft imagining. Still, he feared it was not so.

Her words just now did not bode well at all. There must be a reason she would be praying for him not to hate her.

She complied with his summons immediately, all but leaping from the chair to answer it. "Have you hunger now? Darcy is on her way with your food."

"A plague on the food! Did you or did you not speak to me earlier? What did you say then? Who in God's name are you, woman, and where am I?" he demanded, piercing her with his most threatening glare.

She raised her chin and squarely met his glare with the glowing amber of her own. "Aye, we did speak. I told you that I am Sara, Lady of Fernstowe. That is where you are, sir. Castle Fernstowe, near the northern border of England."

"Yes, yes, I recall your name now," he grumbled impatiently. "But I imagined you said another thing, that we—"

"Are wed, sir. Aye, we are that."

What was this nonsense? She stood near, but far enough away that he could not reach to shake the truth from her.

Richard forced a laugh. "I wed once and vowed never to do so again. If you think you can make me believe you are my wife, you must be mad."

"Nay, not mad. I needed a husband and here you were. The king agreed readily enough. He loaned his priest. He stood by you and assisted you in signing the—"

"He did no such thing! Whatever your game, it will not play, madam!" With all his shouting, Richard's voice quickly receded to a painful whisper. "It will not play."

"We are wed, I tell you. I have the documents if you would see them." She threw out her hands in a gesture of frustration and spun around, giving him her back.

Richard squeezed his eyes shut and pressed his head back against the pillow until his neck cramped.

"No!" he said through gritted teeth. "I sleep. I sleep and am cursed by a fevered nightmare. When I wake, 'twill be to feel the earth beneath me where I fell."

"Would it were so if you're fool enough to wish it!"

"Or my sins were greater than I thought and this is hell," he muttered, throwing his arm over his eyes. "I save a king and this is my thanks?" He scoffed. "Virago."

"Oh, you are most welcome, husband! Welcome to this bed and for my care, you ungrateful wretch!"

"For God's sweet sake, woman," he shouted hoarsely, "would you leave me alone and let me rest in peace!"

"Well, I should have done!" she cried. "But you live. And now you are mine, Richard Strode. For better or worse, you are mine. So make what you will of it!"

The door slammed and Richard knew she was gone.

"Short work of it is what I'll make, you sharp-tongued witch," he muttered. "For I will not be wed. Not to you, or any other."

# Chapter Two

Sara fled to the door of her old sleeping chamber, but before her hand touched the door handle, she changed her mind. No, she would not seclude herself in there like a child rebuked. Her behavior toward her husband had been childish enough.

Had she not expected Sir Richard's anger once he awakened? It was not as though he would thank the angels for the privilege of marrying her. If she'd thought that possible, she would have waited until he knew what he was doing.

The man had been tricked, by her and by his liege. Small wonder he cursed his fate and her, as well. But the marriage was done and he could not undo it, not without demanding annulment and questioning the honor of the King of England to his face. Though her husband's angry reaction to wedding her had bruised Sara's feelings, she vowed she would shed no tears over it.

She had passed twenty-one summers and never wept for any man, none save her poor father when the dreadful Scots slew him six months ago.

Simon, Baron of Fernstowe, had been a man to weep for. How she missed him. If only this knight of hers would come to care for her half as much as her beloved sire had done, she would cry tears of joy for it.

Very little hope of that, she thought, scoffing at herself. Even had this fine knight come courting, cap in hand and contract readied, it would have been her lands that he sought, not herself. Ungainly tall as she was and with her face scarred to the bargain, no handsome warrior like Sir Richard Strode would stoop to win her favor. Foolish even to indulge in any fantasy such as that.

She marched down to the kitchens to see to the making of candles and wiped the foolish wishes from her mind.

All the while she issued orders to the maids performing the noisome work, Sara bent her mind to a practical solution. She would win her husband's respect if nothing else.

And when he bedded her, she meant to make him glad of her attentions. He would find no whimpering virgin twixt the sheets when they sealed their bargain. Untried she might be, but Sara had never whimpered in her life.

She knew full well what to expect. Life in a castle did not lend itself to privacy and she had a curious mind. Though the act itself looked rather awkward, even frightening betimes, so was riding a horse when she thought about it. She had certainly mastered that feat quickly enough, and the rewards had been great. It got her where she wanted to go.

Marriage would be rewarding, she would see to that. She would have protection from the Scots and the husband of her choice. Richard Strode would share Fernstowe and all its profits. And pleasure in the marriage bed, every delight that she could give him.

Sara smoothed her hands over her middle in anticipation, paying little mind to the household task at hand. She watched her women add and stir the bayberry scent to the cauldron of melted wax.

The smell of it always stirred memories of Yuletide seasons, of gifts and celebration and the happy laughter of the children of Fernstowe. She needed little ones of her own, and now would have them.

The sons she would give her husband could be naught but sturdy and wise. She was that way herself and so was Sir Richard, if the king spoke true. Like always bore like. Her husband would be proud then, glad she was no dainty weakling with goose feathers for brains.

She would not dwell upon the daughters she might produce, who would likely top their suitors in height, just as she usually had done.

Her father had loved her despite her tallness and he never seemed to notice the scar after it had healed. Fathers tended to turn a blind eye to their daughters' faults. So she hoped that held true, in the event she birthed a few girls for Richard.

She would allow him some time to bemoan his lot and nurse hurt feelings toward her and his king. He had, after all, been wed against his will and without his knowledge. But very soon, Sara meant to turn his thoughts around for all and good.

Together, applying his strength and her wisdom, they would vanquish her dreaded Scots neighbors and make Fernstowe the strongest estate in the north of England. Together, they would produce children to make King Edward himself turn green with envy.

Sara knew she could make all of this happen if she persevered. Her father had always assured her that she could do anything she set out to do if she would keep her goals foremost in her thoughts and never doubt her abilities.

Her looks were not that important, she told herself with a practical sniff. What was that old saying? *All cats are gray in the dark.* Men said that, meaning they cared little about a woman's appearance in the bedchamber. Any female would please them there. She would do that right enough if she put her mind to it.

Sara moved forward to take over the positioning of the candle wicks, making certain they were exactly centered within the long slender iron cups that would receive the scented wax.

As in the creation of candles, every worthwhile endeavor required careful preparation of the ingredients, a series of steps accomplished one upon the other in precise order, so that the end results justified all the effort.

Her immediate task concerning this marriage was to convince her husband to put aside his pride at being duped. She must point out the advantages for him in becoming the new Lord of Fernstowe. Later, when he was recovered enough, she would encourage him to look past her appearance and take joy in his good fortune.

The next morning Richard rubbed his eyes and then rolled his head, stretching the stiff muscles of his neck. He had slept the sleep of the dead.

Where was the woman, he wondered? He refused to ask about her. "You were here before, I recall," Richard said to the man who had come in her stead.

"Oh, aye, milord. I been seeing to yer, ah, needs. Milady woulda done, but she still be a maid. I didn't think that fitting."

"I quite agree." A humbling thought, indeed, having that woman tend to washing him and such. It was bad enough to suffer anyone doing so, but he could barely sit, let alone stand by himself. "So, who are you?"

"Eustiss, milord. I be Lady Sara's smithy, the only soul about the place strong enough to lift ye."

Richard jerked his arm out of the man's grasp. "I can

do for myself now.'' He added belatedly, ''But I thank you.''

'''Tis well come ye are.''

''You sound like a... Were you born here?'' Richard asked.

The red-whiskered fellow laughed, a booming sound that matched his girth. ''Nay, I'm a Scot. Ye needn't bite yer tongue on it. Least, I *was* one. Broken man now, cast out. Lady Sara's old da found me near the border and took me in. All stove up from a beatin' and left fer dead, I was, nigh on six years past. Home's Fernstowe now, and allus will be, long as I'm allowed ta stay.''

He pointed to Richard's wound. ''Strange, that.''

''What is so strange? It's an arrow wound, nothing more.''

Eustiss pursed his lips, his eyes squinted. ''Scots I knew had little use for bows.''

''The one who did this will have even less use of his,'' Richard remarked with satisfaction.

He suspected this old fellow still held some ties with Scotland, if only those of homesickness. However, it wouldn't pay to raise any question of loyalties at the moment, not when he could scarcely make a fist.

A quick glance about the room told Richard his weapons were not available, either, even if he had been in shape to use them. He hated feeling disabled. How long would he be invalid? Had the woman said a fortnight? Two?

In spite of his former intention, he asked the man, ''Where is...your lady?''

Eustiss cackled. ''Out seein' ta matters at the village, I expect. She goes out most days round this time.''

''That cannot be safe, her wandering about in these times,'' Richard declared, leaning back against the padded bolster the man had arranged behind him.

He knew that Fernstowe Keep lay only a short distance

from the border, probably a favorite target for raiders from the north. Edward's main reason for the visit here had been to judge the extent of the troubles in the Middle March and decide what to do about protection for the estates in peril of attack.

Eustiss regarded him with a jaundiced eye. "Yer worrit that th' lads across the bog'll get her, eh?" He shook his shaggy head and sighed. "More danger's like ta come from th' east. One fine English laddie tried to grab 'er once. She knocked him clean off his horse. Heh-heh. Th' beastie drug him nigh on half a league afore he got his foot loose of the stirrup. Served him right."

Richard had jerked upright at the news and was now paying for it. He grabbed his chest, sure that his heart would pump right out the hole that arrow had made. "Damn!" he gasped.

"Heh-heh," the old man chortled. "Teach ye ta stay still, won't it?" Despite the jab of his words, the smithy's eyes looked sympathetic. "Ye got a ways ta go afore yer mended."

Gently as a mother would, he lowered Richard back against the bolster. "Best ye rest the night now. Milady will see ye in the morn."

"Wait!" Richard demanded, reaching out to grab hold of the man's sleeve. "Tell me about her. She says—that she is my wife. Is this true?"

Eustiss looked him straight in the eye, a thing no one below knight's status should dare. His words were every bit as direct. "Aye, if she says it, then 'tis so. And she's a fine lass, is my lady. Ye'll treat her kind. I'll be seein' ta that. I ain't lookin' ta die fer attackin' my betters, but do ye fergit her worth, I'll see ye straight ta hell afore me." Then he smiled, sweet as you please. "Beggin' yer pardon, milord, I've horses ta shoe."

Richard hid his smile until the door closed. The smithy

might be one to watch, but he had convinced Richard he was no Scots spy here to scout the place for future raids. Pledging lifelong fealty to the family who saved his life spoke well for the man's honor.

Richard's father had taught him that loyalty weighed more heavily in a man's favor than all other virtues combined. Richard lived by it, serving Edward III unto death as he had vowed to do at sixteen.

Richard shifted and winced. He had very nearly met that obligation earlier than hoped. And how had the king thanked him for that? Saddled him with a wife and property he had no use for.

How many times had Richard stated without equivocation that he intended to remain unwed forever? That he wished nothing more than to ride behind his king until he met the reaper or grew too old to sit a saddle? More times than he had fingers, that was for certain. Had the man ever listened?

Richard sighed and closed his eyes again, brushing a hand over his face. Yes, of course Edward had listened. He never missed a word spoken within his hearing by anyone. He heard every syllable, every nuance of meaning, then evaluated, drew his conclusions and acted on them according to his and England's needs. That meant Edward of Windsor had a reason for wedding one of his knights to this woman. A purpose greater than the need to keep one knight content.

There would be written orders. Of that, Richard had no doubt. He would follow them, of course. Had he not sworn? This sacrifice ill suited him, this taking of a wife when the thought was so hateful to him, but he would not protest to the king. Knowing Edward, it would accomplish nothing save to raise that Plantagenet temper. Any man with any sanity avoided that at all costs.

In fact, Edward had likely set this task with an eye to a

twofold result. Fernstowe, a favored keep of Edward's, would gain a watchdog, and the king would see whether he had the unquestioning obedience of the man set to the task. This, then, was a test in addition to a mission.

"Ah, damn you, Ned! How could you doubt me? *Why* would you?" Richard rasped, slamming a fist against the mattress.

That cursed female had put the idea in the king's head. And Edward did hold soft feelings for the married state. He loved his queen—and rightly so—but it gave him the idea all the souls in Christendom should march through life in pairs. *Ha!*

Lying here, useless and groaning, would gain him no answers. But at the moment, he knew he could not drag himself down to Fernstowe's hall, naked as the day he first drew breath, and demand an accounting from his new *wife*.

He was trapped.

Sara dressed with care the next morn. She drew her second finest gown and chemise from her clothing chest and shook out the creases. The pale saffron and emerald green suited her coloring. Father had always liked her in this one.

As she donned it, working her arms into the fitted sleeves, the smooth samite felt light and smooth floating against her bare skin. She executed a whirl as though dancing, and smiled as the billowing fabric settled around her body. 'Twas a childlike thing to do, but Sara had learned long ago to take small pleasures wherever she could find them.

The soft woolen overgown warmed her, calmed her as it smoothed over the folds of the silk. She fastened a belt of golden cord round her hips using a clasp set with pretty stones. The long tasseled ends of the cord swung nicely against her knees when she walked.

Will he like it? Sara wondered as she brushed out the length of her dark mane and caught it up in a twist. The pins carved of bone slid out of her grasp and she had to begin again. Once she had tamed her unruly hair, draping it on the sides to try to cover her scar, she placed a transparent veil of silk over the crown of her head and secured it with a thin circlet.

Hesitantly she picked up the polished silver mirror that had once belonged to her mother. For a moment she studied her reflection, trying to examine her features without noting the scar. "No use," she admitted, making a wry face at herself. She could see naught but the long, thin line from brow to chin, too far from her hairline to cover completely with a wave.

With a sharp huff of resignation, she put the mirror away. He'd already seen the scar anyway. Vanity would be her undoing. She must accept herself the way she was and see to it that her husband did the same. She'd not disguise her faults, not the scar, not her height by stooping or bending her knees, or her willfulness. That last, he'd probably like least of all. But he might as well adjust to the whole of her at once.

Sara went to her writing table and picked up her marriage documents, along with the missive King Edward had left for her husband. With a lift of her chin and a squaring of her shoulders, she went to present herself to the man she had chosen to share her life.

"Will he nill he," she repeated the king's words, and stretched her mouth into a confident smile of greeting.

He was sitting up in bed looping the ties of a loose sark when she entered. Either Eustiss or Darcy had returned his clothing to him, and he was almost fully dressed.

At first glance, Sara knew he did not recognize her. That accounted for the pleasant smile. It faltered at once. "Oh, it's you," he muttered, resuming his task of dressing.

"You should not be up and about yet, sir," she admonished, noting the sweat on his brow and the paleness of his face.

"I am well enough," he replied. "I was about to come and seek you out. There are matters we must discuss."

"No argument there. But I believe I have what you would have sought," she said. Stepping closer, she held out the folded parchments. "Our marriage lines and a letter from the king."

He snatched them from her hand, pushed himself back upon the bed and unfolded the one on top. She watched him scan the bold writing long enough to read the signatures and then toss it aside. The sealed packet took more time.

When he had finished reading that one, he sighed and lay back against the pillows, not resigned, but fuming.

Sara felt she must say something to break the ominous silence. "I regret you are not pleased."

His eyes cut to her and then through her, chilling her to the marrow. "Do you?"

She lowered her head submissively. Now was no time to assert herself with a pithy reply. He looked dangerous. Not surprising, but disappointing all the same. Reason might not work today.

For the present, however, she could remind him of all he had gained by this match. "The king offered me a choice of husbands, you see. This was my reward for saving your life. I asked myself why would any landless knight not welcome rich properties, more coin in his coffers, a strong woman to bear his children?"

He spoke through gritted teeth. "I am not landless, nor do I need your wealth. And I already *have* children."

"Oh, but that's wonderful, sir! Will you bring them here? I adore—"

"Spare me that tripe," he snapped. "I've seen how you

noble women adore! My progeny can do without that quite well, thank you!"

Sara moved to the bed and laid a hand over his. He snatched it away, scattering the papers across the coverlet. "Richard? I may call you so, may I not? I am sincere in this, believe me," she continued without awaiting an answer. "I love little ones, I do. Nothing would please me more than to have you send for them. I do recall the king saying you were father to a fine son. You have more than one child, then?"

Richard grunted, not deigning to look at her.

"How many and how old are they?" she asked, hoping to supplant his ire with fatherly pride. "Come, do tell me!"

"A son of seven years," he said, nearly spitting the words. Then he turned his gaze on her. "And a daughter of eight. A bastard. How will you adore *that* one, madam?"

Sara stood back, folding her hands in front of her and tilting her head to one side. Her husband thought to shock her, mayhap even to humiliate her by demanding she take in his natural child. Foolish man. A real smile crept across her face. "I shall gladly be mother to both if you will allow it."

His expression changed to one of patent disbelief. Then he changed the subject entirely. "The king wishes me to settle the Scots matter hereabouts as soon as I am well. That was his intent in allowing you this marriage to me. So much for your fine reward."

If he meant to disappoint her with that news, he had certainly failed. "I know. Your success in that alone would be reward enough. They did kill my father. 'Twas my reason for choosing you over the other suitors."

"You had others?" he demanded.

She smiled wryly. "Surprising as it is, I did."

"Why did they not merit your grand gesture?"

She shrugged, still holding on to her smile. "One was nigh as much trouble as the reivers and the other probably tied to his lands in Kent. I wrongly assumed you were landless since you travel in the king's retinue as a knight. I thought we would both benefit by this arrangement." She toyed with a tassel on the end of her belt, swinging it to and fro, then feathering the tufts with her fingertips.

He followed the motion of her hands for a moment and then jerked his attention elsewhere.

"That is all it shall be," he announced. "An arrangement. The king wants these lands and this keep made safe, so I shall make them so. But if you expect a loving husband to the bargain, you have made an unwise choice in me. When all is done, I shall remove myself to Gloucestershire and leave you to your precious Fernstowe."

She digested that, losing the smile but holding on to her dignity. "I know I am no prize to covet, sir. My mother warned me well not to expect more than I was due or I would suffer for it. I need nothing from you but your sword once you are mended." She rose to leave.

"Hold a moment. We are not done with this. Where is this mother of yours? Dead?"

"Nay, she took herself to a convent just after my father was slain."

"A right good place for a woman who belittles her own child," he said. "I do hope she acquires a smattering of kindness along with her vows."

Sara jumped to her dam's defense. "My mother was not unkind! She did not belittle me! She merely spoke the truth!"

He sat up straight and swung his legs off the side of the bed. "By disparaging your worth?"

Sara shook her head, uncertain what to say next.

"Do you seek sympathy from me with this tale? Or do

you expect me to gainsay her and shower you with compliments? Very well then. You are beautiful. Beyond compare." He tossed his head and scoffed. "As though you do not know it!"

Sara's mouth dropped open. What did he mean, spouting this nonsense? "You speak of my mother's unkindness and then you mock me?"

He narrowed his eyes and shook his finger at her then, as though she were a fractious child in need of chastising. "You mark me well, madam, I hold beauty in contempt. It means less than nothing, do you hear? *Nothing!*"

"You taunt me, sir," she said, more hurt than angry, but she was that, too. "I accept that you do not want me as wife, but it is a done thing! So let it be!" With that, she whirled around and quit the chamber.

Richard regretted the conversation. Though he believed his ire justifiable under the circumstances, he found no excuse for destruction of the woman's pride. She thought he objected to the marriage because of her face. He did not want her to believe that, but he could hardly give her his real reasons. He didn't even like to admit them to himself.

He covered his eyes with one hand and exhaled all the pent-up fury in his lungs. When he had done so, only despair remained, and that so invasive, he almost prevented himself drawing in another breath. Yet, he could not afford to die. Good Lord, he had too many people dependent upon him; aging parents, his young children, the folk on his father's estate and that of his son. Now, thanks to that king of his, he had acquired a wife and her assorted problems.

Though Richard never shirked responsibility, he did resent shouldering his older brother's load. Had the errant Alan assumed what was rightfully his as he should have done, Richard would never have had the task of managing an estate that he would never really feel was his own. And he would not have had to wed in order to add the necessary pasturage needed to make Strodesouth turn profitable.

Though if he had not married, Richard recalled, Christopher would not exist, and having his son proved one of the finest joys in his life. The other was Nan, of course. Sweet little Nan.

Since he must remain here and do as the king had ordered, Richard wondered who would see to things at home. He had planned to be there in time to arrange for the shipping of the wool. Now he would not.

Richard forced himself to his feet again. He had to recover his strength as rapidly as possible and lying abed was no way to do that. Each halting step wrung new agony from the wound in his chest. He knew from experience that the grunts he uttered now would lessen in frequency as he became accustomed to the pain. The discomfort would sharpen his wits and banish the lethargy that fostered his current feelings of frustration. He needed to move, get things done. God only knows there were enough of them.

"You will come unstitched and bleed yourself out!" came the dulcet sound he both craved and dreaded. She was back again.

He turned too quickly and nearly fell. "What do you here?"

"What else?" She shrugged, holding out both hands, palms up. "To make amends. You must excuse my temper."

"Do not tell me what I *must* do!"

She smiled and rolled her eyes. "Comes from issuing too many orders, I would think. There's been no one else to do so for some half a year now, since my father died."

In trying to quell the urge to fall down and faint, Richard

held his breath for a moment. He released it on a question. "Why?"

"The Scots who killed my father also wounded his steward. He died later of infection. My mother left for the convent immediately after the funeral. The old priest died of age just recently. Eustiss would help me, but no one pays mind to his words. He is a Scot himself, after all, and most resent his telling them what to do. So, everyone looks to me, and there you have it."

*Here he had it.* He nodded. "Sit," he demanded. She did so, appropriating a stool near the fire hole while he shuffled to the chair she usually claimed.

"First of all," he said, "we must address the attacks. I would call to arms all who are able to wield a weapon and assess their abilities. Training will take time, but I have no other recourse than to make defenders of those capable of it."

She nodded and smiled her approval.

"No lord can be everywhere at once and the Scots take advantage of that fact. They attack the most vulnerable, those who would offer the least opposition. We must provide that resistance."

"True," she agreed with another succinct nod. "When would you begin?"

"Immediately, of course," Richard answered, leaning on the armrests and steepling his fingers beneath his chin. "The sooner the better."

"Today?" she asked, unbelieving. "But you are not well enough! How do you expect to train a troop of men to fight when you can hardly stand without assistance?"

"I will do what must be done, my lady, and I, not you, shall decide what that might be!"

She leaped from the stool and paced, kicking her skirts out of her way with each step. "Fine," she grumbled. "Undo all I have done for you, then. Ride out if you will.

Challenge old Alan the True himself if you should happen upon—''

"Who?" Richard barked. "Whose name did you call just now?"

She stopped midstride and turned on him. "Alan the True, scourge of Bannockburn and friend to the old Bruce. Have you not heard of him? I assumed the king knew that he is the one we all dread."

Richard felt his heart turn to cold lead, weighting down his very soul. Edward's test of his loyalty was no longer an idle supposition, but a near certainty. "He may, though he has not mentioned him to me. Question is, my lady, what have *you* heard of this man? You are saying he is the one behind these raids?"

Her eyes took on a hatred so intense he marveled at it. When she spoke, her words contained pure venom. "That one boasted of his name to our men whom he left lying wounded in the wood. After he slew my father, he made certain all would learn of his deed."

Her voice grew quiet with determination. "If you do nothing else when you are sound and hearty, my good sir, I would you brought me this man's head. Do this, and I shall grant you anything that is within my power to give."

Richard clenched his jaw so hard he thought his teeth might crack. He dared not speak for fear of what he might say.

The woman could not know what she asked of him. Or perhaps she did. And he had small doubt that the king knew it also.

Richard wondered if Edward had brought him north for the sole purpose of pitting him against Alan. The wounding had not been planned, of that Richard was certain. However, it did seem fortuitous that the incident had left him in this particular place and with the responsibility of handling this border trouble. This, rather than the marriage itself, was to be his supreme ordeal.

Sara of Fernstowe wanted retribution for her father's death and the king wanted rid of the threat to the Middle March. They could have conspired to accomplish both goals, using him as the instrument. Or all of this could be coincidental.

Not likely. But no matter what the circumstance, Richard could not do what they wished. Leastwise, not the way they wanted it done. Not for his king's approval, not to satisfy his own resentment, and certainly not for this woman's revenge, would Richard slay his own brother.

# Chapter Three

Richard propped his elbow on the chair arm and rubbed his forehead with his thumb and forefinger. But he knew that nothing he did would make this particular ache subside.

His wife, he hoped, had not yet put together the fact that this Alan the True and Alan of Strode were the same man. Richard had heard his brother called both by the family.

Of course, it was possible—even probable—that Alan had ceased using the English name of Strode. It was a place-name, though it had evolved into a surname long before his time. Alan had not been born there, nor had he ever lived at Strode. He might call himself Alan of Byelough now that he was lord of that estate, or simply Alan the True, a name earned by reputation.

Alan had declared himself a Scot, both by birth and loyalty, having had a Scots mother and lived in the Highlands with her family for a score of years. Their English father loved him well, despite that. Even Richard could understand why Alan, more than twenty years his senior, had chosen as he had.

He barely remembered the man. They had not seen each other since Richard was less than three years old. He was not even certain whether what he had of his half brother constituted real memories. His parents had spoken so often of Alan during Richard's childhood, the recollections could easily be their own and not his at all. But Alan's letters were genuine, and frequent, considering the difficulty of getting them delivered.

Somewhere in those hills across the border nestled Byelough Keep, the home Alan had gained through marriage to the widow of his friend after the Battle of Bannockburn. Richard wondered if times had grown so hard there that his brother must now raid the English to support his family.

Should he tell this wife of his about the kinship? She stood there anticipating his promise that he would slay this dragon for her. He decided to wait and see what would happen. In any event, she could not expect him to do anything about it in his present condition.

"He has attacked other properties," she was saying now as she began pacing to and fro. Her action annoyed Richard, for he wished to do the same and could not. She continued, "Though my sire is the only noble he has slain, so far as I know."

Somehow, Richard could not equate the man who wrote such witty and loving missives to his English father with the brutal knight she described, one who would put to death Lord Simon of Fernstowe and then brag of it to all and sundry.

Stealing to survive or taking an enemy for ransom, Richard could comprehend. Senseless killing, he could not.

Though this brother of his had slain a number of Englishmen on the field, the man had been renowned, even among his enemies, for holding to a knight's code of mercy when given a choice.

Richard decided there was surely more to this tale of murder than he had heard thus far.

"So, you will find and destroy him?" his wife asked, interrupting his thoughts. "That should put an end the raiding. I would have done it myself did I possess the skill."

"Make no mistake, I shall find him," Richard answered, glancing up at her.

He did not expect this marriage of his to offer anything in the way of happiness. That would be a foolhardy hope, indeed. But if Sara did not already know, he had to wonder what this bloodthirsty wife of his would resort to once she discovered the man who boasted of killing her sire was her husband's brother.

Sara fought to control the feelings that rose in her breast each time she thought on her father's death. Lord Simon had been the best of men, undeserving of a horrid death at the hands of the marauding Scots. Had she been a man, they would all be dead now. She drew in a deep breath and let it out slowly, regaining her calm.

Her husband appeared preoccupied, but no longer unduly angry. Now might be as good an opportunity as any to attempt the establishment of a friendship. The task would be hers alone, for he would never initiate such a thing.

There was an excellent basis to build upon, however. They had a common enemy and like goals, even if his had been set for him by the king.

Though she wanted more from Sir Richard than he would give, all willing, Sara knew she would get nothing at all if she did not befriend him first.

She reached inside herself and drew out a smile she did not feel. Over the years she had learned that even a forced display of contentment did much to help dismiss agitation within herself.

"I would caution you again not to move too quickly in taking up your duties as lord, lest you overtire," she said.

"But I can see that you must feel better since you have dressed yourself. Would you take your meals in the hall with our folk come the morrow? We could speak more then of gathering the men and planning our strategy."

"Um," he answered, still lost in other thoughts, troubling ones by the look on his face.

"You might sit in the pleasuance a while and take the sun, if there is any to be had. What think you?"

"What?" he asked, finally abandoning his distraction, whatever it had been.

Sara laughed a little. "My, but you do turn a woman's head with all of this attention!"

He attended her than, surveying her head to toe and back again. Only when his gaze held hers once more did he speak. "You seek attention, do you? Of what sort?"

Sara sat down again and smoothed her gown flat over her knees. "Whatever you wish to give, Richard. I demand nothing of you."

He rested his head against the back of the chair and regarded her through narrowed eyes. His long fingers tapped rhythmically against the armrests. "Then let us clearly mark what I demand of you."

Sara bristled, but she thought she hid it well. Was this a test of some kind, or did he mean to order her life as though she were a servant? Many noble women lived as such, she knew. Her own mother would have been one of those had not her father been disposed to kindness.

"Make your list of dictates, then. Are they in such number as I would need to write them down?" she asked, idly twisting the end of her corded belt.

One corner of his mouth rose in a half grin. "You have a sharp tongue, Sara of Fernstowe. Rather cutting when you wish it to be. Unfortunately, that is too often. You might keep it behind your teeth, for a start."

"I might," she said, not committing to it.

He raked her clothing once more with a look of disdain. "And I should not like you garbed in rags again now that I see you possess better."

"As you wish," she agreed. "However, 'tis not thrift in any measure to ruin good clothing. I only dress so modestly when I am about those tasks as require hard work."

One eyebrow rose in question. "Tasks? Such as?"

She smiled sweetly. "Tending the wounded, for an instance."

He did have the grace to show chagrin at that, assuring her he did have a conscience. "Point well-taken. I have not yet thanked you properly for tending me. Be assured, you shall have a gift."

"The king gave me one," she replied with a lift of her chin. "You."

With a quick exhalation of what seemed disgust, he turned his gaze away, blinked hard, and then looked back again. "I repeat, I would you attire yourself appropriately whenever possible."

"Of course." Sara had not thought Sir Richard a man of vanity, but she supposed most men would not like to have their wives give cause for embarrassment should they have unexpected company. What would he have thought if he had seen her dressed for their wedding? A grin escaped her at the imagining.

"What amuses you so?" he demanded, his voice brusque with offense, as though she were laughing at him. Sara supposed she was in a way, but also at herself.

"Life becomes unbearable if you overlook the ridiculous," she advised him with a knowing look. "I would have leaped from the tower years ago had my good humor deserted me. Why so glum?"

Richard scoffed and shook his head. "You need ask?"

"Oh, come now. You say you have property, wealth. Now you have added mine to it. You have children, a great

king to serve. Your health improves by the day. A homely
wife is not the end of the world, you know," she admonished, still grinning. "I might not set any hearts athump
with passion, but I can converse as well as any man. What
say we strike a companionship here instead of suffering
over your dented pride?"

He watched her for a time as he sat there all unmoving.
"You are sadly misinformed as to your appeal, madam.
And a bit mad, I believe," he finally stated.

She laughed outright and let it die to a chuckle. "Aye,
with that dour disposition of yours, you would think me
daft. What has made you as you are, I wonder? Tell me,
have you never a cause for levity?"

Those dark eyebrows made a V over his eyes. "Now
and again, but not since I came here."

With a long sigh and a shake of her head, Sara rose
from the stool and approached him. "Then we must find
you one, for I would see you smile." She reached out and
dared to touch his brow, brushing away the lock of dark
auburn that had fallen out of place. "Can you not?"

With a move quick as lightning, he grabbed her wrist.
"Do not touch me."

While his grip did not hurt, it was quite firm. "Very
well," she whispered, not missing the unexpected flare of
hunger in his eyes. It gave her hope enough to persist.
"But how are we to manage a marriage between us if we
never touch?"

Carefully he moved the wrist he held so that it rested
against her own body, near her hip. Then he released her,
his fingers unclenching slowly and closing in upon themselves as his hand retreated.

In a measured tone, his desire now well concealed, he
replied, "I shall fulfill the king's wishes on the matter of
the Scots. And I will see to your estates as if they were
my own, so long as I remain here."

"But we are not to cohabit as man and wife, is that what you are saying?"

He nodded once, his hands gripping the chair so tightly his knuckles turned white. "You wish me to be blunt? Very well, I shall be. You made a bad move wedding a man who wants no wife."

"What of children?" she offered hopefully.

"Another excellent reason to abstain. I already have some."

She lowered her eyes. "And I do not."

"So be it. You'll have no cause to bemoan the state of your ruined body or your lost hours of idleness."

Sara placed her hand over his, the one that had gripped hers only moments ago. "That wife of yours must have wronged you foully, Richard. I would not."

"Leave me," he ordered, and jerked his hand away. "And do not broach this matter again, for I would not speak of it further."

Sara shrugged. "As you will. But, be that as it may, we could be friends, could we not?"

He did laugh then, bitterly. "Good God in heaven, you are the strangest woman I have ever met! And the most determined. Have you no pride at all? Here I have said that I will not bed you! I have denied you children! And still you want to be my *friend?*"

"I do," she admitted. "It makes more sense than not."

He blew out a huff of frustration, or perhaps disbelief. "You ask for a man's death in one breath and laugh in jest the next. You leap from slayings to beddings without pause to breathe. What am I to think of you?"

"So long as you *do* think of me," Sara declared. "Your anger will fade eventually. I would be a wife in truth, Richard. One who will love you if you let me. Your children, those you have and those we might make, would provide great joy for me, not cause for complaint. Think

me mad for that, if you will,'' she said reasonably, ''but
*do* think of me.''

She watched his face as he took in all that she had said.
When his expression offered her no hope of succeeding in
her mission today, she quietly turned and left him alone.

He would come around to her way of thinking, she decided. It would take time and great effort on her part, considering how wronged he felt, but she would not give it
up.

He spoke of her having no pride, and she supposed it
must seem so to him at the moment. If he only knew that
pride of hers. It would be the thing that kept her at him
until he admitted to himself that he needed her. He might
never love her as he had loved that first wife of his, but
Richard did need her. She had seen it in his eyes.

*Think of her?* That request certainly unleashed all the
dormant humor within him. He felt like laughing uproariously at the moment. At himself. Here he sat, hardly able
to rise from the damned chair unassisted, and yet his trai-
torous body was raging with lust.

Did she know what she had done to him with her uninvited touches? Could she see the turmoil she aroused in
him with her passion for justice, that she compounded it
with merry laughter, even though at his own expense? And
that offer of love, so sweetly made, her crowning touch.
*Witch.*

Richard allowed himself a groan of agony as he pushed
out of the chair. The pain in his chest ought to take his
mind from his other ache, but it did not. He made it to the
bed and lay down. The fullness of his body still mocked
him. Richard cradled his head on his hands and stared at
the canopy above.

Of course Sara knew her effect on him. Women learned
such things early on. They were female weapons, those

enticing tricks. Evaline surely had used hers well enough when it suited her. A man could excuse his gullibility when he was but eighteen or twenty. However, Richard had believed himself immune to those devices at the age of twenty-seven.

Again he studied the length of his body, willing himself back to a normal state. *Control the mind, control the action,* he thought to himself.

The long year of celibacy had no doubt prompted the reaction to this new wife of his. After that one unplanned coupling with a willing chambermaid last Michaelmas at a Dover inn, he had sworn off altogether. Unlike a noble-woman, a common wench might be pleasurable and pleasured, but Richard always regretted such occurrences afterward.

He worried that such women would feel that he took advantage of his station as a noble. He had done that once, prior to his first marriage. The resulting child, labeled a bastard, had suffered for his mistake, even if the mother had gained by it.

His own mother had been a commoner, a former servant of his father's first wife. Richard knew well that the indomitable Janet never let any man use her ill, noble or otherwise. She had wed his father to look after the man, fulfilling a deathbed promise to her lady, Alan's mother.

Though the marriage had proved long and successful, Richard had not failed to note the barbs his mother suffered because of her former status. He had decided never to wed a woman not of his station and cause her that kind of hurt.

Neither had he intended to wed another of his own kind. Without exception, they were either power mad and conniving like the ones he had met at court and in his travels with the king, or else they were like the angelic Evaline.

She had been perfect, of course. Chaste, above reproach,

serene and so lovely it hurt to look at her. Evaline had possessed a cool, passionless nature, which everyone knew was a most admirable trait in a noble wife. By all rights, he should have loved her beyond all reason. Instead of appreciating her natural reserve and dignity, Richard had thought her aloof and cold. He had been at fault, not Evaline. He only realized that after she had died.

Because neither class of woman suited him as wife, Richard had intended to remain unwed forever, but that intention lay in ashes now. And this wellborn wife seemed to be of the conniving ilk. She was in no way reserved, that was for certain.

Question was, what did Sara of Fernstowe want so badly that she would offer her body? Her enemy vanquished for one thing. She had admitted it, but she must know he had no choice about that with orders from the king. A son to inherit her lands? So she said, but he could not imagine a woman suffering so when she would never hold the profits in her own hands. What, then?

His body ached to give her what she asked, for whatever reason she asked it. Why not succumb to her wish and bed her?

Because she would loathe it, that was why. As all noble daughters were taught, Sara would believe it degrading, a necessary evil for begetting. And Richard knew he would hate equally a pretense that she liked it, or a cursory avowal that she did not. Better to do without.

Unfortunately, he did lust after Sara of Fernstowe. If she affected him this powerfully when he felt so weak from a wounding, how the devil would he manage to resist her when he grew strong again?

Friendship, indeed! A gust of laughter broke free and Richard was infinitely glad Sara was nowhere near to hear it, for he knew it might please her. That was the last thing he wanted to do.

* * *

The next morning, Sara halted just outside her husband's chamber. She smiled to herself as she leaned back against the wall and waited for him to immerse himself in the tub Eustiss had brought and filled for him.

Through the partially open door, she had caught a brief glimpse of him unclothed before she stepped back. It would take her a moment to still that wicked heart of hers. Richard's was a finely wrought figure, even viewed from the back.

In a few moments Eustiss came out and passed her with a look of silent amusement. Sara immediately marched in humming and plunked down a fresh change of clothing on his bed, garments of her father's that no one else at Fernstowe could wear.

"Here. Have these. Except for the hunting clothes, which were ruined, yours are much too fine for—"

"God's breath!" The abrupt slosh of water and his shout interrupted. "What do you here?"

Sara walked to the tub, hands on her hips, grinned down at him and leaned over. "Attending your bath, of course."

He had clasped his hands over his manhood, scowling as though she'd come to relieve him of it. "I can bathe myself. Now, leave me!"

Sara tossed her head back and stared at the ceiling as she spoke. "I've seen all you have there, husband. No need to play coy."

"*Coy?* Have you no thought to a man's privacy? Or is there such a thing in this place?"

"Not much of it, I do admit," Sara said, laughing. She scooped up the soap and cloth from the bathing stand by the tub. "Lean forward, I shall wash your back. Mind you keep that wound dry."

"Devil take the wound. Go away." But he sounded less adamant and he bent forward just as she'd instructed.

Sara dipped the rag, soaped it and began scrubbing circles on his back. She dug hard into the bunched muscles. He bit off a groan of pleasure, but not before she'd heard it. Sara smiled, enjoying the small success.

"What do you mean you've seen everything?" he asked carefully. "I thought Eustiss did the bathing before."

"Eustiss? Ha!" Sara exclaimed. "That one rarely bathes himself, much less anyone else. Swears it brings on agues and fevers."

Richard remained silent after that until she had finished cleansing the long, muscled length of his back. Then she tilted back his head and poured water over his hair, working the soap into the thick chestnut waves. How silky it felt trailing through her fingers!

Not until she had rinsed his hair and handed him a length of linen to wash his face did he speak. "Why do *you* do this?"

"To get you clean, of course," she said in a bright voice. "Will you not feel better now? I know I do!" Seeing her husband's body recovering its strength did her heart good. "You are more than pleasing to look at in any case, and 'tis wonderful to see you up and about."

She walked on her knees around to his side and again soaped the cloth, intending to bathe the uninjured portion.

He quickly reached out and snatched the wet linen from her hand. "I shall finish this."

"Fine. I'll just watch."

"You'll just leave!" he demanded.

She paid no heed to the order. Instead she boldly peeked over the edge of the tub and grinned. "Ah. You truly are up and about, my friend! We can remedy that soon enough."

"Sara!" He sounded perfectly appalled at her words. But it was the first time he had used her Christian name and it pleased her to hear it on his tongue. She was definitely making progress.

"Well, if you do not wish me to do it, I could call Darcy. She might be more to your liking. Not a bad sort, though not the canniest lass you'll ever meet."

"Good God, woman!" he blurted in a half-choked voice. "You'd thrust me into another's bed? What of my vows?"

Sara took that as a refusal. Richard not only sounded appalled. He clearly was. "Never mind, then. 'Twas just a thought," she said pleasantly as she pushed herself to her feet.

Richard's restraint gladdened her. She could hardly believe any man would turn down a chance to take his pleasure when he was so obviously in need of it.

Her own father had never been terribly discreet about tumbling a wench now and again. Sara knew that doing so had little or nothing to do with the regard a man held for his lady wife, for her father had truly loved her mother. But still, she felt immensely pleased that Richard would not bed the flighty Darcy.

Of course, he would not bed his wife, either, Sara thought. However, if he believed so strongly in those vows made all unknowing, Richard would soon remember duty. His pride would mend. So would his body. And if he would have none of the round-heeled wenches who worked about Fernstowe, then he must eventually come to her own bed.

Unable to resist, she watched him soaping his mighty arms furiously and refusing to look at her.

"Go below and have some food sent up," he ordered. "When I've dressed and eaten, I would tour the keep and grounds." Then he seared her with a glare and added, "Alone."

"As you will," she answered with a beatific smile and

took her time in leaving. Her reason for intruding on his bath had been satisfied.

Surely, once Richard realized that she offered her friendship sincerely and without reservation, he would not mind her presence so much. And after he grew comfortable with that, who knew what might happen?

Richard found Fernstowe a better keep than he had hoped for in terms of defense. The curtain wall stood in good repair. The place boasted no moat, but the ground sloped away at such a steep angle war machines could not be levied close enough to do harm. If any brigand took the place, he must use either stealth or prolonged siege to starve them out.

"The problem with the reivers lies in the outer reaches of my—our—property," Sara informed him as though he could not see that for himself.

She had accompanied him, despite his protests that she remain within. A light drizzle fell, though the weather remained warm as was usual for July. His luck, to get shackled to a woman without sense enough to get out of the rain.

Richard could not understand the woman's motives for anything she did. First she had all but thrown herself—and failing that, the dim-witted Darcy—at him while he sat randy as a goat in his bath. And in this past hour, she had nearly convinced him she possessed more knowledge of this property than a steward would.

Unseemly, quite forward, and more than a little mad, Richard thought. But Godamercy, she stirred his blood, this woman.

He avoided looking at her after noting what the rain-soaked gown revealed. The soft, wet wool molded her proud breasts like a drape of clinging silk. He cleared his throat since he couldn't clear his head.

"Have the Scots stolen many of your herds?" he asked.

"The cattle that were in their path they slew and left rotting. They were not after food."

Richard halted and stared at her in disbelief. "What purpose in that kind of waste?"

"What does that matter? They murdered my father! Who cares how many—"

"*I* care and so should you!" Richard said, throwing up his hand. The instinctive gesture cost him, but he stifled the groan. "These raids are crimes of hatred, not of need. Or even greed for that matter."

"Why should that surprise you? The Scots do hate us! They made that perfectly clear to me when they killed Father."

"We should bring in those folk who live betwixt here and the border and do it right soon," he suggested.

Sara pursed her lips and sauntered away from him. He knew she bit her tongue to prevent arguing.

"What? The plan's not to your liking?"

She turned, one hand resting firmly on her hip, the other worrying her chin. "Those we bring inside the gates, we must feed. Our stores would exhaust within a week. Aside from that, I doubt they will come willingly and leave their homes vacant." Her amber gaze pinned him with the question even before she asked it. "Why not simply kill the rogue who leads these marauders and be done with it?"

Richard took to strolling the perimeter of the inner ward again, so that she must abandon her challenging pose and follow. "I am but one man and none too hardy at present. Once I recover my strength, matters will be remedied."

How could he admit to Sara that the man she spoke of was his brother? How could he believe it true? If Alan were responsible for the killing of Lord Simon, what was his purpose in doing so? The cattle were there for the taking, the people outside the keep vulnerable to sacking whenever it pleased the Scots.

Yet his wife would have him believe that Alan had lured her father out and horrified everyone along the length of the English border by killing the noble and bragging of it.

It was as though whoever did that deed had deliberately set out to incur King Edward's wrath against him and all his kind. Were the Scots trying to instigate war?

That toady king of theirs had not the ballocks for it. All Balliol had ever wanted was the crown on his head, and Edward had been the one to let him wear it. No, Richard concluded, this was not a collective effort by the Scots.

The issue would not be solved right soon, so he decided not to dwell on it today. Instead, he headed back toward the hall where he could dry himself by the fire. If he went, so would Sara. The henwit looked like someone had thrown her fully clothed into the nearest river.

With a growl of impatience, he stopped her and pulled her cloak together where it gapped in front and framed those pert breasts of hers. The woman had no shame. Likely no one had been looking after her properly since she came of age.

"A wonder you don't catch your death," he muttered. "Go straight to your chamber and change, you hear?"

She beamed up at him, shining droplets caught upon her lashes and her lips. The breath caught in his throat as he watched her mouth come closer and closer still. Suddenly it met his own, brushed lightly and was gone on the instant.

Damn, he thought. He'd not had time to taste her.

Like a sprite tripping through a rainy forest, she gamboled up the stairs to the hall and disappeared inside.

For a long time, Richard stood there wondering how a woman of her height could move so gracefully, as though she trod upon air. And why the devil he should notice or care.

# Chapter Four

More than a fortnight had passed since his wounding. Richard thanked God the Scots had stayed on the other side of the border for the time being. Though he had healed well, he had enough trouble as it was right here at Fernstowe.

As a rule, he rarely dreamed. Now Sara not only invaded his privacy by day, but also by night. In the days following her interruption of his bath, he could not banish the woman from his mind no matter how hard he tried.

The clean, flowery scent of her clung to his pillows as though she had slept there. He would awake with his nose buried in their softness, seeking the phantom source of her essence.

His hands tingled for want of touching that fine, smooth skin of hers. More than anything, he ached to teach that impudent mouth of hers a lesson, to devour it with his own and make her groan with need as he felt like doing. She set his senses afire, waking and sleeping.

On this particular morning, he again woke in a sweat, highly aroused and with every detail of the fantasies fresh in his mind. Before he'd had time to recover, she swept into his chamber chattering. Though nothing she said was in any way provocative, the mere tone of her voice made him burn like a brush fire.

"'Tis dawn! Looks to be a lovely weather. I thought we might hold the court outdoors."

"Court?" he questioned, squinting at the window and its meager light of early morn. He had sudden visions of a daylong harangue between squabbling peasants.

She handed him the cup of ale she'd brought with her. "Not really court as such, though it is the time for it. There are no quarrels to settle that I know about, but the villagers and many of those farming the outer reaches will come today to swear fealty to you. I thought we would make a celebration of it. Nothing grand. Extra ale and sweet cakes, cheese, broken meats."

She whirled around and threw open the lid of his clothes chest. "What will you wear? I'll help you dress."

He thunked down the cup on the table and swung his legs over the side of the bed, careful to keep his body covered lest she see the state he was in. "Go along. I'll be down directly."

She glanced over her shoulder and for an instant vulnerability and uncertainty clouded her features. Then, quick as a blink, the expression was gone, replaced by a blinding smile. "Very well. I am glad you are feeling better."

Carefully she laid down the tunic she was holding and backed away from the chest.

She hesitated when she reached the door and turned back to him. "Richard, would you grant me a favor? Just for the duration of the swearing and the feasting afterward?"

He did not feel disposed to grant her anything after the restless nights she had caused him, but he was curious. "I owe you for tending me and you know it. I always pay my debts. What is it you wish?"

She banished the blush she wore and met his eyes directly. "Hide your displeasure with me for the day?"

Richard could clearly see what the request had cost her. She bit her lips together and stood as straight as a lance, but her knuckles gleamed white on the one hand that clutched the other. He noted a tremor shake her ever so slightly as she awaited his answer.

"If you wish," he agreed, watching her closely.

She nodded once. "My thanks." Then she turned quickly and left, silently closing the door behind her.

Richard began to dress, wondering all the while why he should feel so guilty. Had he treated her any worse than she deserved? What could a woman expect when she tricked a man the way she had done? But his cursed conscience bothered him all the same.

Sara had believed him landless. She thought he also would profit by their marriage, so he could not complain that her motives were entirely self-serving. And save for an occasional flare of temper, the woman did act kind and cheerful, almost desperately so. Patient with him, too, even on the occasions when he had deliberately set out to raise her ire.

He shrugged and put his mind to dressing himself as befitted a lord about to assume the rule of a new estate and win the confidence of its people.

No reason to air his grievances about his new wife publicly, Richard decided. By rights, what lay between the two of them *should* remain private. In any event, he would never disparage Sara before Fernstowe's people. But he would make an extra effort to appear congenial toward her now that she had asked it of him.

When he arrived in the hall, he saw Sara in an earnest discourse with two of her men. In truth it appeared to be more an argument than a discussion.

Richard recognized Everil and Jace, two of the most

vocal among Sara's men-at-arms. He had become fairly
well acquainted with most who resided at Fernstowe now,
and had appraised the force available to him for defense.
At present, both guards were disagreeing hotly with something she had just said.

Richard approached, stood close and laid his right palm
at the back of Sara's waist. The men immediately fell silent. They regarded him and his proprietary gesture toward
their lady with sharp curiosity.

"I trust nothing is amiss here," Richard said evenly,
favoring each man with a pointed look of warning.

"Nay, milord," the man called Jace assured him. Then
he smiled. "Milady says we should ride to the outer
reaches this morn and escort in the folk who bide there.
Ev and I, we thinks they'll be coming without our prod-
ding. They know it's court day. We'll stay here." The
other fellow, Everil, nodded in agreement.

Richard raised an eyebrow and pinned both men with a
glare that promised retribution if they balked further. "If
your lady says ride out, then mount up and do it. Her word
is mine, and you will obey her every command hereafter.
Or *else*. Am I understood?"

They left immediately, all but stumbling over each other
in their haste to reach the stables.

Richard removed his hand from Sara and propped it on
the hilt of his sword. "Have you had problems with those
two before this?"

"Not really," she answered with a short laugh. "'Tis
only that they find it loathsome to risk the others appropriating their added portions of ale while they are gone."

"And they do not like a female issuing directives," he
guessed. "We cannot have that. If they question your orders again, I shall put them on the road."

"It is good of you to support me so," Sara said with a

shrug of embarrassment. "I did not expect it, but I do thank you."

"My duty," Richard replied. When he glanced down at her and saw the frank gratitude in her beguiling eyes, he added, "And my pleasure."

Now why the devil had he said that? Her artless appreciation of it made him uncomfortable. Next she would be treating him as though they were boon companions or some such. Or worse yet, taunting him in his bath again, as if they were lovers.

Why did she persist with this idea that they could be friends? A ridiculous notion. He could never be friends with anyone he did not trust, and he knew without doubt that Sara had some ulterior motive in befriending him.

She wished him in her bed. He knew very well that it was not for want of him as a man. Nobly born women only suffered that duty for one reason and he supposed that was as it should be. Sara wanted a child, probably to insure that his own son did not inherit Fernstowe.

The fairness of her thinking struck Richard fully for the first time. Fernstowe should belong to her and hers. Neither he nor his son had any use for this place. Christopher already owned one twice the size that had been his mother's dower portion. And, unless Alan decided to claim Strodesouth at their father's death, Chris would also become heir to that estate in Gloucestershire.

Richard slid a glance sidewise at the lovely woman who daily sought to seduce him with good humor. True, she was ambitious, at least for the unborn child she wanted, and she needed a protector to hold this place safe. Mayhap she had been too presumptuous in choosing him to provide those things, but she was no villain.

Everything he had demanded of her thus far, she had done willingly and without complaint. Her comely appearance did them both honor. She wore no jewels but the fabrics were fine. The clothing she chose was fashionable. He had found no fault with that since the day he had ordered her to dress as a lady should.

Truth be told, he found no fault with Sara at all, except her claiming him when he did not wish to marry. Yet beneath all his anger about that, Richard could not help feeling flattered that she had chosen him. That was a vanity best kept well hidden.

Did she really think he was fooled by this come-hither game she played? He had to wonder just how far she would carry the pretense of wanting him. No further than his capitulation, he would wager. Only far enough to make him beholden to her. Sara was not to blame for that, of course. It was simply their way, these gentlewomen. They were taught it was the only way to be.

Evaline had also offered promising smiles when they first met. Pity the poor man who believed they would deliver on the promise of any shared passion. He'd not make *that* mistake again.

At the moment, Sara was speaking with one of the kitchen maids who suddenly made a comical face at her and groaned. Sara laughed aloud and hastened the maid away with a pat on the back.

She was always touching. A friendly pat here, a handshake there. Not a standoffish woman, Sara. Not with underlings, and most assuredly not with him.

God knows she made him want to touch back. Even now he could feel that lively body of hers against his palm as he had lent his consequence to her orders earlier.

Could he ignore his pride and anger and give this wife of his the heir she wished for? He should, for it was only fair. But could he bear it when she lay motionless beneath him, merely enduring his attentions in order to get the child she wanted?

No, not under any circumstance would he suffer that

again from any woman, no matter how much he desired her.

"Why do you shake your head so?" Sara asked him. "One would think I had just proposed that *you* milk the goats in Ethel's stead!" She gave his arm a fond squeeze.

Touching again, Richard thought with a scowl.

"Come and sit with me. We'll have bread and cheese to break our fast while we make plans for the day."

He itched to fling her hand off his arm and curse her for her merry nature. He yearned to kiss that sunny smile off her face and force her to feel how she tempted him. He ought to haul her back to the bedchamber, and make her feel as undone and as trammeled as he was.

That would never happen, Richard knew from experience. Oh, she would allow his advances right enough. Then when it was too late for him to stop, she would stiffen with disgust, bear his attentions like a stoic and then calmly ask a huge favor in return for her trouble.

The game of marriage was conducted that way, but Richard refused to participate this time. Right and proper it might be to everyone else's thinking, but he misliked it intensely.

Instead, he bared his teeth in what he hoped passed for a smile and followed Sara's lead. For the day, at least, he had given his word to play sweet.


All of those who were coming for the monthly court day had arrived by midmorning and Sara formally introduced Richard as their new liege.

His way with her people amazed her. Though he appeared pleasant, even benevolent, not one of them would ever believe her new husband a weak lord. He offered strength of sword and strength of purpose.

Whatever his feelings toward her, Sara knew she had

chosen wisely. He would protect Fernstowe and see that all went well in the areas where she could not.

"What a fine day," she commented happily as they sat together at one of the tables set up in the bailey. Some of the people milled about and some sat to visit as they ate. All seemed content with the way things were. "The swearing went well."

"None appeared reluctant," he agreed. Richard tore off a piece of the special bread she'd had prepared for this day and offered it to her as was fitting.

She took it and inclined her head in thanks. "They will thrive on your leadership, I expect."

"And have not done poorly under yours, so I see."

"Why, thank you, sir." Though she knew he forced the smile, Sara lauded his effort. All day he had kept his word. Not once had he glared in anger or given any sign that he resented his position here, either as her husband or as Lord of Fernstowe. By standing always near her, discreetly stroking her back or taking her arm, he had exhibited his claim upon her and thereby upon Fernstowe.

Now he had just paid her a very high compliment, indeed. Since no one else was near enough to overhear his words, Sara regarded them as genuine and not for show. How heartening.

She watched the movement of his large, capable hands as he cut a bite-size portion of meat and held it out to her on his eating knife.

His gaze fastened on her mouth. Sara reached out and touched his wrist lightly as though to steady his aim and felt his pulse quicken beneath her fingertips. Desire flamed in the green depths of his eyes as it often did when they came close.

If only she could persuade him to act upon that impulse, Sara thought she might make those smiles of his become real. Though she knew her limitations as a temptress, she also understood his needs. She could meet them if he would only let her.

No woman at Fernstowe, including the promiscuous Darcy, would dare usurp her place in Richard's bed. Not unless Sara herself suggested it to them.

Her offer of Darcy had been made only to see whether the man would ever seek another. His reaction to it reassured her. Richard did not hold with infidelity.

Sara hoped that he would relent in his attitude toward her if they became intimate. Surely two people could not share such closeness and remain strangers for long.

Aside from that aim, anticipation flowed through her veins like warm, sweet wine each time he was near. Sooth, even when he was not, she thought about it.

When she had received the bite of meat, Richard abruptly turned away. But Sara did not worry overmuch. His reluctance would fade one of these days. He still felt trapped. She would grant him time enough to come to terms with all that had happened. No need to hurry.

She quickly sought a topic of conversation that would lighten his mood. "Your messenger will have reached Gloucestershire some while ago. Should the children not arrive soon?"

He nodded and concentrated on his food. "In a few days, if all goes as planned. Both ride well and will not need to come by cart. My father will send them under escort. I've requested two of his knights and I expect they will stay on here. You could use more men accustomed to arms until the border problem is resolved."

"Do tell me about them." She leaned toward him, eager to hear.

"The knights?"

Sara laughed. "Nay, your children! I do not even know their names."

He looked suspicious. "Why do you pretend interest?"

"No pretense, Richard," she assured him. "I *am* interested."

"Why?" he asked, idly stabbing at his trencher with the knife.

"Because I look forward to being a mother."

For a long moment, he was silent. Then he acceded, though his words were gruff. "Christopher is seven and big for his age. Has the look of me, they do say. It is past time he began training as page, but my mother has put it off."

"Then we shall begin his instruction as soon as he has settled in. Now, what of your daughter?" Sara asked.

Richard's hand stilled. Then he carefully laid down his knife and turned to face her. "She has suffered enough, my Nan, so do not think I'll let you make a servant of her."

Taken aback by his sudden vehemence, Sara shook her head. "Oh, Richard, I had no such notion."

"See that you do not. Nan shall be taught a lady's skills so that she might marry well one day. Her birth is not to be discussed in her presence. Not by *anyone*. Is that understood?"

"I agree," Sara said. "Does she know that she is your natural child?"

He snorted with disgust and looked away. "People have beaten her about the head with that fact since the day of her birth. Always behind my back, be assured. But if it happens here, I shall know it and there will be consequences."

Sara smiled with relief and delight. "You love her."

He sighed heavily and rested his elbows on the table. "She has no one else."

Sara reached out and encircled his arm with her hands, unable to help showing how much she admired him. "Rest your mind on that score, Richard. Your Nan will have me, as well.''

That earned her a wary look of hope. He did not quite believe her, but she could see that he wanted to. That was progress.

Sara determined then and there that no matter what his children were like, she would make them as welcome as if she had birthed them herself.

She patted his arm fondly and let go of him. ''Now, finish your meal and go above for a rest. We must get you completely well before Christopher and Nan arrive. Nothing troubles a child more than seeing the father less than hardy. I speak as one who knows.''

He rose and accompanied her toward the entrance. It felt almost natural now, this walking side by side in step, her arm looped through his. Progress, indeed. Yesterday, he would have stalked away and left her standing there.

''Your father was often ill?'' he asked, his voice almost conversational, as though they truly were companions and he cared about her answer.

''Healthy, for the most part, but I have seen him wounded a few times. Father was never the most cautious of men.'' She remembered well her feelings whenever she had seen her sire bedridden. ''As a girl, I much feared he would die and leave me.''

''And so he did,'' Richard reminded her. She heard the sympathy in his voice, even though he tried to sound blunt. The man had a good heart, but worked so devilish hard to hide it from her.

She frowned up at him. ''Aye, he died. But I was no longer a girl when it happened. Though one is never prepared to lose a father, I was able to keep things going much as he would have done.''

He pursed his lips and nodded. ''Until you found you must marry.'' As they climbed the steps, he asked, ''Those two suitors of yours cannot be the only bids for your hand in all these years. Why did you wait so long? Most women are wed, or at least betrothed, at half your age.''

Sara pulled open the door, not waiting for him to do her the courtesy. "I grew old awaiting the right man," she said brightly. "And, lo, I have found you."

She grinned up at his dark expression and fiercely indrawn breath. Good Lord, why did she feel so obliged to bait him? Must be because he always reacted so obligingly, she thought.

Her wicked teasing would one day be the death of her, but somehow she could not resist. "You are entirely too grave, Richard," she admonished playfully. "I did but jest."

"I failed to find humor in it."

"Well, I guessed that right away. What must we do to make you laugh, I wonder?" She sidled away from him and then turned toward the kitchens.

His eyes remained on her back until she was out of sight. She could feel the heat of his glare. It warmed more than her heart, she thought with a secret smile.

Richard watched Sara's hips sway as she left him standing in the hall. She did that apurpose, he knew.

With those long legs and slender curves, the woman had to work at that enticing, follow-me saunter. She usually moved with a firm and purposeful stride. She continued to taunt him, now without any words.

Despite knowing that, he was still watching when the hall door burst open just behind him.

A breathless lad he'd met earlier gasped, "Milord...banners. Royal. Quarter league distant. A herald rides hard for the gates."

*King Edward.* Richard groaned beneath his breath. He was not looking forward to this.

# Chapter Five

Richard reached for the boy's shoulder and gave him a gentle push toward the kitchens. "Go and inform my lady the king's almost here. She must join me in the bailey to greet him."

Richard had barely made the bottom step before Sara caught up and passed him in a flurry of skirts. No foolish prancing now, he thought, hiding a grin. She ran like a courier with news of attack.

He calmly observed her sending everyone about her into a state of panic.

Several moments later, he saw that he'd been mistaken. Every soul left in the courtyard had been given a specific task to perform and each was about it.

By the time the king and his retinue arrived, Richard wagered the tables still standing from the earlier feast would be laden with more food.

He had to admit, Sara of Fernstowe did not wait upon fate. She caused things to happen. And wasn't *he* a case in point?

A short time after, the gates opened to admit Edward and a score of troops, many of whom were comrades Richard had known and served with most of his life.

All would know the tale of his hasty marriage. Probably found it amusing to one degree or another. Richard decided to put a good face on it, just as he had done for Sara's people.

He threw up a hand and smiled winningly, as though content with it all, then bowed low to Edward.

He noted Sara had smoothed her hair, sucked in a few deep breaths and had a pleasant expression firmly fixed on her face. She curtsied at his side as was proper and looked fully prepared to meet the devil himself. "Well-done," he heard himself whisper.

She flashed him a brief but heartfelt smile before she composed her face into a mask of earnest welcome for their royal guest.

"Ha, there he stands, by God! Alive and well!" the king shouted as he dismounted. He ignored all the bows and murmurs of Fernstowe's people and marched forward.

Richard rose from his bow. "Well come, my liege."

"And glad are we to hear you say it," Edward replied heartily. He took Sara's hand and bade her rise from her curtsy. "My dear Lady Sara. Has this knave made you regret saving his hide?"

"Not for a moment, sire. He does me all honor," Sara said demurely.

Richard did not miss the wry twist to her lips or the twinkle in her eyes as she said it. Neither did the king for he threw back his head and laughed uproariously.

They thought this a grand jest, the two of them, to marry him off while he was in a stupor. As much as he resented what they had done, he knew better than to complain. Instead, he pursed his lips and nodded, granting Edward his drollery, acknowledging that he could play the fool with good grace.

The king's laughter trailed off as he trained his keen

gaze upon Richard until tension trembled the air around them. Then he spoke. "We must speak together."

Sara beckoned. "Come inside, please, sire. The solar will be comfortable." She led the way to the steps.

"Madam, forgive us," Edward said courteously. "I would speak to your husband in private."

"Oh, of course," she said with a small shrug. "Shall I send in wine and food for you?"

"No, we shall join the company out here anon. Meanwhile, do not let my men inconvenience you. We will take our leave within the hour."

Richard did not insist that they remain here any longer than necessary. He ushered the king into the solar, eager to have done with their discussion. It surely involved the trouble with the Scots, probably the activities of his brother.

"Why have you come this way again, sire? You know it is not yet safe hereabout."

"You dare question my moves now, Richard?"

"It's a fair concern on my part. Last time you were here, you nearly met death. Who is to block the arrows for you if I can no longer ride beside you?"

"Who, indeed?" The king strolled over to the cushioned chair usually reserved for Sara and took a seat. Richard remained standing until Edward motioned impatiently for him to sit.

He pulled up a sturdy bench and straddled it. One always sat lower than the king. "Where is young John? Did he remain in York?"

The king looked away as though uncomfortable. "I knighted him. I knew you would not mind. He is almost eighteen now, after all. His father wished it and John was ready."

Richard did mind. He had fostered John of Brabent for over five years, since the lad was thirteen. It was Richard's place to say when knighthood was in order. Lord Brabent had not wanted his son to return to this troubled part of the country, that was the gist of it. Probably wise of him, since his son was not as ready to don spurs as the king thought.

"How are matters in York?" Richard asked, brushing his disappointment aside.

Edward scoffed. "Same as ever. Unruly nodcocks." He leaned forward. "Richard, I am come because my conscience will not let me sleep. I fear I've done you a wrong you do not deserve."

Did he dare reply to that? Did the king mean setting him against his Scottish brother, or did he speak of the unconventional marriage?

"The queen was not amused," Edward admitted. "She writes that she spoke to the archbishop on your behalf. The marriage can be undone," he said, answering Richard's question in as apologetic a tone as he'd ever heard the king use. "Unless you have bedded the girl. Then I suppose you would feel honor-bound to stay with her. You have not, have you?"

"No," Richard admitted, feeling very uneasy when he should be delighted.

"Because you've not been well enough, or because she displeases you so much?"

"It is true that I did not wish to marry," Richard equivocated. Now was his chance. Why wasn't he jumping at it, grabbing at the opportunity for an annulment? He would. "What will happen to her if we invalidate the marriage and I leave here?"

The king lifted one shoulder and cocked his head. "I shall give her to someone else."

"Who?" Richard demanded.

"Lord Aelwyn, I expect. He's best prepared to hold the place since his own lies close."

"No!" Richard almost shouted, then carefully lowered his voice. "Not him."

Edward chuckled. "Do you know the man? Is he unworthy?"

Richard had to admit he'd never met Sara's suitor, nor did he wish to. "No, but Sara did not want him to begin with and should not be forced to wed where she will be unhappy. You did promise her a choice."

The king waved that away as unimportant. "Aelwyn must want her right badly for some reason. Likely to increase his property. Many would not persist in a suit as he has done, once they saw that face of hers."

"There's nothing wrong with her face! So she has a scar. It is hardly noticeable. The woman is beautiful. You just told her so yourself."

The king flapped his hand again. "Courtesy. You know I have to say things like that. 'Tis expected. Even if you disregard that fault, there is her height. She's eye to eye or taller yet than almost every man I know, save the two of us. Sara the Tower is what they call her behind her back, you know." He shook his leonine head sadly.

Richard decided to hold his tongue before he said something that might get it removed from his head. He ground his teeth so hard his jaws ached. Did Edward think to rule his life in each and every quarter? Marrying him off, knighting his squire, now ridding him of Sara as though she were some ugly inconvenience?

"So, shall we request a dispensation? I'll give witness you were unconscious and did not consent. That's perfect grounds. Without a consummation, there should be no problem at all."

Richard knew he had to stay. If he put Sara aside this way, she would always believe it was because of her appearance. How shallow would that make him in her eyes?

And Aelwyn of Berthold would have her whether she wanted the man or not. Obviously she did not.

"I will remain," he said. "If Sir Aelwyn could handle the problems, he'd have done so by now. You need me here, and so does the lady. The raiders won't hold still long, even though they've been quiet since you were here last. As for the marriage, I would guess the word of it has spread throughout the Marches by now?"

Edward rose abruptly. "Truly spoken, on both accounts. Very well, it is your choice to make. I admit that your presence at Fernstowe will ease my mind with regard to the Scots. If you left now, I would have to station more men here in your stead. As it is, you are capable of organizing those who have suffered hereabout and form your own offensive."

He laid a hand on Richard's shoulder. "But when you have all that settled, you may still have your freedom if you wish it."

Richard merely nodded thoughtfully, wondering why he did not relish that idea more than he did. Guilt assailed him for wanting to put the marriage aside. And pride prompted him to do it. Yet Sara would suffer such a blow to her own dignity, he could not bear to think about it.

"That is, *if* you do not bed her," the king added in an offhand manner as he headed for the door. "Do that, and you might as well accept your lot."

Richard cursed under his breath. If only he had taken Sara to bed before this wretched visit, he would not need to wrestle with such a choice.

"Refraining shouldn't cause you much loss of sleep. If I had taken time to regard her appearance more closely that night, I would never have countenanced the match between you in the first place. The pockmarked Aelwyn no doubt will suit her better."

Richard almost wished he had stood aside that day and let that cursed arrow find its mark.

Sara paused in her conversation with one of the visitors when she saw the king exit the hall. Richard followed, fists clenched and face dark with brooding. He looked fit to kill. She could guess why. Richard had voiced his objections and still the king meant to make the marriage stand.

"Look to! We ride," King Edward shouted, his long stride eating up the distance from the keep to the saddled horses. Then he turned and raised his hand toward her husband. "Farewell, old friend. I will be at Morpeth Castle this next month. Send us word of any progress."

Richard executed a stiff bow and nodded once.

The royal men-at-arms hurried to mount. None had approached Richard, though some had called out their good wishes. She had not missed the teasing tones and silent smirks some affected. Neither had her husband, she was sure. Thankfully, the entire party soon rode out through the gates and left Fernstowe in peace.

Sara heaved a long sigh of relief.

"Your business with the king did not go well?" she asked as she strolled over to join Richard. Might as well prod a wild boar with a tree branch, but she never hid from a confrontation. There would be one over this, so they might as well have done with it now.

He still stood there, glaring at the gates while they swung shut. The portcullis lowered with a grinding squeak as the people within the bailey went about their business.

For a moment, Sara thought Richard would tell her what went on in the solar, but then he merely shook his head.

For a long moment thereafter, he studied her face, every aspect of it. His intent gaze traveled her entire length and back again where it met with hers. The anger had not abated one whit. Richard suddenly swerved and stalked away without a word.

Sara released the pent-up breath she'd been holding and allowed her shoulders to slump. He and the king *had* spoken of her. She knew it as well as she knew the sun rose that morning.

Richard had asked the king to let him out of the bargain and was refused. That was the only thing that could account for the surliness of his mood.

One short visit and King Edward had undone all her progress in making friends with her husband. Now she must begin again to win Richard over.

Damn the royal hide. Why couldn't the king have returned to London and let them be?

Berta, the best among her weavers, approached her. "Lady Sara, is your husband angered that we did not do more to please the king? I'm afeared the women made themselves scarce whilst all those knights were about. Last time they came, there was a bit of sporting."

Sara turned and smiled down at the small, plump woman. The ever-friendly Berta always spoke her mind and Sara admired her for her pluck. "His mood has nothing to do with that. I think the king's concern over the border threat weighs heavily on his mind."

Berta grinned, showing a missing tooth. "Good thing they left so quick. We used up most of the bread and the ale's running low. Cook's all atwit wondering what to fix for supper."

"You took much upon yourself without my direction helping out today, Berta. I thank you for it," Sara said sincerely.

It occurred to her that Berta had always done this. She seemed to feel as much pride in putting Fernstowe's best foot forward as Sara did herself.

The weaver's cheery nature and willing hands might be a godsend in yet another matter.

"Tell me, Berta, do you like children?"

The round face brightened even more. "Oh aye, my lady. I do love the lambs. Got none of my own, y'know. Old Morgan never gave me a one in the ten years we had together."

Sara nodded, recalling the wiry old villager who had died of ague last winter. Berta was not yet thirty. She might remarry and have those babes she wanted, but Sara decided to make use of her talents now.

"Would you like to help me look after my children, Berta? It would mean moving into the keep."

"Oh, my lady, aye," Berta fairly breathed the words, awe shining in her dark eyes. "When the day comes, I would be honored."

"The day is coming sooner than you think, Berta," Sara said, laughing. "They should be here within a week if the roads south are in fair condition."

"Lord Richard's get?" Berta guessed.

"Son and daughter, of an age to train. What say you now?"

Berta grinned with delight, grabbed Sara's hands to squeeze in thanks and rushed away to tell her friends the good news.

Richard might have arranged for a nurse to accompany the children, but Sara didn't think so. If that were the case, a cart would have been necessary. She meant to surround those two with all the goodwill and affection she could muster, and Berta could provide that when duty took Sara in other directions.

Pleased with herself for latching onto a happier subject than Richard's foul mood, she turned her efforts to clearing the bailey of the trappings of the day's events.

\* \* \*

Six days of turbulence followed the king's visit. Sara worked everyone to within a hairbreadth of exhaustion, getting Fernstowe prepared for Richard's son and daughter.

Her people cleared the keep and grounds of all objects that might prove a danger to curious children. She added swings to her garden for their pleasure. Late into the night, she sewed and stuffed poppets for Nan to cuddle. She set old Tam to whittling tops and toy horses for Christopher. With loving hands, Sara sanded and waxed a small, blunt wooden sword her father had given her as a child and ordered another fashioned exactly like it.

The memories summoned by these activities made Sara miss her own father, who had gone to great lengths to see to her happiness as she grew to womanhood. If only she could live up to his standard as a parent, she would be happy.

"A mother, finally," she often crooned to herself with anticipation.

Richard ignored her for the most part, never commenting on the efforts. He generated a bit of exhaustion himself, insisting that the men train daily and for long hours. Each day, he spent longer and longer exercising his own muscles, regaining his strength. He bathed in the bathhouse with the men, preventing a repeat of her intrusion on his ablutions.

She left him to his own devices, content with her arrangements to welcome those whom he loved. Other than greeting each other in passing, they spoke only at the evening meal, and then of inconsequential things.

Except for that sixth night. Then Richard broached a dreaded subject Sara had almost dismissed from her mind. The Scots.

"Word of our marriage must be widespread now. I've

had a message today from Alan the True to parlay," he announced.

"You cannot!" she exclaimed, horrified.

He speared a section of apple, combined it with a cube of cheese and ate it as though he did not intend to answer.

"Mark me, Richard, this is a trick."

Calmly he chewed, swallowed and set down his knife to indicate that he was finished. "Do not speak to me as though I have no wits. 'Tis unseemly for a wife."

"What will you do?" Sara asked, weak with fear for him.

"Meet on an open field, under a flag of truce, two days hence. The messenger assured me the man's eager for peace."

She snorted. "Pardon me if I think those wits of yours have gone begging. He will kill you!"

Richard smiled, an expression so alien to him, and so captivating, Sara nearly forgot the subject of the argument. Before she could recover her faculties, he rose from the table.

She scurried to follow, catching his sleeve with her fingers. "Wait! Tell me what you plan to do. *Exactly.*"

"Go into the solar where we may discuss privately," he said pleasantly. "Unless you'd like all and sundry to hear us."

Sara nodded and rushed ahead of him, her thoughts tumbling every which way, casting about for a solution that would not mean his death.

He took his usual seat beside the fire. When she sat and leaned forward anxiously, he began. "First of all, I shall have archers stationed in the nearby wood with arrows trained upon this delegation. I shall ride out, as will the Scot. Knowing one's adversary is important. I would see this man to gauge his intent."

Sara ran a hand through her hair, raking it back from

her aching forehead. "My lord, Richard, we *know* his intent! The man's a murderer without conscience and he leads murderers. What more do you need to know?"

He drew his fine lips into a line, a habit she'd noticed he employed while judging his words. She wished he would simply spit them out and say what he meant.

To her surprise, he leaned forward and took her hands in his. "Do not worry, Sara. I am no greenling unused to treachery. This Scot may have nothing to do with what happened to your father, and be one who wishes to establish peace."

Not for a moment did she believe that, but railing against this plan of his would not deter him. She must use reason. "Will you tell me what the message said?"

He drew back, reached into his sleeve and drew out a small parchment. "Read for yourself. You do read?"

She snatched it from him. "Of course I read."

"Meet me alone in the Meadow of Dispute in two days' time. I come in peace," Sara read. She scoffed. "He signs it simply *Alan*. That is passing strange."

"He offers truce, at least for the day," Richard said. "I cannot tell you why as yet, but I believe he means me no harm."

"Ha!" Sara threw up her hands. "Obviously he has heard of you and wants you dead. Meet with him and it will happen!"

"Be calm, Sara," he said easily. "I do not intend to die." Then he added, "But I shall meet with him and see what he has to say."

"And you think he will honor that truce of his? Ah, Richard, you are green if you believe so." Tears threatened, but she willed them away as they clouded her vision.

He watched her for a moment, then stood and nudged a fallen log farther back into the fire hole with the toe of one boot.

She knew he would go in spite of anything she might advise. Knowing that, she left her own chair and approached him from behind. Tentatively she slid her arms around his waist and leaned close against him, resting her face on the muscled planes of his back.

His words vibrated in her ear. "You fear I will be killed and you'll be obliged to wed another? Is that what troubles you?"

"I fear for your own sake, Richard. Not my own."

Richard sighed, a rushing sound as he braced his arms against the stones of the mantle. "Go to bed, Sara."

"Come with me," she whispered.

He gave no answer.

Slowly, accepting that he would not, she withdrew her arms and left him there. She silently made her way from the solar, up the stairs and into her chamber.

He was not yet ready, but he could not mask the desire that burned in his eyes like green flames or the way his body tensed every time she touched him.

Sara knew if she could hold him in her arms, he would understand the depth of her feelings for him. And in the dark, he would not have her marked face to contend with. He could forget his troubles for a time and only know her caring and her touch.

Richard might not know it yet, but he badly needed someone to care for him. It did not matter if he never loved her. She only wanted him to accept that she loved him. Without doubt, she *did* love him. There was the attraction between them, but beyond that, Sara greatly admired his love for his children, loyalty to his king and his bravery. What drew her more than anything, however, was his loneliness. How would she bear it if he died?

# Chapter Six

Richard never planned to go alone as the message had requested. Despite what Sara thought of him, he was no fool. Alan would receive him in peace, of course. But who was to say how much control his brother had over the men who would ride with him. Alan would not venture across the border with no troop to protect him. He was no fool, either.

And so, six would accompany Richard as they rode north. They were few enough to signal that Richard intended no attack. Yet these carefully selected men could comprise a considerable defense if need be.

The Meadow of Dispute was a clearing, a narrow strip of a mere dozen acres that had shifted ownership so many times no man had memory of the original claimant. Neutral territory, where no one lived, planted crops or grazed cattle.

"Beware of the Scot, Richard," Sara warned him as she offered up the stirrup cup. "If you insist upon this mission of madness, do take utmost care."

"I shall be home to sup," he said. He drank the ale and handed down the empty chalice.

"Go with God," Sara said.

"Bide in peace," he replied formally.

Richard waited until she stepped safely back from his destrier and then guided the huge gray mount to the head of the waiting column of men, three archers and three horsemen schooled in close fighting. None of these were knights, but all had served in battle at one time or another. Richard had been pleased to find them among the men-at-arms Lord Simon had collected to Fernstowe over the years.

If put to the test, the archers could fell at least a score of men before they reached Richard in the open meadow. As Eustiss had pointed out to him, the Scots were not overly fond of bows. If there was an attack, it would likely be with swords or pikes.

Though Richard had prepared, he truly did not feel his brother would betray him. Not that man who had written those letters full of love and kind regard for his parents and younger brother. Family loyalty surpassed a man's politics. Just as Richard would refuse to kill his brother if King Edward commanded it, so would Alan hold his peace. They were Strodes and lived by the same code. Alan had proved that once to their father when he saw him safely to England when their two countries were at war.

Alan's invitation was no trick, as Sara thought. Richard did not believe his brother meant to kill him, any more than he believed Alan had killed Lord Simon.

This meeting would give them an opportunity to have their reunion after so many years apart. Together they could try to determine who had slain Sara's father and accused Alan of instigating the border hostilities.

He would not have chosen to meet Alan this day, when his children might be arriving, but a refusal might have indicated to his brother that he was unwilling to parlay with him at all.

Richard and the men rode due north for near an hour.

The sun had burned off the early morning fog and provided ample warmth.

"So, here is the place, my lord," Markham said in a low voice and pointed. "Through that copse there."

Fortunately there were enough close-set trees surrounding the meadow to provide adequate cover for his men. The day and location could not be finer for an encounter such as this.

As captain of Richard's guard, Markham assumed the duty of stationing the men where they would remain hidden, yet able to go swiftly to Richard's assistance if need be.

"Let me come with you, sir?"

"No, Markham, you stay. He did ask that I ride alone. I will stay within the tree line until I see him. The banner?"

"Aye," he said, transferring the pennon displaying Richard's colors, blue and black. Above it he had added a wide banner of white. The soft, shifting wind gently waved the fabric to and fro and stirred the leaves above his head.

Richard waited for some time between two low-hanging oaks until he spied a sleek brown horse emerge from the opposite side of the clearing. A surprise, that. Richard had heard that the Scots generally rode the rougher galloways or what the local folk called bog-trotters. These were wide-muscled, surefooted mounts able to navigate the wastes or ingates through the Cheviot Hills and bogs. This one looked too clean and without the rough coat Richard had expected to see.

Suspicion nagged at him, but he cast it away. Alan must have decided to impress his younger brother with his fine taste in horseflesh.

Atop the prancing steed sat a warrior dressed much as he was, in mail hauberk and chausses. He wore and carried identical colors to Richard's.

Though the man had covered his head, Richard marked a long nose and short, dark beard beneath the mail coif and half helm. The right hand lifted in greeting, and to show that it raised no weapon. Richard did the same. Both rode slowly toward the center of the grassy pasture.

Something felt wrong about this, Richard thought once again, as the man drew closer. Very wrong.

Richard had provided cover for his back as any prudent man would do, though he knew no knight with any honor about him would violate a truce. Alan of Strode had been well renowned for his honor by both Scots and English alike for the past twenty-five years, a near legend.

A horse whinnied in the wood behind him, breaking the silence. He heard several thumping sounds and a strangled cry. *Ambush!* Richard wheeled quickly, drew his sword and raced back to aid his men.

*Too late.* Markham lay in a heap, bleeding from the head. Likewise, Bryce, one of the horsemen, and all three archers had been knocked senseless—or mayhap killed— where they stood. Newson was nowhere in sight.

Five armed men stood in a semicircle around Richard's fallen companions. Two more, mounted, barred his only route of escape, and the man he'd met in the clearing was behind him. In the distance he heard hoofbeats tearing through the forest, in the direction of Fernstowe. Had Newson made it to the horses?

Richard instantly decided not to fight. Even though he had healed and was in fair battle form, he could not hope to best eight men. That was likely how Sara's father had died.

If these men had come here to kill Richard, he knew he would be dead already. He would lull them into thinking he accepted defeat, and then make his escape. Failing that, they would ask ransom for him. This was his first time to be captured thusly, but many knights had been. It was not at all unusual.

"So, we meet at last," said a deep voice behind him. "Drop your sword. No one has died yet this day, so do not make me kill you."

Richard kept a grip on the hilt of his sword, but lowered it as he slowly turned in the saddle. "Where is Sir Alan?"

The man he had met in the meadow smiled beneath the half helm. "Why right here, where I promised I would be, *brother*."

The crackle of leaves underfoot warned him of a mount's approach on his blind side. He whirled and set to with his blade, connecting solidly with the cudgel aimed for his head, full knowing he had not a prayer of winning the day.

The horn upon the north tower alerted Sara that the guard had spotted riders. She rushed from the solar to the bailey at once to await Richard and the men.

"Only one comes, my lady," young Fergus called down from the top of the wall. When the gates opened and the portcullis ground upward, Newson rode in. If she had not recognized his straw-colored hair and his horse, Sara would not have known the man.

He hung on to the pommel of his saddle until his mount came to a stop. Then he released it and slid to the ground in a heap.

Sara ran and knelt beside him, lifting his head into her lap. "Newson, where is my husband?"

"Don't know what they done to 'im." The poor man struggled to open eyes that were near swollen shut. He sucked in a pained breath to speak further. "They waited in the trees, Lady Sara. Jumped down upon us after Sir Richard rode out to meet that bastard Scot. I made it to the horses, but they caught me."

"You escaped after they beat you like this?"

"Nay, my lady. They did that when they caught up, then put me on my horse and let me go. They said I was to tell you to wait. They'll be sendin' Sir Richard to you."

"Oh, God save him," Sara groaned. She knew well how they sent their victims home. "Why would he not listen to me?" she cried, covering her face with her hand. Her body shook with grief, but tears would not come. The sorrow ran too deep for them. Bone deep.

Several of the women gently moved her aside and took over the care of young Newson. "Come away, my lady," Berta said. She took Sara's arm and helped her stand.

Again the horn sounded. Sara shook off her inertia, jumped up and dashed to the open gate, expecting to see the other men bringing Richard draped over his saddle. Dead. But no one traveled upon the road north. Instead, a party of travelers approached Fernstowe from the one curving south.

Six mounts, four riders, she counted. Two packhorses, two small palfries, and two destriers.

*The children.* "Oh, Lord, not now!"

She could not greet them this way, distraught and mourning. And for Richard's sake, she must not foist this grief upon them yet. Not while they still wore road dust and suffered the weariness of their journey. Poor, poor babes. "I am all that's left to you," she whispered. Then she took a deep breath, drew on her strength and called for Berta.

"My lady?" Berta said comfortingly. "You cannot be certain 'tis as bad as you think."

Sara brushed the meaningless words of comfort aside. "Look there, our children are coming. As soon as they ride in, I shall make them welcome. But I must be brief about it. You will take charge, see to their baths, make them comfortable."

"As soon as may be," Berta assured her.

Sara glanced toward the gates which still stood open after Newson's arrival. "I must speak with these knights my husband sent for and see if they will help to find him. No word of this must trouble Christopher and Nan, you understand?"

"They will hear it, my lady," Berta argued. "This is no secret that can be kept. And they *should* know, don't you think?"

"Once they have bathed, eaten and rested, I shall tell them. Until then, not one word!"

"Aye, you have the right of it. Poor sweet lambs. This news will affright them, that's for certain."

Sara knew that Berta and everyone at Fernstowe believed her husband dead now. So did she, but until she saw his body, she would hold on to hope. If the Scots knew that Richard had ridden in the king's personal guard, they might decide to ask ransom.

Suddenly one of the small riders broke free of the approaching group and rode hell-bent for the gates. Sara cried out in fear, terrified that the palfrey had bolted and the child would bounce off and break his neck. One of the knights kicked his horse to a gallop and followed. The huge destrier lumbered along, unable to catch the nimbler horse.

"Papa!" a shrill voice called. "Where are you, Papa?" Halting in a flurry of dust, the rider swung off the saddle, turned loose of the pommel and jumped the few remaining feet to the ground.

Bright green eyes focused on Sara. "Where is my papa?" demanded the red-haired scamp. "I want to see him *now!*"

Sara took in the thick padded jerkin and woolen trews. The small boots were replicas of Richard's. "You must be Christopher," she said, forcing herself to smile at the child.

"Not so, I am Nan!" the imp declared hotly.

Sara tried to hide her surprise. And dismay. Her husband's offspring—at least this one—possessed a willful and reckless nature. But Sara could not bring herself to chastise the girl at first meeting. She must be kind and understanding, especially knowing what the little one might soon have to accept.

"I am Lady Sara of Fernstowe, your new mother." She reached out to brush a hand over the springy curls.

The girl dodged her touch. "My mother's Annie Causey and she's dead. Now where is my papa?"

The big, heavily bearded knight who had followed Nan dismounted and approached them. "Mistress Nan, your father might not be best pleased with these manners you display. Now stand away until I introduce you."

Nan shot him a belligerent look. "No need for it. She knows me now."

The knight blew out a weary breath through his teeth. "My name is Sir Edmund Folway, my lady. And this is Mistress Nan. Please forgive—"

Sara nodded, distracted, as the rest of the travelers came through the gates.

The lad calmly rode up and addressed her while still mounted. "I am Christopher Strode." He jerked a thumb at the knight who accompanied him. "That is Sir Matthew Turnsbridge. You are my father's wife, the Lady Sara?"

"I am," Sara replied, her smile firmly fixed. "I bid you well come to Fernstowe, Christopher."

"She didn't curtsy and call you 'my lord,'" Nan observed.

Christopher shrugged and slid off his horse. "I'm not a lord," the boy said patiently to his sister. "Not yet."

He marched up to Sara, reached out and snatched her hand. Before she knew it, he had planted a hasty kiss on the back of her knuckles and released her. "There. Done and done. We are hungry."

The knights exchanged a harried look. Sara could well imagine the trying trip those two had just endured. One thing Richard's progeny did not lack was a sense of self-importance. She would have to establish her authority immediately or these rapscallions would take over the entire keep.

"Children, you will go with Mistress Berta. She will bathe and feed you. Remain in your rooms until I come. We must talk."

Nan laughed merrily, pulled a wry face and nudged her brother. "She thinks to bathe us, Chris."

The boy pursed his lips, looking for all the world like Richard at his haughtiest. "My father is not here?"

"No," Sara answered, trying hard not to show her grief. "Not presently. Now go with Mistress Berta and do as I say."

"I will not!" Nan announced, crossing her arms over her chest and thrusting out her chin.

Christopher stood close to her and assumed a like pose. "We will wait for Father here."

Sara leaned over, her head between theirs so only they could hear her words. "Notice my size, if you will. I can lift you both bodily, one under each arm, and haul you into the keep like naughty pups. Or you may walk in a dignified manner befitting your station. The choice is yours. Will you do as I ask?"

"Well, since you *ask*," Christopher said with a sniff of disdain. "We only take orders from our father."

Berta beckoned and led the two away, marching in step like little soldiers.

Once the young ones were out of hearing, Sara quickly turned to the knights. "My husband has been taken by the Scots. He might have been killed this day." Without pause, she told them what she knew from her short conversation with Newson.

Sir Edmund protested her suggestion that they attempt a rescue. "If the Scots let him live, they will not have him where we can find him. Even if we should discover his whereabouts, they would kill him the moment we approached. They said to wait and that is what we must do. If they do not want ransom, then he is already beyond help."

When Sara would have spoken, Sir Edmund held up a hand to still her words and continued, "My lady, your husband and I have been friends since we were children. I fostered with his father. If there were any chance at all of saving him by hunting down these scoundrels, I would be the first to ride out."

Sara released a shuddering breath. There was nothing any of them could do now. "We wait," she agreed. "You and Sir Matthew come to the hall. Have some food and wine." She pointed toward the long building set against the inner bailey wall. "There's a place for you in the barracks when you're ready to rest."

Sir Matthew, the younger knight, fell in step with her, speaking for the first time. "Sir Richard's a resourceful man, my lady. If there's any opportunity at all, he will escape."

Sara nodded. But she feared Richard's condition after the wounding had left him with less than his full strength. He would not escape. If indeed he still lived, he would remain at the mercy of the Scots until they decided what to do with him.

And now she must tell this to his son and daughter, who very likely believed their father invulnerable.

Leagues distant, Richard awoke with a start. He blinked away the ale someone had just doused him with and tried to determine where he was. No place he knew. A stone passageway of some sort within a keep. Near the kitchens, for he could smell roasting meat. Someone stooped behind him and blindfolded his eyes.

The memory of the altercation in the woods by the infamous meadow returned forthwith. *Captured.*

His head felt like a coshed melon and his body ached abominably as a result of his resistance. He'd meant to go peacefully until he could catch them off guard and escape. But when he'd chanced to hear the man behind him with the cudgel, he had turned and blocked the blow. From there on, he only recalled red rage and pain, both suffered and dealt out. That cudgel must have found him after all.

"Ah, back amongst the living, I see!" his host declared.

Richard grunted, much afraid he had not the wind to complete a real word. He lay prone, trussed up like a Christmas goose, but he turned his head toward the speaker as though he could see.

For some reason, this man had come to the meadow in Alan's stead. And Richard did not believe him a Scot. For one thing, he did not sound like one of them. Though many Scottish nobles received their educations in places other than Scotland, a trace of their birthplace usually remained on the tongue. Not so with this one.

If this truly was his brother, Richard knew he had sorely misjudged both the man and the situation. He should have paid more attention to Sara instead of trusting in blood ties.

Whether this was Alan or not, Richard decided he had best play the game out. He was in no condition to bolt even if he were untied.

"What do you want," he managed to grunt. His ribs ached and breathing hurt like hell. His eyes stung from the ale.

The man laughed. For the first time, Richard paid heed

to more than the words. The voice sounded too youthful, he thought, for the fifty years his brother had lived. Or hope was deceiving.

If only he could see the man's face, surely he would know if this was Alan. How many times had Richard's mother sworn that Alan resembled their sire? Yet one thing like unto the family's description of his brother was this man's laughter. It was said that his brother laughed often.

Richard's host poked his shoulder with a boot. "I'd like a goodly fortune from your lady wife, of course. That will do for a beginning."

"Ransom." Richard spat. "For family?"

The man chuckled. "But surely I am due some of the riches you have gained as an Englishman! That only seems fair, *brother*."

"You chose to stay in Scotland," Richard said, wondering who the man could possibly be, if not Alan. It was not common knowledge to any but the Strode family that Richard even had a half brother. The family and the king.

"You could still swear to Edward and accept the lands and title when Father passes on," Richard told him. "The choice remains yours."

For a few moments, silence reigned.

Then the voice boomed, "Take him away!"

Apparently, they had nothing further to discuss.

Richard steeled himself against the rough handling of two minions as they dragged him down stone steps and tossed him in a cell. One stood guard with a sword while the other cut the bonds on Richard's wrists and ankles. Neither spoke.

He quickly removed the cloth from his eyes. The closing door shut off all light save that of the torch the men had carried down with them and were now taking away. He watched the square of the barred grate in the door as even that weak illumination disappeared upstairs with his captors. Now he could see nothing.

Richard stretched his limbs to regain feeling in them and began to explore his injuries. They were numerous—cuts, massive bruising, an enormous lump on his head—but none seemed life threatening or even all that serious.

Even so, had they left the door standing open, he doubted he would be able to walk out under his own power, much less make it up the stairs. Not yet.

Sara would pay the ransom, of course. Whether that would save his life remained to be seen. This man who called himself Alan had no honor. And apparently no familial feelings toward him whatsoever if he was a brother. He could as easily collect the ransom and dispose of his captive with none to chastise him. Until King Edward found out. There would be hell to pay then, and Alan would be the one to pay it, guilty or not.

Richard used up the last of his resources as he crawled around the cell to find what it contained. A bucket for slops, another full of brackish water, and a frayed blanket that fell apart in his hands. He lay on his side and rested his head on one arm to recover his breath.

Even after all that happened to him, he still refused to believe Alan would betray him so. How many reasons had he conjured today why this man could not possibly be his brother?

Was he right? Or was this merely an unwillingness to admit his own mistake, his all too trusting eagerness to meet with Alan?

Why hadn't he listened to his wife, who knew the Scots' treachery far better than he? Pride had cost him dearly, and now it would cost her, as well.

No doubt Sara would be questioning her fine choice of

husbands once she received the ransom request. Richard could hardly blame her for that.

Whoever the man was—Alan or some other—he would receive a damn sight more than a cursed ransom if he released this captive, Richard vowed.

# Chapter Seven

Fernstowe's folk settled in for the night after a day of worry. Berta told Sara their younger arrivals had offered only token resistance to bathing and donning fresh chemises in which to sleep. Their appetites had proved hearty after their long journey.

Sara joined them in Christopher's chamber to tell them of their father's dilemma.

Now she listened with amazement to the rapid conversation between the two.

"You call all the men together, come morn," Nan ordered her brother, ticking off their plans on her fingers. "Our knights and hers." She inclined her head toward Sara.

"And send word to the king, too," Chris replied with a succinct nod. "Whom should we send? Sir Matthew?"

Nan hopped up on the bed beside Christopher. "Does he know the king? Sir Edmund does, I think."

"Hold a moment!" Sara interrupted. "Will you not hear the rest of what I know?"

She could scarcely believe these two. She had expected tears and worry. They sounded as though they arranged rescues every day.

Admittedly they did plan well together. Nan neither deferred to Christopher because of his maleness or his legitimacy, nor did she lord it over him because she was a year older. Christopher treated her as equally as he would have another page of like years. They seemed the best of friends and obviously did not care who knew it.

That alone was highly unusual, given the status of Nan's birth. Sara was surprised such as this had been allowed by the baron and his lady. Richard must have taken a strong stand on it.

Both children resembled their father. Their eyes were exactly like his, bright green, piercing, and missing nothing. Christopher's chestnut hair waved the same and was only a shade lighter than Richard's, while Nan's was a fiery red-gold. Sara sympathized with the girl for the wildly curling mass, which, like her own, must be difficult to control.

The two were of a size, though Chris was a year younger. Only Nan's bright locks kept them from appearing as identical as two could who were not born twins. Handsome, both, and as canny for their ages as any she had ever met.

Richard Strode truly sired fine-looking, intelligent children. Her heart swelled with pride for him and for herself, now that she would be mother to them.

Neither seemed unduly alarmed that their father might be dead already. Not that she had mentioned that possibility. She'd merely said that Richard had been captured. Still, fear of the murderous Scots ran rampant, even in the south of England. They must believe Richard invincible, just as she had feared they would. What in heaven's name would she do if they were proved wrong?

"The message said to wait," she informed them. "If we send men to try to free your father, the Scots might…hurt him."

"Kill him, you mean," Nan said, pursing her small pink lips and sucking in a deep, steadying breath before she spoke again. "Would they do that, Chris?"

"No, of course not!" the boy answered immediately. Not denying it out of fear, but with certainty. "If they kill Father, King Edward would destroy them."

He looked from Nan to Sara, his eyes older than his years, and wise, like Richard's. "I believe they will ask for gold. Grandfather told me that is what happens when a knight is taken in a battle. The enemy asks gold in exchange. When we give it to them, they will let Father go."

Nan nudged his shoulder, grinning. "And then *he* will kill them!"

"Just so," Chris agreed.

"We know not where they hold him," Sara volunteered. "So, even if we wanted to rescue him, we could not."

She did not add that she had set someone to gathering that information in secret. A force of troops tearing off across the border at this point would serve no purpose at all.

"Then we will wait," Christopher said evenly. He tilted back his head and peered at her through narrowed eyes. So like Richard's considering look. "You have much gold?" he asked.

Sara was not about to discuss the state of her coffers with a seven-year-old child. But neither could she dismiss these two as ordinary children. They were no more commonplace than the man who fathered them. And not much more affable, come to think of it. They only suffered her presence now because they must.

She understood why they held little regard for her yet, because thus far, they thought she'd done nothing about their sire's situation one way or another. They had sense enough to know they needed her at the moment to help insure Richard's return.

Some inner wisdom prompted Sara to treat Richard's children with adult respect—despite their tender ages—if she planned to receive like courtesy from them. She recalled how she had hated being treated as a brainless, bothersome pet when she was young. Most children had sharp minds and they used them, regardless of what their elders might think.

Nan and Christopher probably thought her some aging feather-wit by the condescending tones she had used to tell them about their father. No more. Henceforth, she would deal with these two as straightly as she would any ally sharing a common cause.

"We have sufficient coin," she assured Christopher. "The king is in Morpeth now, but it will take too long to send for him. Even if he came, there is nothing he could do that we cannot. This incident could cause a small war and put your father in even more danger. We must manage this on our own."

"You do not weep for Father," the boy noted. "Why is that? Do you not care what happens to him?"

"Of course I care! He is my husband!" Sara declared. "What good would weeping do? You shed no tears, I see." Then she recalled to whom she spoke and softened her words. "But I certainly would understand if you and your sister did so. Your father is a fine man."

Nan shot Christopher a knowing look. "Loves him," she said with a wry little snort of disgust. "My gran used to call it *making sheep's eyes* whenever my mum spoke of Papa in that way."

Christopher squinted and leaned closer, examining Sara's face. Then he straightened, sighed and nodded.

Sara didn't deny it. What could it hurt for them to know how much she cared for Richard? If anything, it should make them feel more secure than not. "Do you mind if I love him, too?" she asked, keeping her voice friendly.

They consulted silently. She could almost see their thoughts shooting back and forth. Then they turned as one, their expressions solemn. Chris spoke for them. "We shall see."

"Reserving judgment, hmm?" she said, nodding. "Prudent. Your father would approve that, I believe."

The two smiled at each other, but they were brief, tight smiles. More in mutual support than self-satisfaction, Sara thought.

She continued, changing the subject. "We should all rest now so we might wake early. There may be word of your father come the morrow and we must be clear of mind." She turned to Nan. "I will walk with you to your chamber."

For the first time, Nan's pluck abandoned her and she appeared truly uncertain. Her worried gaze flew to her brother.

"Nan stays here," he declared calmly, but Sara sensed his apprehension. He feared she would deny them the solace of each other's company in this troubling time. "Father charged me to look after my sister when he left us last. She will sleep upon the trundle." He pointed down to indicate the servant's cot slid beneath the bed where they sat.

Sara had already sent Berta to her new pallet in the hall in order to speak privately with the children. Now she felt loathe to leave them alone. They were unused to this place and far from the only home they knew. Despite the bravery both of them exhibited, she knew they must be terrified of what the morrow would bring. She certainly was.

What courageous little souls they were. It had taken every whit of her own energy to keep from flying apart in the face of this day. How hard it must be for Nan and Christopher, especially now that darkness had fallen.

She joined them on the bed, sitting only a little way apart from them. Richard's admonition about making a servant of Nan rang in her head. The trundle was there for that purpose, to allow an attendant to sleep nearby. Well, they must make do, she supposed, but Nan should not sleep there. What if the girl told Richard when he came home that Sara had ordered it so? Despite the circumstances, he might resent it.

*If* he came home. She must believe that he would.

"Would you mind if Nan and I took the bed, Chris? Surely, as a future knight, you would grant us women the comfort of it. Will you take the trundle in Nan's stead?"

Both sighed with obvious relief even as Christopher gave his shrug of assent. They no more wanted to spend this night alone than did she.

"Let us have prayers for your father, then," she suggested. "Then we will sleep."

Surprised when they did not object at all, Sara felt a swell of relief. She felt almost like a mother already.

But that relief did not salve her real worry at all. Her new children might find themselves fatherless when tomorrow dawned.

Richard remained patient as the hours wore on. Sara would need time to gather the ransom and deliver it. He could not expect a release overnight.

Hunger pains gnawed at him and his thirst grew unbearable. The tainted water tempted him, but he resisted the urge to drink it. Though exhausted by the exertion of fighting and pained by his injuries, he fought sleep. With this infernal darkness, he would lose all sense of time.

He felt feverish. The rank, moldy odor in the airless cell made his empty stomach roil. Wadding the old blanket to pad the stones, he sat upon it and leaned against the damp wall.

Doubt crept in to keep him company. Would Sara pay to free him after all? Why should she? Upon recalling their conversations, he could not think of a single reason why she would.

She must have realized by this time what a poor choice of husbands she had made. All she need do was leave him here to die in this godforsaken place and choose another.

*No!* He would not believe that of Sara. True, she had tricked him into the marriage, but did that not mean she wanted *him* and no other? She *had,* but mayhap not now. At the time, she hadn't known how unwilling and surly he would be. Yes, surly. He had to admit he had behaved abominably. His reasons for that seemed pettish now, unchivalrous and mean.

All she had wanted was his protection from the Scots. And a child. God help him, he had failed her on both counts. Her second request, he had denied out of foolish pride. However, if he *had* granted that last wish, he would never be free of her.

But did he want to be?

Despite his intentions, he soon slept as though drugged. And when he awoke, doubt sat there waiting to assault him again. Would Sara pay? And was the man demanding the payment his brother?

Now that he had slept, he had only a fair notion of how long he had been shut up. Captured yestermorn, held overnight and well into the next day, he thought, judging by his thirst and hunger. No one had brought any food and his belly cramped unmercifully. He decided to chance drinking a bit of the water and hope he would not sicken from it.

What must have been hours later, the two guards who had brought him to this place returned. They blindfolded him again, bound his hands in front of him. The front was a good sign for they must intend for him to ride. Then they drew him to his feet, each holding one of his arms in a tight grip. He had allowed the binding, assuming the ransom had been paid and that they were about to release him.

Then his captor entered the cell, spurs scraping the stones.

"Well, look at you!," the man said, laughing. "Not so fine a knight today, eh? More like a beggar. What would the king think to see you brought so low? Not to mention your lady wife. Though I'll wager she'd be surprised to see you in any guise."

Richard raised his bound hands to the blindfold.

"Remove that and you will die here," the man assured him.

"The ransom?" Richard asked before he could stop himself.

Again, that nasty laughter. "The lady paid only half. I should kill you now and be done with it, but unlike her, I've decided to show mercy." He paused. "This time."

Richard ground his teeth. He wanted nothing more than to break his bonds and then this devil's neck. After that, he would take care of that wife of his. Half, indeed! Sara *must* want him dead. Or could it be that her coffers were short of gold? For her sake, he hoped that was the case.

As though the man could read minds, he addressed Richard's thoughts. "Sara of Fernstowe is a wily one, make no mistake. By delivering a portion of the ransom, she can tell the king she made the effort to reclaim you. Yet she knows it is not enough to save your hide. Devious, eh?"

He prowled the cell restlessly. Richard could hear the scuff of shoes on the rough stones. "However, I do not

choose to involve myself in fratricide at the moment. I will
release you. On condition.''

Richard checked a sigh of relief. ''And that is?''

''I require your word the rest of the ransom will be
forthcoming when you return to Fernstowe. In fact, I demand a like amount each quarter. Two hundred marks, left
in the same spot, at the tree line on the Scots side of the
meadow. Any attempt to apprehend or question the one
who retrieves it will prove fatal. No one outside the boundaries of Fernstowe's outer wall will be safe if you interfere
with my man. I will kill them all. Every one, and all their
beasts as well.''

''Two hundred per quarter? That's madness!'' Richard
exclaimed.

''Refuse me and I shall salt your lands and slay everyone and everything you own. Pay, and we shall leave you
be, you and yours. Agreed?''

Richard pretended to consider it. If he refused outright,
he knew he would die without seeing the light of day
again. If he made the promise, then he would have to keep
it. A vow was a vow, even one made to a madman.

He allowed himself to sigh as though defeated. Then he
turned to the sound of his captor's voice and nodded once.
''I vow that I will deliver what is due you as soon as is
humanly possible. And I'll not detain your courier when
he comes to collect. Will you grant time to arrange for the
payment?''

''You have exactly a fortnight, no more. On Friday after
next, you will pay, or else suffer the consequences. Now
our business is concluded.''

The devil addressed one of the men holding Richard.
''Alfred? See that Sir Richard is returned to Fernstowe as
was his man. You may exact the toll for your brother's
death at his hand if you wish, but do leave this good fellow
alive. I cannot collect from a corpse, now can I?''

The minion chuckled with delight.

"Give my regards to your lady when you see her," his captor said. "Tell her the ploy to get rid of you was masterful, even though it did fail." He laughed madly as he turned and left the cell.

A meaty fist to the midsection doubled Richard over, but he'd expected it. He immediately brought his clasped hands hard up beneath the man's chin, then kicked out and connected with something he thought was a knee. A powerful blow to the back felled him, but he rolled, kicked again and sent one dolt sailing. He snatched off the blindfold, but the other man fell upon him then, obstructing his sight and pinning him to the floor. A sudden clout to the side of his head and the world went black.

When he came to, his eyes were covered again. The two oafs he had scuffled with in the cell were lifting him to a saddle. He grasped the pommel and shook his head to clear it.

Just as his feet found the stirrups and he secured his seat, one of the men planted a fist in his face. Richard tasted blood. A loud slap to his horse's rump warned him to hang on. It reared and set out at a frantic gallop.

By the time Richard settled the startled mount to a trot, he realized he was riding alone.

He released the pommel, pulled down the cloth that obscured his vision and tried to judge his whereabouts. Behind him lay the Meadow of Dispute.

*Cursed place,* he thought darkly, as he tugged left on the reins and headed toward Fernstowe.


"He comes! He comes!" shouted keen-eyed Fergus, leaping up and down and pointing out between the merlons. A number of men had been standing watch on all sides of battlements since the ransom had been delivered.

Sara and the children had walked the wall themselves

for most of the day, eyes trained upon the north road in anxious expectation.

She could see the steed now, and though it was not Richard's destrier, it was one of Fernstowe's own, one of those missing since the injured men had come home long after Newson. A rider clung to it, bent over as though injured, fists tangled in the mane.

"Ride out and assist him," Sara shouted to the two knights Richard's father had sent with the children. "Bring him around and in through the sally port. In case the Scots are nearby, we'll not open the main gates."

She rushed across the ward to the small, stout door set into the back wall, an opening just large enough to admit one man and horse. Christopher and Nan flanked her as she ran. Their short legs worked furiously to keep pace with her much longer strides.

They stopped and waited by the open portal like sentinels, silent until Richard and the two knights came into view at last.

"Papa's hurt!" Nan screamed, and dashed outside. Christopher lunged, grabbed the back of her gown and hauled her back. Both landed in the dirt, arms and legs flailing.

"Goose! They'll trample you flat!" Chris cried, wrestling Nan to keep her on the ground.

"Let go of me, you bleatin' goat!" Nan hollered, landing a fist on Chris's chin. Doggedly he held on to her skirts.

"Right yourselves *at once* and make ready to greet your sire!" Sara demanded while she untangled and held them at arm's length. "Mind me *now!*"

Both glared, sniffed and pouted, but began brushing at their clothes and running hands through their hair. By the time the riders approached, they looked fairly presentable. And sorely worried.

They had good cause to worry. Blood trickled from his nose and one corner of his mouth. It covered Richard's lower face and had soaked the breast of his filthy surcoat. He attempted to speak, but it seemed beyond his power. God help them if he was bleeding from the inside where she could not reach to heal him.

"Take him to my solar," she ordered the men. The children looked dumbstruck, as horribly frightened as she was herself. She had to remove them somehow so she could think only of Richard's care.

"Nan, hurry and find Berta. Have her fetch my basket of medicaments. Chris, to the kitchens. Tell cook we need hot water and the tub brought down. Then go to your father's chamber for fresh clothing, his bed gown will do. Bring his special soap. Make *haste!*" She shooed them about the errands.

Sara walked beside the horses, easily keeping pace, but unable to reach Richard and determine the extent of his injuries. They moved slowly so as not to jar him unnecessarily.

"How bad, do you think?" she inquired of Sir Edmund, who rode to Richard's left, supporting him with one hand so he would not fall.

"Not so good, my lady," Edmund answered. "Barely conscious."

"But alive," Richard grunted angrily. "More than you bargained for, eh, *wife?*" He shifted slightly in the saddle and grimaced. "You will...pay for this," he gasped.

Sara stiffened at the accusation and warning. Did Richard believe her responsible? Here was not the place to argue about it, not in front of his men, and not when he could hardly draw breath to speak.

Edmund clucked to the horses and walked them a little faster. He obviously did not intend to take sides in this, nor did she want him to.

Sara thanked God Richard was coherent enough to say anything at all, even if it was not something she wished to hear.

The knights assisted Richard down from the horse and half dragged him up the steps to the hall and on to Sara's solar. Berta had a thick, soft pallet readied beside the fire.

Chris and Nan hovered nervously while the knights placed their father on the makeshift bed. Then the men stood aside awaiting further instructions.

"Papa?" Nan whispered. She dropped to her knees beside Richard and gently touched his swollen cheek with one finger. Chris yanked her hand away and she let him. "You fought them hard, Papa?" she asked softly.

"Yes, sweeting," he said, reaching out to find her hand. "Chris? Lean closer so I may see you. Both of you...well?"

Sara, kneeling on his other side, heard his breath catch and watched him wince. "Hardly *well,* husband. They fear you are dying. We must show them you are not."

She smiled at the children. "He will be fine. You two go with Berta into the hall and wait. We will see to your papa's hurts and then you may visit with him."

When they started to object, she guided them away from him. "Do as I say and he will be the better for it." Sara dropped a hurried kiss on each head. "I will not let him die, I promise you that on my soul. Go now."

Reluctantly, the two left with Berta. They peered over their shoulders as they went, obviously trying hard to banish their doubts and trust their father's life to a woman they scarcely knew.

"Sara—"

"Hush," she demanded. "If you've a bone to pick with me, husband, do it later when you have the breath for it. Is anything broken?"

"Ribs, mayhap," he rasped. "Nose?"

Sara gingerly felt his ribs and then his nose. "Badly bruised, but not broken. The nose could be cracked, but it should heal straight. Open your mouth."

To her surprise, he did as she asked. A cut on the inside of his cheek accounted for the blood loss from the mouth. Sara nearly fainted with relief.

The nosebleed must have caused most of the gore. She had feared a broken rib might have punctured his lung. She sat back on her heels and covered her eyes with one hand, offering a hasty prayer of thanks.

"Undress him," she ordered Sir Edmund. "A hot bath will help, and then I will bind his ribs. I believe they are sound, but I could be wrong."

Richard grabbed her arm, his grip surprisingly strong. "Why, Sara? Why did you only pay half?"

"What?"

"The ransom," he muttered from behind gritted teeth.

Shocked speechless, she looked from Richard to Sir Edmund and back again.

"She paid all, sir," Edmund said. "I saw the demand myself. I carried the gold and placed it where they said. 'Twas the full amount, in truth, I swear."

Richard closed his eyes and pressed his lips together hard as if enduring a harsher wave of pain. Then he cursed the Scot, whispering a string of words Sara thought might scorch her ears ere he was done.

He finally ended the tirade and addressed her, his voice still brusque and angry as ever. "I was wrong...about everything. About...you...the marriage—"

Sara chuckled and shook her head. "Poor fellow. They beat the charm right out of you, didn't they? I mean to say, before this you were so courteous! So gallant I could hardly stand you. But now, so gruffly wooing!"

"Hush," he gasped. "Do not make me laugh."

"Hurts, does it?" she asked, grinning. "Let's get you

well, then. We have some debts to pay across the border, and I do not speak of gold. We will see if you can match actions to those nasty words of yours. Sir Edmund? Disrobe him now and let us get him clean. Those hellions of his will not wait long to see whether—''

*"Hellions?"* Richard demanded, his voice much stronger than before. Sara had to grab his shoulders to keep him from rising.

"A jest, Richard, merely a poor jest," she assured him with a kindly pat. "They are truly the most wonderful children ever born. I dote on them, I do. And they on me. We are in perfect accord, Nan, Chris and I."

Sir Edmund scoffed and Sara shot him a threatening glare. He cleared his throat. "Accord's the word, sir. Perfect accord, the three of 'em."

Richard lay back, apparently mollified for the moment, and allowed himself to be tended.

Sara watched, trying not to sigh too noticeably as the older knight bared the body of the man she wanted above everything in the world. The Scots had pummeled him unmercifully, but he would heal.

She hugged herself with relief. Richard would recover soon. They would begin afresh, this time with an understanding that theirs would be a real marriage. Surely that was what he'd meant when he said he was wrong.

# Chapter Eight

Nothing much could be done this day to settle matters, so Richard lay abed for the duration of it. In all truth, he had sustained worse injuries in tournaments and gone on about his business as though nothing was amiss.

The bruised ribs pained him, of course, but he doubted they were broken as he first believed. His body would heal without all of this coddling. His face looked a fright with a blackened eye and the swelling of his nose and cheek. That also would return to normal in due course.

But he liked Sara and the children fluttering about him the way they did, so he remained where he was and thoroughly enjoyed the comfort of it.

Once Sara had bound the ribs with strips of linen, Edmund had helped him to his chamber. If Richard had expected solitude there, he certainly hadn't gotten more than a scant few moments of it after Edmund left.

Ensconced in the large poster bed, he gladly endured Sara's cold compresses on his face and Nan's awkward attempt at grooming his hair. Christopher stood by with a tasty potion in a spouted sickling cup and dosed him regularly.

Twice, he had nearly died in service to the king. Not

even the royal physicians had tended him with such zeal as did Sara and the children.

He recalled some of Sara's later efforts when he'd been wounded by that arrow, but had been too furious about her news of their wedding to appreciate them at the time. She had saved his life, and he had been worse than obnoxious to her.

"Hop down off the bed now, Nan," Sara said, smiling at his daughter. "Your wriggling about shifts the mattress."

"No, I'm not finished," Nan argued, plying the wooden comb with added enthusiasm. It tangled in his hair and Richard stifled a yelp.

Christopher lunged forward to drag his sister off the bed and spilled the cup of medicine all over Richard's arm.

Sara grabbed a struggling child beneath each arm and set them on their feet a safe distance away. He marveled at her strength of arm and purpose. Would she punish them?

To Richard's amazement, she kissed them soundly on their cheeks instead, one after the other before she turned loose of them. He watched her walk them toward the door, her hands guiding them by their shoulders.

"What a fine job you have done, both of you!" she said proudly. "Now your father needs you to see to his things while he has a good sleep. Nan, you go and tell the laundress to soak his surcoat and gambeson in cold water to remove the blood. Chris, you must act squire and check his mail for damaged links so that we can point them out for repair. I will meet you in the hall in two hours so that we may plan for tomorrow's duties."

Richard felt burgeoning admiration for his wife's mothering of them. "Well-done of you," he remarked after the children had rushed out to obey her.

She laughed merrily as she returned to the bed, took up

a linen napkin and began wiping up the potion Christopher had spilled. "They were about to kill you with kindness. But they needed to be near you awhile. To see that you would live."

"And I wanted them here. Thank you for allowing it, Sara. Most women would have shoved them out immediately."

Her ready smile warmed him. "I have no notion of what's proper in this instance. My own mother never attended a sickroom. Nor did she favor children about her in any case."

"Why did she leave?" he asked. "You were no longer a child, but a woman grown when your father died."

"I cannot say for certain why she wanted to go. We were not close. I think she was always unhappy here. Father loved her well, but she only tolerated him. I disappointed her, of course."

"You disappointed *her?* She is the one who left you here to preside all alone. In your grief," Richard snapped, his contempt for noblewomen reaffirmed. Hopefully, Sara had learned what *not* to do, by her mother's poor example.

Sara sat carefully on the edge of the bed and busied herself straightening the covers over his legs. "I acted as chatelaine long before Father died. Without those chores, grief would have consumed me."

Richard sighed and closed his eyes. His wife confused him at every turn. By rights, she should be furious that he had accused her of betraying him in the matter of the ransom when she had not. She should be soliciting his sympathy for the hardships of managing Fernstowe without help. And she should resent the intrusion of his unruly children in her life, especially the baseborn Nan. Yet she did none of those things.

How would she cope if he did leave her once he had settled the matter of the Scots? Admirably, he suspected.

Sara would accept the annulment the king had offered him and hold her head high, ignoring the disgrace.

And she would believe he had set her aside because he found her unattractive, scarred, too tall and in no way appealing. Despite her determined show of self-confidence, Sara saw herself that way. Richard could not envision hurting her so, even if it meant relinquishing his freedom forever.

At the moment, marriage did not seem all that confining. Certainly not as it had before.

"I find that I quite like you, Sara," he said aloud without thinking to do so.

She leaned toward him and took his hand in hers. "Because I have you at my mercy," she said, teasing.

Richard smiled at her foolery. "There is that." He turned his hand palm up and grasped hers. "I must trust you with something. Can you keep it between us?"

"A secret will remain with me," she answered seriously.

In this, he did not doubt her. "I do not believe the man who captured me is the one called Alan the True."

She frowned. "Why ever not? The message came from him. He was there to meet you."

Richard still felt reluctant to tell her of his kinship with Alan, but he must determine the identity of the man who would extort riches from them and threaten Fernstowe's people.

"First of all, he did not speak as a Scot."

She shrugged. "Many border Scots sound the same as we do, especially if they are well educated. That is not significant."

"He wore his helm when we rode out to meet. After my capture, he had my eyes covered. Still, I believe this man is too young to be Sir Alan. Judging by his build and his voice, my captor is not more than thirty, I would guess. The Scot is nigh fifty years of age,'' Richard said.

"How do you know this?" she demanded, still frowning. Her color had heightened with excitement. The scar stood out like a thin ivory line, beckoning his finger to trace its length. He barely resisted. "What else do you know of him?" she demanded.

Certainly more than he would tell her at the moment, Richard thought. "Never mind that now. He wants a like amount of gold delivered in a fortnight."

"What!" she exclaimed, her body stiffening with outrage.

"And that much again each quarter day as surety against attack."

"Damn him straight to hell! He'll not have it!"

Richard grinned, painful as it was to do it. "No, he shall not. I mean to rid you of that scourge as soon as I can ride again."

She disentangled her hand from his and slipped off the bed. "You rest. I must speak to Sir Edmund and the men."

"Wait!" Richard ordered. "No need to— "

"No need?" She rounded on him and began pacing beside the bed. "We'll find that cursed keep of Byelough and wipe out the lot of them."

"Sara—"

She stopped and shook a finger for emphasis. "They have murdered my father, nearly killed my husband and now they would beggar our estate? I have had *enough!*"

"Hot rage will not serve," he said firmly. "We will do this together. When the time is right."

She clasped her arms beneath her breasts. Her chest rose and fell with each harsh breath as she fought to tame her fury. With fingers clenched upon her elbows, she stopped pacing. At last she nodded reluctantly and agreed. "As you will then. When the time is right."

"Friends?" he asked, raising his hand with the offer.

She marched toward him and took it, the clasp of comrades before a battle. "Friends."

Richard felt the uncommon power in her grip. He saw the fervent determination in her eyes. And a wave of the strongest lust he had ever felt for a woman rushed through him on the instant. Freedom be damned. He wanted this woman and he knew without a doubt she wanted him.

Desire quivered between them like a living, breathing entity that would not be dismissed. Somehow, Richard could no longer imagine Sara lying passive, listless and merely yielding beneath him.

"Not yet," he whispered, determined to do her justice when they did succumb.

Her lips stretched into a wide, provocative smile and she caught her bottom lip between her teeth for just an instant. The small gesture stirred him like a hot hand on his body.

She raked his entire length with a slumberous gaze and undoubtedly noticed his aroused condition. One perfect eyebrow rose in gentle mockery. "As you will."

Richard groaned deeply as the door closed behind her and it had nothing whatsoever to do with the pain in his side.

The next morning, as Sara directed the laying out of the morning meal, she saw Richard descend the stair, cross the hall and head out of doors. He wore no mail or weapon save a short sword, so he obviously did not intend to ride out.

He moved carefully, as though determined not to favor his injuries by limping or listing to one side.

She raised her hand in salute. He nodded acknowledgment and smiled. Not an invitation to join him on his morning jaunt, but good sign, nevertheless, she thought.

Apparently, he did not intend to regain his strength by lying in bed all day. She approved his decision, since she now knew he had no terrible wounds requiring that. She turned and contented herself with seeing the food properly arranged.

As was custom when no guests were present, no one sat for the morning repast. A single table was set up, supplied with trays of bread, meats and cheese. Residents wandered in as they began their day, helped themselves and then went about their duties.

Sara chatted with Berta as they ate. "The children are settling in. Making themselves at home in the kitchens, I notice."

"Ach, those two! Dearlings, they are, but they are a double handful, my lady," Berta said as she chewed. "They are harrying cook this morn to make marzipan. Say they got it every day back home."

Sara laughed. "Could be that's so, but I doubt it."

The two scampered in then, each wearing a goat's milk mustache. "Good morn to you both," Sara called.

They gave no answer as they marched quickly past her to welcome their father, who was returning from outside. When they reached him, they stopped abruptly. Christopher bowed and Nan curtsied.

Gone was the openness they had shown toward him when he lay abed, injured and in need of care. Today they approached him as one might the king. She had not expected this, but apparently it was their usual way.

Though she smiled as the three approached the table, Sara reflected on how formally Richard dealt with the children. He had clasped hands with Christopher as he might a comrade, then patted Nan once on her fiery curls.

They followed him like pups, matching their short

strides to his long ones, looking up at him and longing for his approval. Did he not see?

Sara noticed that neither had acquired the easy way she'd had with her own father. He offered no teasing, no swinging around in the air, no hand on the shoulders to mark how glad he was to see them.

Nan did not employ the nonstop chatter and boisterous affection she displayed toward her brother. Christopher acted even more adult than usual.

Both needed hugging and praise and a father's loving jests. Yet he seemed aloof, some sort of godlike figure they adored above anything but were afraid to embrace. Judging by their behavior toward him just now, she suspected the three were not as close as they should be.

Unless Richard's present mood was not his usual way with them, Sara clearly saw her mission. Richard needed frequent embracing as much as did his children.

His reserve had cracked a bit when he had come home injured yesterday. Sara had seen the overwhelming love in his eyes for Nan and Christopher as they worried over and tended him. Yet even then, she recalled how he held himself apart, allowing them near as though it was a one-time occasion.

Even if Richard never learned to love *her,* Sara meant to leave no doubt in the children's minds how much he cared for them.

"Welladay," She greeted him, smiling. "You are looking much improved."

"Go with your nurse and finish eating," he ordered Nan and Chris, not unkindly, yet firmly.

Though reluctant, they allowed Berta to herd them out of earshot without argument.

Richard helped himself to a chunk of bread and a slice of cheese, stacking them neatly so that he could reach for a cup of ale.

"Come, let's go to the solar," Sara suggested. "It will be warmer there and you can sit down. Do your ribs still ache?"

"Some, but at least they are not broken. Have you eaten?"

"While you were out. Is something amiss?" she asked as they strolled toward the smaller room. "You seem troubled."

He grunted in agreement. "With good reason. But the ransom issue will go begging today I am better, but not yet ready to make a war."

"Wise of you," Sara agreed, relieved that he would wait on that. She took her chair before the fire and waited until he joined her to suggest a topic for conversation. "We should speak of the children."

Richard looked heavenward and shook his head. "What have they done now? You might as well tell me."

"Not a thing they shouldn't, but I—"

"Then let's not borrow trouble, eh?" He smiled winningly, abruptly casting aside his dour mood. "What I'd really like is to know more about you."

She had not expected this. "What would you hear?"

He hesitated a moment, filling the time by sipping his ale and perusing her face. "Why don't you tell me how you got the scar?"

Sara almost dropped her cup. Her free hand flew to cover the side of her face. No one ever asked her that. They pretended not to notice or frowned with pity and turned away. But they never asked.

"Come now," he said, still smiling, "do not hide it. You seem to think it detracts from your beauty. It does not, you know. If anything, it adds character to what might otherwise be but a lovely face."

Sara was appalled that he would show such callous disregard for her feelings. "Why do you mock me?" she whispered.

"Mock you?" he asked, a picture of disbelief. Slowly he leaned forward as though he might attempt to touch her. "I would never do such a thing, Sara. But truly, you make too much of it."

He sighed. "If it distresses you to tell me, then do not. But I confess I do wish to know what happened. Shall we trade tales of valor? Just here," he said, bumping his thigh with one elbow, "I caught a blade to the bone. Almost lost the leg. Now that," he said wryly, "is a truly ugly scar. Yours is not. I find it...intriguing."

Sara let out the breath she'd been holding and stared into the low-burning fire. Why not confess it? What did it matter now who knew?

"A man who wanted to wed me marked my face. I had my father refuse the betrothal. My suitor said, as he did this, that no other man would have me so disfigured. That I would have to wed him after all."

Richard remained silent for a time. She could feel him looking at her, feeling sorry for her maiming. Sara hated pity, but she endured it, just as she had from others.

"How old were you," he asked, his voice deceptively light.

"Fourteen," she replied. "He had applied to Father for my hand. I refused, as was my right. He was angry."

"Your father killed him, of course," Richard said, taking a bite of his cheese.

He was attempting to act naturally, Sara knew, as though they spoke of nothing consequential. Mayhap to him it was not, but she suspected he felt rather strongly about the matter. She hoped he might, for that would mean he cared about her.

"I never admitted to Father who did it. I feared it would cause trouble between the families. Mayhap a small war."

Sara forced a laugh. "That sounds as though I felt dreadfully important. But you see, I was an only child. My father loved me well and might have sought revenge."

"Well he should have," Richard agreed. "I certainly would." He finished his food and washed it down with the rest of his ale. Carefully he set the cup on the floor beside his chair. Without looking at her, he asked, almost idly, "What was his name, this fellow handy with the blade?"

Sara was no fool. She smiled to herself, treasuring this attempt Richard was making to avenge her, even as she refused to let him. "You will never know it. That secret will go with me to my grave."

His gaze met hers and burned with all the fury he had been hiding. But she knew well that the anger was not for her.

"I dealt near as good as I got," she said, hoping to placate him, "so do not see me as some faint heart, weeping into my sleeve."

Sara warmed to the story no one else had heard from her lips. "You see, I had sneaked my pony out the sally port to ride alone. Not a wise move, I do admit. I fell asleep by the stream while my pony grazed nearby. That blackguard came upon me and carved me up ere I came awake."

"Good Lord," Richard whispered, grabbing her hand as though to comfort the child she had been. "What then?"

Sara shrugged. "My blood frightened me witless. I thought I would surely die from loss of it. And there the fool was, sheathing his wicked knife and threatening me with lack of a husband. As if I cared to marry! I would shortly be dead!"

She laughed at the memory, knowing it got better. "So angered I was that he'd killed me, I grabbed my eating knife from my belt and lunged for his eye."

"Took it out, I hope!" He squeezed her hands so hard, Sara felt the bones grind.

"Almost! I thought as much and so did he. Now, by this time, prudence suggested I run home to do my dying, and so I did."

"Oh, Sara, Sara!" Richard grasped her head with both hands and kissed her on the mouth.

A benediction. A blessing for her bravery, though she had not been brave at all, just foolhardy and mad as the devil. Her lips smiled beneath his.

When he backed away, he still held her head, his fingers laced through her hair. His gaze burned into hers for the longest time.

Then tenderly, he lay his mouth upon the thin, white line and traced it with his lips. "A wondrous mark of valor," he whispered against her face. "Wear it proudly. Always. Each time I look upon it, I will remember how courageous you are."

Sara's heart swelled with happiness. Richard did not mind. He did not mind the scar. He had kissed it. And even now he was looking upon it as though it pleased him. She smiled into his eyes. "Thank you."

"I did nothing." He moved away from her then and stood, hooking his thumbs in his belt as he walked over to the window. "Tell me, did you ever see him again?"

"Yes, years later," Sara admitted. "He still has the eye, for my blade missed the mark."

Richard swerved around to face her. With the morning sunlight behind him, she could not see his features, but his stance looked determined. "Tell me his name, Sara. I *must* know it."

"No, Richard," she replied, every bit as determined as he. "You must not."

Moments passed as neither moved or spoke. Sara

thought he would grow more demanding and press her for an answer.

Instead he broke the silence gently. "I would avenge you for the hurt, Sara."

"I know and I thank you for it, but there is no need. The man is no danger to me now."

"He may be more of a threat than you know. He might have held a grudge against your father for turning away his proposal. Suppose he killed Lord Simon and is the one behind all this trouble."

Sara sucked in a breath of disbelief. "Impossible. It could not possibly be him!"

"Why not?"

"Because the man I spoke of is not the Scot!"

"That is my point, Sara. Every man with a reason to slay your father and hate you is suspect. Give me the name."

"Never," she swore again. "Why are you so set upon proving the man who has done all these things is not Alan the True?"

"When you have a name for me, let me know," he said as he headed for the door. "Now, if you will excuse me, I should be about the day."

Sara fairly leaped out of her chair. "You come back here. We are not finished," she demanded.

Richard turned and smiled. "Thank you for reminding me."

He crossed the distance between them, moving so quickly she had no time to retreat. Before she realized what he was about, he embraced her and kissed her so soundly her head spun.

One of his large hands caressed the back of her neck while the other pressed her lower body flush against his own. His tongue invaded her mouth and she surrendered to the unique sensation.

Just as she began to savor his taste and respond in kind, he released her. She clung to the front of his tunic where he had trapped her hands between their bodies.

He reached up and gently freed himself, his fingers and palms hot against the backs of her fists. "Good day, my lady fair," he said, raising her knuckles to his lips in a gentle, final salute.

She stood there, wits cast to the winds, and watched him go.

"Lord grant me mercy!" she mumbled, fanning herself with one hand. She dropped back into her chair, her entire body humming still.

Sara clenched her eyes shut and relived that kiss, her first involving such definite promise of things to come.

"Grant mercy *tonight,*" she whispered for good measure.

# Chapter Nine

Sara thought this might be the longest day she had ever spent. Richard had teased her with his presence a number of times, always smiling confidently, making her wonder what would happen once they were alone.

He joined her to observe the children's first lessons under her tutelage, though he spoke little during the session. They shared the noon meal, and later he returned to the hall to collect Christopher for a short lesson in swordsmanship. At Sara's insistence, he reluctantly included Nan.

Other than the engaging smile he offered, Richard behaved as though nothing had passed between them that morn. Apparently he found enough going on about him to provide distraction. Not so with her.

Yet Richard said or did nothing further to indicate that he would follow through with what he'd begun with that rousing kiss of his.

Either the man had completely forgotten the moment, or now he expected her to suggest they take things further. Would that be seemly?

Sara seriously considered it and then decided that he might not feel well enough yet to pursue the matter past kissing. Last evening he had said "not yet." Or he could have changed his mind altogether, in which case she would not court humiliation any more than she already had.

It vexed her that he could kiss her senseless, and then calmly walk away. Mayhap she should simply put the entire matter aside for now as he seemed inclined to do.

Being mother to his children presented enough challenge at the moment. The trick was keeping them busy and making their efforts seem important. Only rarely did she need to resort to an outright command. They were headstrong and a bit spoiled, yes, but affectionate and eager enough to please.

Richard had watched with apparent interest how she dealt with the children. And she had observed him in like manner. Not once had he bade Nan or Chris to do—or for that matter, to cease doing—anything. Whatever they did seemed to suit him well whether their actions were appropriate or not.

In fact, he acted as though he had never had anything to do with their upbringing. 'Twas possible, she supposed, for he must have traveled on progress with the court much of the time.

As they sat together at supper that evening, she questioned him. "You are remarkably tolerant of Nan and Christopher's behavior. As their father, I would think you'd exert more...direction."

"Discipline, you mean," he replied, calmly slicing a portion of lamb into bite-size morsels. "No, I shall leave that to you."

Sara inclined her head toward Christopher, who had wandered away when he should have been serving wine to those seated on the dais.

"I hate to play the wicked stepmother, but I shall have to reprimand him yet again. He acts as though he is merely doing me a gracious favor by carrying that flagon about."

Richard chuckled and tore off a piece of his bread.

"Chris is unused to serving, that's for certain. But it is my lady's duty to train the pages."

"I shall cut short his sword practice as penance," she warned, knowing Richard probably enjoyed the weapons training he had begun as much as the children did. Sara admitted she had a mind to punish her husband a bit for his indifference, both toward his children and her.

Richard reached for her hand, which lay on the table between them. "Why not send him to bed early instead? Nan, too, for she plagues Mistress Berta even now." He nodded toward the lower table set at right angle to their own.

Sara glanced toward Nan and the nurse. Berta's admonishing gesture toward the shared trencher, and the girl's mulish expression indicated a whispered argument over food.

"She's refusing to eat her beans," Sara guessed, thinking back to her own childhood transgressions at table.

"A right horrid offense, surely," Richard commented. "I mislike beans as well. See, I have left mine all untouched."

Sara glanced down at the trencher and frowned at him with pretended rebuke. "So you have, you wasteful lad."

"Will you put me to bed early then?" he asked with a grin.

A playful suggestion it was, so unexpected and so utterly unlike Richard, Sara could scarcely believe he had said what he'd said.

His hand tightened around hers, his thumb caressing her palm. She clearly understood the question he had really put to her. The question she desired above all to answer.

"You beg a punishment for this naughtiness?" she asked primly.

He grinned. "I beg an undeserved dessert, my sweet."

"A tart, mayhap?" she asked, suppressing her laughter.

She saw she had shocked him. He very nearly blushed, but still wore the smile. Sara was entranced that a full-grown man would color at so mild a play on words.

He cleared his throat and released her hand. "My chamber, then? Or yours?"

"Yours," she answered without hesitation. "In one hour."

He frowned. She hoped it was the delay he objected to.

"Prayers," she explained. "Nan and Chris will want those. And a tale to make good dreams, as well. Would you join us?"

"No," he said, avoiding her eyes and returning his attention to his food, though she noticed he did not eat. "Come when you are ready."

"When I am *ready?*" Sara reached out and fondly pressed his arm as she got up from her chair. "A mother's duty calls, else I would race you to the stair," she whispered.

His look of pure astonishment made her laugh with delight as she went to collect the children for bedtime.

Richard poured himself another cup of wine as he awaited Sara in his bedchamber. Her response to his banter confused him. He had not thought for a moment that she would refuse his invitation, but he had expected a show of shyness, for form's sake if nothing else.

Women should never admit to eagerness, he thought with a shake of his head. They had to know they lost the advantage once they abandoned their role of the pursued. That was why it was called *bestowing favors*. How could they make any demands of a man if they gave all so freely? Had her mother taught her nothing? In all truth, he hoped not. And yet, her unusual behavior troubled him because he did not understand it.

Should he greet her in bed, already disrobed? Or should

he wait, offer her wine to soothe her fears and then undress them both?

Hell, one would think *he* was the terrified virgin here. Nothing had prepared him for dealing with this wife of his.

Was Sara as inclined toward this as she sounded? She certainly showed none of the trepidation a woman should show in facing a first encounter with intimacy. Or any encounter with it, judging by his first wife.

In truth, she acted more like Annie Causey than Evaline. Yet even the sprightly Annie—certainly no virgin at the time—had shown some hesitancy their first time together. And decorum, as well. Sara had shown little of either tonight. Nor had she ever. Richard suspected she was a law unto herself.

He must decide how to begin this, for the candle had burned almost an hour down. Soon she would arrive and find him pacing like some timid, untried lad. That, he most assuredly was not.

Though he had become much more circumspect since his unfortunate marriage, Richard could not count the number of women who had shared his bed after he came of an age for it. And not one of them had been anything like Sara. She was nobly born, yet did not behave like any of that ilk he had ever known. Nor was she common in any way, except mayhap in her forwardness.

"Richard?" came the mellifluent greeting from the doorway. "I am come." He loved her voice.

"So I see," he replied, trying to sound unaffected. "Enter, please." Feigning nonchalance, he sauntered toward the table by the window and refilled his cup. "Would you care for some wine?"

Her laughter sounded as shaky as he felt. "That would be most welcome. As many times as I have been here, I find this visit flusters me more than a little."

Richard smiled sincerely. Sara might be blunt, but at least she did not dissemble. "You are direct."

"Ever so," she said succinctly, accepting the wine and peering into the cup as though she sought something important inside it.

Then she looked up at him, almost reluctantly. "Are we agreed this is the right thing to do, Richard? Suddenly, I feel very guilty that I have pushed you to this point."

She had done exactly that, he thought. That might be what bothered him about it. He should have been the one to do so now that he'd decided to stay with her. Richard shrugged. "We are wed, Sara. 'Tis expected."

"But not desired?" she pressed. "If we do not...if we abstain, likely the king could be persuaded to...once you have made the border safe hereabouts, he might allow—"

"An annulment?" Richard supplied. "Yes. As a matter of fact, he offered that when he came."

Her mouth dropped open and she stared at him as though he were an apparition.

"I've rendered you speechless, I see," he said, still smiling. "An amazing feat, that. But, yes, Edward did say we might dissolve the marriage." He took the cup from her hand before she dropped it. "I refused."

"Why?" she asked, barely breathing the word.

Richard reached out and cupped her cheek, running his thumb over the scar she hated so. Since she had told him the story of it, the mark fascinated him even more. Her badge of courage.

"I want you," he whispered, losing himself in the dark gold of her eyes.

"Why?" No sound emerged. Only her lips moved.

"I think you know," he answered, sliding his arms around her and drawing her close. Embracing Sara felt inordinately natural, just as it had earlier in the day. Right, somehow.

The sweet, pure scent of her invaded his senses. Her softness settled against him in all the right places. He reveled in the sigh of pleasure that warmed the curve of his neck. "Because you are so beautiful. Because I desire you. Just because…"

He did not miss her almost inaudible hum of disbelief.

Instead of using words to convince her, he lowered his mouth to hers and employed all his powers of persuasion.

Surely no man had kissed her before him, leastwise not with passion and purpose. He could tell by her innocent response this morning, and especially now. Relief that he did truly excite her made him bolder than he might have been.

How sweet she tasted, how warm and willing, as he explored the depths of her mouth and coaxed her to reciprocate.

Suddenly her tentativeness disappeared altogether and she came alive in his arms, all impatience and energy. Richard hummed with surprise and with pleasure. Sheer, sharp and heady pleasure that shot through his body and heated his blood to a boil.

He raked up the hem of her surcoat and released her mouth only long enough to slip the heavy garment over her head. Again he kissed her, as madly and as deeply as he had ever kissed a woman.

She tugged at the fastening of his belt and he heard it drop to the floor behind him. Her hands dug into the front of his tunic. He whipped the thing off and tossed it aside.

"Everything," she gasped against his mouth. "I want to see you."

He cast off his sark while she pulled loose the points of the hose. All the while, he fought to hold her mouth captive with his.

His body burned for her. Ached with eagerness to have her, to make her his. When all his clothes lay scattered, he felt her hands upon him, felt the soft silken slide of her chemise against his skin.

"To bed," he growled, and scooped her up in his arms.

She laughed nervously and clung to his neck. "I am heavy! Do not drop me!"

"Light as thistledown," he muttered as he settled her on the mattress and followed, trailing kisses on whatever part of her he could reach. Her neck, her shoulder, the delicious curve of her breast.

She arched, offering more, and he fastened on the rosy tip, tugging it deeply into his mouth. Her moan swept through him, as much felt as heard, an echo of his own.

He must slow this madness, Richard thought, but he could not. She urged him on with lips and fingers and sinuous shifts of her hips against his.

Some ragged remnant of his mind warned him she needed gentleness, coaxing and soft words. His unruly body ignored the cautioning. It had been too long without.

"No," he groaned, lifting himself away from her, determined to do this the way it should be done.

"Yes," she hissed, grasping his hips and holding him against her. "Please."

Richard surrendered. With a growl of defeat and sweet victory, he brushed her chemise aside and guided himself home.

Her maidenhead gave way with the first thrust as she took him into her with a sharp cry of welcome. Her long fingers flexed on his hips, a sensation he thought might unman him on the instant.

"Wait," he gasped, attempting to hold her body still with the weight of his. But Sara would not have it. She pushed up with all her strength to take more. And Richard was lost.

Again and again he thrust, deeper and harder, absorbing

the heady feel of her inner muscles grasping, taking, giving.

Suddenly she tore her mouth from his and cried out his name in wonder. The shudders within her body demanded answer and he gave it, pouring himself into her with a wordless shout.

Unable to stir, other than to fight for breath, Richard pressed her into the soft mattress, his face buried in the silken curve of her neck. Her curls tickled his nose and cheek. The feel and the scent of her tickled his mind. He felt an urge to laugh aloud with joy, but had not the strength or breath for it.

Her purr of satisfaction went straight to his heart. Richard knew he should move off her, but was loath to leave her body. To think, he might have missed this altogether if he had decided to set her aside. Thank God, he had come to his senses. Or lost them completely. He was not certain which, and at the moment, did not care in the least.

With a major effort, he slid one hand up to her face and brushed the tangled hair aside so that he could see her features. Her lazy smile made him swell inside her when he should have been spent for the night.

What did a man say to such a woman? Rather, to such a wife? Had she been some trollop who'd set out to please him so, he would promise more coin than she asked. To a mistress, he would offer a special gift. But to a wife?

In truth, no woman at all had ever met him with such ardor or pleased him half so well.

He must have frowned, for she said, "Regrets already?"

That startled a laugh from him. "Regrets you would not credit. Regrets that we have wasted so much time."

Sara cradled his head with her hand and turned to kiss him softly on the forehead. "No more. You are mine now and I will not let you be sorry for it."

Her lower body rose invitingly beneath him as he grew

hard again inside her. He closed his eyes and savored the feeling. "Slowly, this time," he promised as he began to move. And she allowed it.

Dawn finally lighted the chamber just enough for Richard to see the silhouette of Sara's face as she slept. He wanted her once more. During the night, he had wakened her, but he would not do so again. Richard crossed his arms beneath his head and waited. He would not trouble her for other than a morning kiss, but neither would he leave her here in his bed to wake alone.

Her hand on his thigh startled him. He grasped it just in time to prevent an exploration of things best left undisturbed. "Sara!"

"Richard!" she answered in like voice, taunting him with pretended shock. Her seductive laughter disconcerted him.

"Where is your shame, woman?" he asked, half-meaning it.

"Gone by the wayside with your freedom, I should think," she replied with a contented sigh. "Are you having second thoughts?"

"Are you?" he asked, turning toward her though he could not yet see her expression.

"Now there's a proper jest! I did not mark you as having such a bent toward humor. You never cease to surprise me, Richard." With that, she wriggled her hand free of his and continued the quest he had tried to halt. "Um, what have we here? Yet another surprise?"

Richard grasped her wrist and moved her hand away. Slowly, because only his mind was involved in the attempt. Her fingers left a trail of fire he both welcomed and fought to ignore.

He must not give in to his greed again. She had been a virgin and should have time to recover. "You tempt me, Sara, and last night was more than enough."

Again she laughed, soft and cajoling, as she rolled to her side and pressed her body against his. "*He* doesn't think so."

"He?" Richard groaned, giving in to her insistent fondling and rapidly losing his determination to be chivalrous.

"Sir Eager Fellow there. I suspect he welcomes as much attention as he can get." She squeezed gently and wriggled her body even closer to his. "Shall we indulge him? He has been so *good!*"

Richard's breath caught on his wordless, mindless sound of encouragement. Before he realized what she was doing, Sara had rolled atop his body and positioned him at her entrance.

His hips arched upward beneath hers, seeking surcease for sweet torture, not awaiting permission from his brain. He gasped her name as she seated herself firmly upon him.

Sinuously she moved. More of the dawn's light crept through the window as he opened his eyes and regarded her with wonder. Thrown in sharp relief, her features appeared surreal. Her breasts quivered near enough to kiss. And so he did, drawing upon her as though he wished to devour.

She pulled away and settled higher, riding him, controlling him as though she would a mount. Heaven help him, he had no wish at all to reverse matters and wrest the power from her. Let her have it. Let her have him. He must be dreaming anyway.

But all too soon, she quickened the pace, and he felt the end approach. For the life of him, he could not prolong this, could not deny the overpowering urge to end it. She tensed above him, all around him and drew his life force within her until he was no more.

She melted atop his body, draped over him like a coverlet of contentment. He held her as tightly as his boneless arms could grasp while his heart pounded furiously against her breasts. Those sweet, incomparable breasts.

"So," she said, her voice a breathy shudder against his neck. "I should arise soon, I suppose." Reluctantly she moved off him and once more snuggled against his side.

He drew in a deep breath, again uncertain what he should say to her. Words of praise? She did not seem to need those. Besides, he could think of none quite grand enough to fit the occasion.

Everything that came to mind seemed so inadequate as to be laughable. She surely knew how adept she was at pleasing. *Adept?* He nearly laughed at what an understatement that would be.

But if he was so satisfied by what they had done—and he definitely was—then why did he feel such unease with it? Had he not wanted her to participate? His greatest dread had been that she would silently endure this duty. Well, she assuredly had exceeded his wildest hopes and laid those fears to rest right enough.

Sara of Fernstowe was beyond any female of his experience. For the first time since he had lain with the cold, unhappy Evaline years ago, Richard was unsure of how to proceed with a woman. For totally opposite reasons, of course, but he still felt confused and at a loss as to what he must do next.

He hated that sensation, but he would gladly suffer it in return for all the others he had enjoyed these past hours.

Sara left the bed and began to gather up her things. Her nakedness did not trouble her overmuch, though she knew Richard watched her every move as though he were hawk and she the prey.

He had liked her body well enough in the darkness, now he must grow accustomed to it in the light. A man and wife should not hide one from the other and conceal their faults. It would take him time to get used to her looks, of course. She was not built as daintily as most women.

"You are even lustier than I imagined," she commented as she pulled on her wrinkled chemise.

"Such observations are not becoming, Sara," he muttered.

"Why ever not?" she asked, shaking out her surcoat while she shot him a flirting glance. "'Tis true enough, so why not say it? I am mightily impressed with your stamina and your expertise. Surely you must be a legend among the women you have enjoyed."

Richard released a harsh breath that spoke his exasperation and ran a hand through his tousled hair. "Saints, Sara, you cannot possibly know about such things, nor should you speak of them."

She chuckled and resumed dressing. "Oh, you would be astounded at the way women talk about their men. And I assure you, I have used my excellent hearing."

He stiffened and sat up. "You would never..."

"Speak thusly of you?" Sara grinned at him. "I'll not need to say a word. Everyone will see the stars in my eyes, the languor of my satisfaction, the—"

"Cease this prattle on the instant!" he ordered, climbing out of bed and snatching up his tunic. Hurriedly he donned it as though it were armor. It covered him to the thigh.

Sara sighed at the sight of his bare legs and feet. "You do have marvelous knees," she said truthfully, "among other things."

"God's teeth!" he shouted. "Will you leave me be and let me dress?"

"Until tonight," she murmured sweetly, and swept out of his chamber. Good Lord, he was wonderful! And so modest. It was one fault she knew she could repair, but was not altogether certain she wanted to do so. Teasing him proved irresistible. And as much as he might protest her outrageous compliments, Sara knew that beneath all that propriety of his, he welcomed them.

The morning progressed much as the last had done, only slower than ever. She longed for the night. If she'd hoped Richard might unbend and court her favor a little during this day, he had not yet done so.

He regarded her as if he thought she might accost him at any time. Sara might have found more humor in that if she were not so tempted to do it.

How handsome he was, even with his eyes still wearing the shadows of the blows the Scots had dealt him. His nose looked fine after all, unbroken and straight as a lance. She knew his side must ache, for it bore harsh bruises from the kicks.

Last night's activities probably had not helped him heal, but he had not seemed to suffer much at the time. She had pleased him well and she knew it. And she would do it again first chance she got.

"I do not see why I need add four rocks and two rocks," Nan said, distracting Sara from more worldly thoughts. "I can see that there are six." She heaped the pebbles together on the table.

"That's wonderful that you can see that, dear," Sara said, exasperated by the child's constant questioning. "But see here. If you had forty sheep and wanted to purchase twenty, you would need to add them to know that you would have sixty."

Nan rolled her eyes. "We haven't sixty sheep. We have six rocks. I could number the sheep if we had them. I can already count." Her bottom lip protruded and her ruddy little eyebrows drew together. "This is a foolish game!" With that, she dashed all the pebbles to the floor with a sudden sweep of her arm."

Sara looked to Richard to correct Nan, but he merely

watched, propped against the wall, arms folded complacently across his chest. Christopher sat in silent imitation. Neither smiled or frowned.

"Pick them up," Sara demanded finally.

Nan glanced at her father and brother, saw that they did not command it, and refused. "No."

"Fine," Sara said as she crouched down and retrieved the scattered rocks. "No swordplay for you today."

"Papa?" the child cried and immediately leaped off her bench. "She hates me. Make her go away!"

Richard uncrossed his arms and knelt on one knee as Nan ran to him. He lifted her and brought her back to the table where he plunked her down upon the bench. "Do your sums, Nan, and you may practice with us."

Sara bit her tongue. She wanted to knock him over the head with a stool. They would have words about this, but not in front of Nan. The lesson continued without incident, except for Nan shooting an occasional superior look across the table.

When she dismissed the children to prepare for the noon meal, Richard started to follow them out. "A moment, sir," she demanded. "I would speak with you."

He turned, chin lifted. "Would you? Do you plan to limit *my* play?"

"Be assured, I would like to do just that!" she retorted. "Never gainsay me when I seek to teach a lesson, do you hear? How is Nan to learn obedience if you—"

"Obedience?" he thundered. "You mean to make her march to your rule, do you? Have her cower on command?"

Sara set her hands upon her hips to keep them from choking him. "She had better learn to obey *someone,* my lord, or you will have a wild, unruly woman on your hands one day!"

He leaned toward her, towered over her, mimicking her

pose. "I have one *now,* thanks to you! How can you chastise Nan when you show twice her wilfulness? What do you know of training children?"

"What do you? Nothing, obviously!" Sara exclaimed. She threw up her hands and sat down heavily, leaning her back against the edge of the table.

She heard Richard expel a deep breath. Then he joined her, his thigh brushing hers as he made room on the bench. "You are right," he admitted. "I shall leave her to you. Henceforth, I will stay away when you teach them."

"Oh, Richard, do not. They work hard for your approval. 'Tis all they get from you." She turned and lay her hand on his arm. "Give them more."

"More?" he asked, genuinely curious. "What more would they have?"

"Hugs," she replied fervently. "Kisses. Shared laughter. Be with them as a *friend,* not some stern overlord."

He looked sad. "But I am not their friend, Sara. I am the father, and fathers should be stern."

"As you were just now with Nan?" she asked wryly.

He sighed. "Point taken, and a sharp thrust it was. Tell me what I must do, then, to make it right."

"Speak with Nan. Reason with her and explain why she must attend to her work," Sara suggested. "And warn her that if she acts so again, there will be no practice for two days."

"Seems harsh," he commented.

Sara patted the muscled arm beneath her hand and then squeezed it softly. "A child needs bounds, Richard."

"So does a woman," he replied. "Do *you* recognize any, I wonder?"

Aha, he did not refer to her mothering talents—or lack of them—now. He spoke of their night and early morning games. He believed he wanted control of her in the bedchamber, but she would not surrender it all. The moment she became the subservient wife, he would grow bored with her and regret their marriage again. She would never allow that.

Sara grinned at him as she leaned on his shoulder to rise. "If I happen to overstep my bounds, you must let me know, husband. Punish me if I do."

"Punish you?" he asked, frowning up at her.

"Put me to bed early if I deserve it."

Then she winked and departed swiftly before he thought to limit her own play.

## Chapter Ten

Richard remained in the solar for a while, waiting for his arousal to subside. Was the woman mad, or merely cursed with wicked humor? It was highly improper to jest about relations with one's husband. It should be a serious matter, indeed, but Sara seemed to find it highly amusing.

Richard smiled in spite of himself, then rubbed his hand over his mouth to erase the inappropriate expression. How did a man deal with this? Jest with her, chastise her or leave her alone? Well, he could not leave her alone, that was for certain. He rarely made jests. Chastisement, it was then. His smile grew.

He would send her to bed, by God. This very night. Early.

The matter of the children bothered him more than Sara's irreverence at the moment. Fatherhood confused him, always had. His own sire had indulged him shamelessly, which Richard had determined not to do with his own children. His mother had ruled with an iron hand he had resented mightily. Though he loved her dearly, Richard did not want to emulate her attitude of intolerance, either.

Managing children might be much like training squires.

However, even there, he had little experience. John of Brabant had come to him at fourteen, his first lord dead of wounds and John already well accustomed to taking orders and following rules.

Richard supposed he must trust that Sara knew more about raising offspring than did he. At least she had a good example to mind. She had loved her father well and Richard wanted his children to feel love for him.

Trust came hard for Richard. He could not bring himself to rely fully on his wife. Her patience and tolerance with Nan and Chris could be an act to gain his goodwill.

So could her bold enthusiasm for bedding with him, but Richard didn't want to think so. Despite the way she unsettled him with her unusual behavior, he had to admit he could scarcely wait for more of it.

For the moment, he needed to put aside these family worries and see what he could discover about larger and more threatening problems.

Later, when he returned to the hall for supper, Sara noticed that Richard seemed more preoccupied than usual. Something troubled him, but instead of confiding in her, he talked only of mundane things.

He waited until they had finished eating to involve her, but then he went directly to the heart of it.

"I have decided it is time to attend to this issue of the raids," he said.

"What are you planning?" she asked.

He glanced around, as though marking the number of folk still milling about and talking. Since the weather was unusually mild and the hall comfortably warm tonight, many seemed disposed to stay and visit a while before seeking their beds for the night.

Richard reached for her elbow and guided her toward the solar. That room had become her favorite place. She hoped he would kiss her again and forget dealing with the border problems until he felt completely well.

"Let us speak in private," he told her. "I need some answers."

Sara entered the solar and took her usual place. She leaned forward, her elbows resting on the chair arms, hands clasped before her. "Question away."

He sat in the chair facing hers and leaned back, stretching his long legs out before him so that his shoes nearly touched her own. "Tell me what you know of your father's death."

She drew in a deep breath and began. "The survivors of the fight brought him in, tied across his saddle. The Scot had run him through with a blade."

"He was not answering a summons such as I received?"

"No," she replied. "Word arrived that several of the lords were meeting at Kielder, toward the western March. They were to discuss the thieving and whether it warranted a complaint to the king. He and our men were ambushed as they rode to the appointed place."

"Near the Meadow of Dispute," Richard said, as though he already knew.

"Some few leagues south of there, I believe."

Richard paused to think for a moment. "You believe that messenger came from Alan the True instead of the other lords?"

"Who else?" she asked, scoffing.

"Who else, indeed." Richard rose from his chair and paced, restlessly. "Did you know the meeting at Kielder was actually held?"

So lost in grief was she at the funeral, Sara had never thought to ask. "I supposed it was a ruse."

"No, it was planned and carried out the day your father died. The question is, how did the Scots learn of it? How did they know he would be on the way there in time to waylay him?''

"Chance?" she suggested, doubting it herself.

He stopped just before her chair, his green eyes keen upon her. "I have questioned those men who brought Lord Simon's body home. They never saw the face of the man who slew him. Even though he boasted of his name, he never removed his coif and helm. And he certainly cared whether I saw his features on the day he captured me. Could that mean he feared your men or I might recognize him as someone they knew?''

"None had met the Scot before that day, so they told me."

"Yet from what they say of him—his armor, his minions, his horse—it was the same man riding beneath the same colors."

"Blue and black with a silver device," Sara affirmed, wondering what point he meant to make.

"The same man who killed your sire was the one who took me for ransom," he restated. "That much is clear."

"Of course," she agreed. "And the same as attacked six more villages lying near the border."

"Whose lords have paid hefty bribes to this man to forgo further attacks upon them. Bribes such as he asked of me."

She had not heard of that. "How do you know this?"

"I sent Sir Matthew to ask them if it was so. He returned this afternoon and confirmed it. That is how I know of the meeting at Kielder."

He sat again and reached out to take her hands. "Sara, the man was extorting money from some of the estates here in the March, even before I came. Those who do not pay, he makes to suffer until they do. Two had complained to the king, which is why we came north in the first place. That, and your father's death, of course."

"You seem to know much more than I do about this. Why question me at all?" she asked, angry with herself for not sending inquiries long ago.

He paused a moment as if searching for words. "Sara, why would the man who held me wish to set me against my own wife? Why would he tell me you had paid only half the ransom? If Sir Edmund had not also read the demand and delivered the gold himself, I might not have believed you had played me true in this."

"You do believe me, don't you?" she asked, fearful that even now he had doubts. He could kill her for such as that and none would condemn him.

"Of course I believe you," he said, dismissing her query as ridiculous, "but what would be gained by my not believing? Who would benefit from it if I punished you or cast you out?"

She replied, truly puzzled, "Not a soul that I know."

"Certainly not the Scot," Richard prompted, placing his hands on her arms.

He spoke softly now, entreating her to consider his words carefully. "For that matter, what had the Scot to gain in killing your father? A few raids here and there never draw royal attention, but the blackmail of nobles and a baron's murder brought the king's wrath north. Ask yourself, Sara, for what purpose?"

She did not mistake his reason for his question. "You really do not think the man responsible is Alan the True, do you?"

"No," Richard admitted with a heavy sigh. "I cannot believe that he is the one."

"You know this man," she guessed, reading the answer in his eyes. "Who is he to you, Richard?"

He ducked his head for a moment and then met her gaze again. His looked infinitely sad. "Alan is my brother, Sara. A brother I have not seen since I was three years of age."

"And you would not know him now, would you, husband?" she asked gently. "Even did you come face-to-face."

"No," he replied, almost inaudibly. "In all truth, I would not know him now."

Sara leaned forward and kissed his furrowed brow, for she knew nothing else to do for him.

Richard had not intended to tell Sara about Alan, but he found he couldn't lie to her outright when she asked. Truth be told, he felt relieved now that she knew of it.

"Someone has purposely set about to make my brother the villain in all of this," he explained.

Sara said nothing, but the sympathy in her eyes told all. Clearly she still thought Alan guilty. At least she had not railed at him for keeping the information from her so long.

"His mother was a Scot," Richard volunteered. He figured he might as well get the worst of this out of the way. There would be no more secrets between them. "So is mine."

Her eyebrows rose at that, though she still remained silent, her hands soft upon his face.

"A commoner," he added for good measure. If Sara would ever turn from him, it would be now.

"Oh well, that explains it then," she said, releasing her hold on him and folding her hands in her lap.

"Explains what?" he asked, girding himself to defend his birth.

She shrugged and smiled. "Why Christopher was allowed to befriend Nan. 'Twould not be permitted in most instances. Your mother must have encouraged him."

Richard scoffed and sat back in his chair. "She did nothing of the sort. For the most part, she ignores the child. She despised Nan's mother, Annie."

"Why should she do that," Sara asked, appearing genuinely interested.

"Annie Causey was my leman for a time. My mother thought her unworthy, even of that dubious honor."

"But you cared for her," Sara said.

"Yes, I did," Richard acknowledged. He had truly liked Annie Causey, though they had never mentioned marriage, not at the outset or even after she conceived. His long-standing betrothal to Evaline aside, he could not have wed Annie. Their alliance had made her life better, however. And now he had little Nan.

"That you did care speaks well of you." Sara's gaze drifted toward the door to the hall where the children could be heard laughing. "Christopher is to be commended for his good heart. To show such care for a natural sister against his grandmother's wishes took courage, I believe."

Her smile grew tender. "He is so much like you, Richard. You must be very proud."

"Not only of my son," he declared, frowning.

"Oh, Nan, too," she quickly agreed. "She's a Strode, through and through."

Sara stood then, smiling down at him. "If we are finished, I think I should go. It grows late and the children really ought to be abed."

Richard caught one of her hands when she would have swept past him. "We are not done, Sara. You distracted me with this talk of the children. I have not finished my questions about the other matter."

"Let me go now and settle our little brood for the night. I will come to you in a while and we will talk more of the Scots, if you wish."

Reluctantly Richard released her hand and nodded. He had no further questions for Sara about the Scots, but he did need to tell her of his plans. She wouldn't care much for them, he knew.

Just as well that could wait for morning. He doubted there would be further discussion of anything when she came to his chamber again. More likely he would fall upon her in a fit of lust if he did not keep tight rein on himself.

Or she would fall upon him. That idea both excited and disturbed him. Sara did not fit his notion of a lady, that was the problem, he reasoned. She should not be judged by another's measure. But, rightly so or not, Richard did judge her. He could not help feeling she had some motive other than desire.

He wished he could simply throw himself into this passion of theirs without thinking so much about it. But there, at the back of his mind, lurked the fear that her eagerness to bed with him might be but a gambit. And if her desire was indeed as real and fervent as it seemed, then he worried that something was woefully wrong with Sara. Appetites of that nature did not bide in women of quality. Did they?

To his own discredit, he possessed very little will to correct her if that was so. What kind of husband did that make him if he took full advantage of her unwitting impropriety?

Richard wondered if his own conception of women, noble and common alike, might somehow be skewed. And if so, how and by whom? The church? His parents? Annie? Evaline? Indeed, *he* might be the one wrong-thinking, and not Sara.

Tonight, he would cast aside these misgivings, and all of their other problems, Richard decided. Be damned to all these qualms about her, the border trouble, and his concerns for the children. He could shoulder all of those again when necessary, but for now, he only wanted Sara in his arms again.

This time, however, he would not wait for Sara to come to him.

Sara struggled to contain her excitement as she wriggled out of her clothes and donned her bed gown. Her rush

through the children's prayers and the brief tale she spun
for them gave her but a moment's guilt. She told herself
the poor dearlings were exhausted anyway and should go
to sleep. Christopher willingly slept alone now that he felt
more at home, and Nan had Berta to keep her company in
her own chamber.

Richard needed her more than did the children tonight.
He must be worried that his kinship with the Scot would
alter how she felt about their marriage. And also that his
mother's common birth might make a difference to her.
Neither made any difference at all.

Richard was his own man. She knew her husband to be
as honorable as any ever born, and none of his kin could
ever change that. She must convince him of her absolute
loyalty and show him how much she cared.

Sara hurried across the corridor, pushed open the door
without knocking and almost fell against him.

He caught her by the arms to steady her. "I was on my
way to you," he said, sounding faintly disgruntled.

Sara laughed and pushed past him into his chamber.
"No, no, my bed is far too small. And given our turbulence last time, it might not stand the test!"

He pinched the bridge of his nose and shook his head.
"Sara—"

"Oh, does your head ache? Come," she ordered, tugging him by the hand. "Lie down and I shall remedy that
right soon."

His resistance only fueled her determination. If he
thought she would demand too much of him, she must
reassure him. "Stretch out now, I shall rub your temples.
Father swore it soothed him, and so it shall you."

Richard gave in, though warily. First he sat on the edge
of the large mattress, regarding her with suspicion. Sara

smiled and gestured toward the pillow. He lay back, his gaze locked upon hers.

"Close your eyes," she suggested. Then she climbed up beside him and knelt. Leaning forward, she slid her fingers along his brow to smooth out the furrows there. The poor man was holding his breath.

"Try to think on pleasant things," she said, keeping her voice low and soft. "Breathe deeply." She began a circular motion with her fingers at the outer edge of his brow. Again and again, she stroked and kneaded until he sighed with relief. Then she continued down the line of his cheekbones to the hinge of his jaw. He clenched the damned thing too often, she thought, loosening it with her slow, steady pressing.

She could see the cords of his neck, tight with tension, and trailed her hands along them until she reached the muscles that held them so. He shifted slightly, allowing her access.

After a few moments, Sara parted the heavy woolen bedrobe he wore and slid her hands inside it to reach his shoulders. "So tight," she whispered as she dug her fingertips into the smooth, hot skin. "You feel so warm," she commented, realized as she did that she shared the heat.

Richard's eyes opened, their heavy lids only emphasizing the lambent look of desire in the green depths. Her breasts swelled with anticipation against the softness of her velvet bed gown.

Sara released his shoulders and stroked downward to his chest. The flat nipples peaked beneath her palms and she made a slow rotation touching only their distended flesh. His sharp intake of breath spoke more than words. She repeated the caress.

He grasped her wrists and his eyes narrowed. "Why? Why do you do this, Sara? What is it you want of me?"

She pulled one arm from his grip and brushed her hand down his stomach, to settle upon the hardness below. "This," she told him truthfully. "This is what I wish of you."

Her wish came true, almost before she knew what happened. With a sudden surge, he sat up. He pushed her backward and rose above her. Sara yanked his robe aside and then her own. With one knee, he parted her legs and lowered himself to her entrance.

She grasped his hips and raised her own, meeting force with force. He thrust hard, retreated and thrust again. She cried out in welcome, accepting the pace, increasing it.

When she opened her eyes, Sara reveled in his fierceness. Head thrown back, teeth gritted and chest heaving, Richard had abandoned his worries.

Savage ecstasy seized him, even as she watched. With one final thrust, he swept her with him. They flew together, a wild swirling, almost frightening in its swiftness and fury. Then they drifted like two leaves clinging together in the wake of a storm.

When she could gather breath to speak, Sara whispered in his ear, "Feel better now?"

## Chapter Eleven

"Only *you* would ask such a question at a time like this." His voice was soft but held an underlying tone of exasperation.

Sara knew she had angered Richard again.

It was not her attempt at humor that bothered him, and Sara knew it. He misliked her taking the lead the way she had done. Some wicked imp inside her had driven her to it, she thought with a sigh. The same imp that believed Richard would change his mind and leave her when he'd completed his business here, unless she bound him fast with the passion that flared between them.

That ploy had failed miserably. Rather than drawing them closer as she'd hoped, this intimacy was driving him away from her. He hated wanting her. And because she made him do that, he might grow to hate her for it.

Her boldness repelled him, at least after the fact. Yet she knew no other way to be but bold. Too late in her life to play the weak and simpering damsel now, nor did she want to. Not even for Richard would she stoop to that. If he could not accept her as she was, then she would have to do without him.

Richard had not truly *chosen* to stay with her as he

would have her think. He was merely attempting to gain back some of the control that she and the king had wrested from him when he lay wounded. If he convinced her and everyone else that he wanted her as a wife, then he would not appear quite so misused.

Leaping at King Edward's offer to annul the marriage would have constituted an admission on Richard's part that he had been made the butt of a royal jest.

Now, even as she held him in her arms, Sara knew that she must let him go. He wanted out of this bed, out of her home and out of her life, she did not doubt.

There was no hope of winning that heart of his. You could not force someone to love. Sara realized now that she should have learned that lesson with her mother. No matter how zealously she had worked to please that woman and become deserving of her affection, Mother had continued to deny her that and find fault in everything she did. Richard would do the same. Sara clearly saw that now.

Richard Strode would never love a woman like her. She had been a fool to try to make it happen by sheer force of will. Why did she court such heartbreak? Her wits were all she had to take pride in. Had she lost them?

"No," she muttered, abruptly withdrawing from Richard's side. "No more. I will not do this again."

"What did you say?" he asked, rising on one elbow and reaching for her hand.

Sara jerked it away before he could grasp it. "Leave me be, Richard."

"Come back to bed, Sara," he demanded impatiently.

"No," she said, pulling her bed gown about her and heading for the door.

He bounded off the bed and caught her arm, turning her toward him. "What is this about? Why are you leaving?"

She looked at him, watching the candlelight flicker on his face and tease the shadows of his body. Her sadness almost overcame her, but she did not weep. She never wept.

"You do not wish a wife, Richard. I release you."

"What do you mean, you *release* me! This is a done thing, Sara!" He glanced toward the bed. "We have already—"

"No one will know. Accept the king's offer to dissolve the marriage. We are not suited."

For a long moment, he stared down into her face. She saw his feelings then, clear as though he named them while they marched across his features. Disbelief, acceptance, fury.

The first two, she could understand. He could not credit that she would offer him his freedom. But then he took her word that she would. She supposed the anger was for the blow to his pride. Even though he did not want her, he must think she could not survive without him.

"That damned pride of yours," she whispered. "You will be free, is that not enough?"

He released her arm and stepped back from her. "You are through pretending, I see."

She nodded. "Yes. I no longer delude myself that you might come to care for me. This was a mistake. So kill the Scot and then go home. Or tag behind your king collecting arrows for him. Go to the devil for all I care, but I am done with you."

"No, by God, you are not *done!*"

"Do not make this more unpleasant than it needs be, Richard. Take what I offer. Do what you came to do and begone!"

He stood straight and crossed his arms over his chest, glaring down at her. Sara wished she could see him as ridiculous, standing there wearing naught but a frown, but he looked majestic. Virile and desirable.

"So, you think two nights enough to put a babe in that

belly of yours, eh? That *is* what you were after, is it not? I should have known—"

"I did wish for a child," she admitted. "Now I want nothing from you, Richard." She forced a smile she thought might crack her face. "Not one thing."

"Not even *friendship?*" he taunted. His smile looked more faked than hers felt.

Sara shook her head, backing slowly to the door. She caught the handle in her hand. "No," she said softly. "That should be earned. And freely given, just as caring should. 'Tis no thing to ask for or try to take. I see that now." She stepped through the door.

"Why are you so angry of a sudden? All I said was—"

Sara tried to close the door between them, but he caught the edge before she could. Yet he did not finish what he had begun to say. Nor did he ask her again to stay. He simply stood in the half-open portal and held her gaze for a long moment.

She sighed wearily, broke the tenuous connection and left him there. There was nothing else to be done. It was over.

Richard could only guess at what had caused this. One moment she was lying sated in his arms and the next, she was quit of him.

One thing about Sara, she never did anything half-measure. "And that is God's truth," he muttered, raking his hands through his hair and shaking his head.

He wandered back to the bed with its tangled covers and scent of loving. She expected him to sleep now, after her throwing that fit of pique? Of course not. Sara thought he would follow her, beg her to return to bed and convince her that he would stay. Well, he would not. If she needed reassurance, she should have asked him for it outright. He hated games.

Tomorrow he would simply tell her to cease all this foolishness and behave herself. If they were to have any kind of decent marriage, she must come to heel.

*Like a hound?* The question popped into his mind uninvited.

He smiled at that as he settled back into bed, trying to imagine Sara doing as he bade her. Impossible. She would likely bite him should he issue commands. This wife of his was no pet to be subdued and trained to his hand. Nor did he wish to try.

Whatever had set her off—surely his admonishment about her asking how he felt—would seem trivial in the morning. He would tease her a bit. She would laugh about it then, that sensuous laugh of hers that he craved to hear, and admit how ridiculous her actions had seemed. And when night came again, all would be well.

*Annulment, indeed.* He burrowed into the pillow and closed his eyes. He and Sara were so bloody well married, the Holy Father himself could not dissolve this union.

But when morning came, Sara did not laugh for him as he had hoped.

"Come now," he coaxed as he followed her out of the hall and down the steps. "We have precious little time to spend at odds with each other. Cease treating me like some stranger who wandered in uninvited."

"You *have* overstayed your welcome, sir," she replied. Her lips were tightly drawn and her eyes flashed with fire.

Richard fell in step with her. "What of the children?" he asked. "Have they overstayed? Shall I go and take them away?"

Her pace altered, slowed. She shook her head. "No, of course not. I would love to foster them, though I know you do not trust them to my care."

"I do trust you," he argued. He caught her arm. "This

is absurd, Sara. Will you please be still for a while and let
us discuss this?"

"Discuss what? The marriage or the children?" she demanded, glaring up at him.

"Both. And tearing across the bailey, all outraged,
serves no purpose. Besides, it looks undignified. Come
back inside."

Sara jerked her arm out of his hold and turned away. "I
plan to ride out. If you wish to talk to me, then come. If
not, I bid you good morn." She was off again. He followed.

Obviously unwilling to wait for the stable lad to do it,
Sara saddled her own mount with rapid precision. Richard
was hard put to keep up with her, she moved so fast. In
moments, they were mounted and headed through the
gates.

Once they were on their way across the open fields,
Richard observed how well Sara managed the large, spir-
ited mare. He hated that the man who had captured him
had kept his warhorse. But the easy-gaited gelding he had
chosen from Sara's stables promised a pleasanter ride. Unless the conversation prevented that. Thus far, however,
neither of them had spoken. He wondered if mayhap they
should keep it so.

They splashed through a small stream and Richard recalled the outing on which Sara had received her scar. Had
this been where she stopped to rest and fell asleep?

Richard ventured to ask, "Did you mean to ride out
alone today, Sara? You should remember that is not safe."

"I should? First you order what I should do. Now you
tell me what I should remember? Save these *should*s of
yours for the next unfortunate who falls under your spell."

He smiled at the admission. "Are you under my spell,
Sara?"

"Not any longer," she growled. A lioness, his Sara. And not disposed to suffer his cautioning.

She urged her mare to a gallop that soon shook loose the braid wound round her head. Free of its confines, her hair streamed in the cool wind like a dark, shining banner. He remained several lengths behind her just to watch how the sun caught it.

This was the first time he had seen her on horseback. How magnificent she was! An accomplished rider who obviously enjoyed speed and challenge. He encouraged the gelding to catch up and ride abreast. She quickly outdistanced him.

"A race?" he called out.

She rode on as though he did not exist. Richard finally gave it up. Her mare was of a size with his mount, and clearly the younger of the two. No point exhausting the old fellow he was riding. Instead, he kept Sara in sight until she paused to rest and then joined her.

She dismounted before he could, flung her reins over a bush and found a boulder upon which to sit.

"You ride very well," he commented, figuring she could not take offense at that.

"I know," she answered, folding her arms just beneath her breasts.

Richard secured the gelding in a good grazing spot and then sat down beside her on the rock. "Whatever I said to anger you this morn, I did not mean it to have that effect."

"I know," she repeated. "You believed I would continue ignoring your criticism and try even harder to please you. Well, I have had enough of that in my life, thank you. Henceforth, I please myself."

Now what could he say? "You must admit that you are different, Sara. Like no woman I know. I confess I hardly know what to make of you," he stated honestly.

She looked him square in the eye. Her own eyes

snapped with defiance. "You will *make* nothing of me, sir. Nothing more or less than who I am. So do not think to try!"

"Agreed," he said, holding up both hands, palms out, in surrender. He knew better than to argue with a woman in this mood. He must concede this battle if he was to win the war. "Now would you please stop this talk of annulment?"

She sniffed and glanced away. "Take care of the Scots. Then we shall see."

"I shall," he promised. "In fact, I have a plan to get things under way."

Her head snapped around. "What?"

Richard hid his smile. He had her full attention now. Could it be that if he got her so engrossed in these plans, she would forget this snit of hers?

"I need to speak with the men whose properties are directly involved. We are going to attend Lord Harbeth's wedding feast day after tomorrow," Richard told her. "He sent us an invitation by Sir Matthew when he made the round in questioning the border lords."

She looked disgusted by the idea. "Harbeth? No, I fear I must decline. I would feel obliged to urge the poor bride escape. He puts me in mind of a clumsy hound on the scent, sniffing and dodging about. Comical, yet not so when one is the game, I trow."

Richard laughed with delight at her description. He had never met the man, but now he wanted to. "We do not go to help celebrate, though I suppose we should do that, too. As I've said, we'll attend because I need to talk to the others who are affected by this threat we are under. And I must speak to a minstrel who will be performing there."

She swung around, interested, anger abandoned for the nonce. "A minstrel? Why so?"

Richard leaned closer, as though to impart secrets. "He

has played at every keep within riding distance. Both sides of the border. Word has it he even visited Byelough, home of our infamous Alan the True.''

"He admits as much?" Sara asked, aghast. And, to Richard's relief, no longer of a mind to argue.

"He is French by birth," Richard confided. "Sir Matthew heard that the minstrel refuses to be caught up in squabbles betwixt the Scots and English. One of the barons thought to press him for Byelough's whereabouts, but the old singer says he'd not reveal it on pain of torture."

Sara laughed without mirth. "And would refuse to sing if abused, I'll wager. He plies his power well."

Richard dug at a tuft of grass with the toe of one boot. "The fellow is elderly and well respected for his talent. Much in demand, so I hear. Melior is his name. Do you know of him?"

Her eyebrows rose in surprise as she turned to him. "I do! Father misliked hiring players, so I have never met this particular one, but I have heard others vow he has the voice of an angel."

Richard gave Sara a questioning look. "Will you come with me?"

She shook her head vehemently. "No, I never attend such gatherings."

"Why not?" he asked, knowing the answer full well. "Ah, it is because you believe someone will look askance at your scar, am I right?"

She did not have to answer. Her face turned crimson, causing the colorless scar to stand out against it.

Richard snorted. "Where is that courage of yours now?"

"My appearance offends," she explained. "'Tis not only the scar. Men shy away, put off by my height." Impatiently she flung her dark, tangled wealth of hair back over one shoulder. "Unkempt. And I have no grace at all.

My own mother said as much. I merely wished to spare others discomfort. But I assure you, I am no coward!'' she announced.

"Prove it, then, and come," he dared, pointing at her with his fore and middle fingers. "Anyone who looks at you with less than adoration, I will poke out his eyes."

Her laughter brightened a day already rife with sunshine. Richard laughed with her and enjoyed a rare moment of warm camaraderie such as he had never felt with another.

"Please do, Sara," he entreated. "If naught else worthwhile takes place, at least I may dance with my wife at last."

She turned away, but not before he saw the wistful yearning in her eyes. Did Sara love to dance?

"My very *graceful* wife?" he added with a grin. "The only woman whose nose does not bump against my chest."

"Oh, very well," she said with a stifled chuckle. "If you insist."

"Never that," he corrected, pretending to be insulted. "I invite. I encourage. I implore."

"And I relent," she said with a wry look and a shake of her head. "Now we must go home. The children will be ready for lessons."

Richard congratulated himself. Dredging up a bit of charm had worked. Sara seemed appeased.

But even as he smugly patted himself upon the back for his success, Sara pulled away from him sharply when he would have assisted her to the saddle.

He was not firmly back in her good graces yet. Never again would he take for granted that Sara would simply ignore his censuring asides.

The smallest of those had set her off, and at the worst possible time. Or possibly, she had noted all of his remonstrances and that last one had tipped the scales. Here-after, he would mind his tongue.

Sara could not think why she had agreed to go to Har-beth's wedding. She'd thought only overly zealous priests flogged themselves for no good reason. Yet, here she was with whip in hand. She had agreed to go, however, and go she would. To excuse herself now would only brand her a weakling in Richard's eyes. And whatever else she might be, she would not be counted one of those.

Many who would attend, Sara already knew from the times her parents had entertained their company at Fern-stowe, and visited in return at other castles. None were *her* friends, of course.

The women disdained her because even her mother had done so in their presence. 'Twas no secret among them how the Lady Eula despaired of her scarred and gangly daughter. Sara shuddered as she recalled snippets of con-versation overheard, some of them meant to be.

The men avoided her because she was taller than most of them. They would look ridiculous walking with her, or dancing. Her father's ceaseless bragging about how adept she was with weapons had not helped her cause, either.

Lord Calpern had actually called her Simon's Boadicea, after the ancient warrior queen who led a war against the Romans. She had pretended to be proud of that, but it had made her feel unwomanly. God grant he had forgotten that sobriquet by this time, but Sara held little hope of it.

Would Richard dance with her as he suggested? Would he really defend her, or would he join in the jests as her mother had done? No, he would simply ignore them as had her father.

Something inside Sara insisted that she go and find out, no matter the hurt that might ensue. What happened there could very well determine whether or not she remained a wife.

Richard declared he would stay with her, but did he mean it? After this event at Harbeth's, would he still wish to? She might not want that herself if he proved less than respectful of her feelings.

She spent the entire ride home dreading what she must face in less than two days' time.

"Such a frown," Richard commented as they arrived back at Fernstowe's stables. "I do hope it was not the company."

Sara looked away as though she had not heard. She would tear out her tongue ere she admitted her fears to him again.

He gave her no chance to avoid him when he held up his hands to assist her dismounting. She allowed it grudgingly, tugging away from him as soon as possible. Her thanks were hardly more audible than they were sincere.

Why could he not leave her alone? Her entire body shivered every time the man touched her. From that grin he wore, she suspected he knew the cause. But no matter how much she desired him, Sara reminded herself that she must not show it. She drew in a deep, calming breath. Never again.

"And King Alfred got so caught up in planning his battle tactics, he allowed the woman's cakes to burn," Christopher recited.

"Should have been watching them while he was thinking," Nan said with a knowing nod. "I expect he went hungry."

"What sort of king was he, unable to think of two things at once, Father?" Christopher asked. "Good King Edward could have done both, I should think."

Richard nodded with approval and remembered to smile

as Sara had suggested. "I shall tell His Majesty you said as much. He will be delighted with your faith in him."

"He is very wise, then?" Nan asked, for she had never met the king.

Richard happened to glance at Sara and saw her look of patent disdain. She obviously did not care for at least one of the king's decisions. Was it Edward's granting her the choice of a husband in the first place? Or was it the king's offer of the annulling the marriage? Richard wondered.

"Some believe him wise, Nan. Those who live beyond our time will tell the tale, for his reign is not yet over. The far-reaching effects of his decisions have yet to be realized."

"As with King Alfred," Christopher added.

"Just so, and a canny comparison, Chris. Nan, whom would you consider our greatest queen?"

"Boadicea!" she announced proudly.

Sara gasped. Richard looked at her, wondering what had caused it. "Do you not agree?"

"H—how did you learn of *her?*" Sara asked, her face ashen.

"Papa told us!" Nan said, excited now that she was the center of attention.

"When?" Sara demanded, glaring at him as though he had committed a crime.

"Yesterday," Nan said, "while we practiced with our swords."

Sara shot him a killing look and got up from her stool. "Continue as you will. I am done here."

With that, she left in a flurry of skirts. And slammed the door.

Nan tilted her head and remarked, "She must favor some other queen."

Richard didn't think that was the problem. But what

was? Why should the mere name of a long-dead queen upset her so?

"Put away your tablets and the stylus," he instructed the children as he got up from the table. "I need a word with your mother."

"She is not *my* mother," Nan grumbled.

With effort, Richard held his patience. He walked over to Nan, crouched and placed a hand on her shoulder. "She will be if you'll only allow it, daughter."

He included Christopher with a nod toward the boy. "Your mothers are no longer alive to provide what you will need in future. Lady Sara seems right willing to do that. Should you not grant her that chance?"

"Do you command it?" Nan asked, her bottom lip aquiver.

"No," Richard assured her. "I only wish you to be fair-minded about this."

"I heard her tell Bertie I was *obsalant*," Nan confided. "Is that truly bad?"

"*Obstinate*," Richard corrected. "And you should never eavesdrop, you know. But obstinate is not necessarily bad. It only means stubborn, which you must admit is true of yourself."

Christopher sniggered behind his hand.

"She said you are *arrogant*," Nan informed her brother, and then turned to Richard. "Is that stubborn, too?"

He mused. "That means prideful, not a bad thing to be," Richard assured them.

"Well, that's good," Nan said, "because she said you are those things, too."

Richard lowered his head and smiled to himself. "I suppose we must learn to embrace humility when the need arises." Then he straightened and stood. "Now get you out of here and enjoy the sunshine. That, I do command."

He laughed at their mad scramble and followed them out.

Obstinance and arrogance aside, he really did need to have words with Sara and find out what perturbed her now.

# Chapter Twelve

"You and Papa are *leaving* us?" Nan demanded to know. She climbed upon the bed and sat, legs dangling over the side. "We want to go with you."

Sara closed and locked the chest she would take with her to Harbeth's. "We will only be gone for two nights. The keep is small and there would likely be no room for you to sleep."

"Chris and I could stay in the chamber with you and Papa."

"We shall have no place to ourselves. The ladies will sleep in the solar, the men in the hall, I expect. Both will be crowded."

And a relief that would be, Sara thought to herself. She would have a perfectly good excuse to sleep apart from Richard for at least one more night. He had not come to her bed last evening or the one before, but she knew it was only a matter of time before he did so.

He had suggested that she join him in his chamber again, but she would not be doing that unless he demanded it outright. Never again would she give him chance to remark upon her forwardness, or to call her unseemly and different from the other women he had known.

For the past two days, he had been unfailingly patient and agreeable. Even charming at times. Sara figured she must be doing something correctly for a change in distancing herself from him.

Nan jumped down from the bed and scampered toward the door, distracting Sara from her thoughts.

"Papa will let us go. I shall remind him the Scots will get us if he leaves us behind."

Berta shook her head and chuckled as she motioned for the lad waiting to take Sara's chest down to be loaded on the packhorse. "That child! I told her we will be having many of the men remaining here to protect us."

Sara struggled with her braid, trying to pin it up in some kind of order with the long bone hairpins. "We shall let her father handle this matter, I think. If he changes his mind about their going with us, I believe I shall stay behind."

Berta laughed again. "Do not ask me to go in your stead. I can well imagine the havoc those two could wreak at a wedding! Nan with her saucy tongue and young Chris with his many questions! La, I hate to think on it."

"There!" Sara said with a final pat to her braid, now properly secured and covered with a veil. "I am ready to go."

"You look beautiful," Berta declared.

Sara grunted. "Hardly that, but 'tis of no consequence."

The maid halted her exit with a tug to her sleeve. "If you'd not mind a word of advice, my lady."

Surprised at Berta's daring, Sara looked down at the woman. "Advice?"

"They will see you as you see yourself," Berta said.

"What do you mean?"

Berta hesitated only a moment before answering, "I've lived at Fernstowe all my life, as you well know. We at the lower tables saw how they was when they come here, these neighboring folk. They but followed your mam's lead in how they treated you, those ladies.''

"And the men?" Sara asked with a tight smile. "What do you suppose stole all of their gallantry?"

"Old Clootie," Berta said with a laugh. "Aye, the devil hisself made 'em tease you." She raised one eyebrow and clicked her tongue. "That, and they was none too sure of theirselves when it come to looking up to a woman."

"So I noted, and they still must do that unless I decide to walk on my knees," Sara said wryly.

Berta patted her sleeve. "You walk proud, Lady Sara. There's no lady there can compare with yourself. All of us think so."

Touched almost to tears by those words, Sara could only nod her thanks. She wished she did not have to face those nobles ever again. But since she had to do so, Sara determined that she would hold in her mind that her own people loved her no matter what she looked like.

They did not care if she was overly tall, or that her hair curled wildly or that her face was blemished with the scar. And neither did her husband. He might not love her, but she now felt fairly certain that was not due to any physical defect. Richard only objected to her bold ways.

She could not change that part of herself, either, but mayhap a bit of boldness would serve her well these next two days.

On the ride to Harbeth's keep, Richard regretted the unpleasant departure from Fernstowe. He wondered if the memory of Nan's tantrum and Chris's silent pouting caused Sara's troubled frown. More likely, it was dreading their arrival at Harbeth's that fostered her worry.

"All will be well, Sara," he assured her.

"Of course," she replied, smoothing out her brow and forcing a smile. "Why would it not?"

He wished he could make her believe it, but he was not certain he believed it himself. The smithy, Eustiss, had felt compelled to warn Richard of what he might expect once they reached their destination. The tales of former events held at Fernstowe gave little hope that things would progress any differently unless Richard took a hand in matters.

Yet what could he do? Flatten every man present who insulted her? And what about the women? How would he manage that? Somehow, he had to prevent them from hurting Sara with their thoughtless words. He felt terribly responsible because he had made her come with him. He knew she could never resist a dare, a challenge to her courage. Any pain she suffered would be his doing.

They had left before dawn, though they needed to travel less than three hours, keeping a moderate pace. The wedding would take place soon after they arrived, about mid-morn.

Richard wondered whether they should stay for the feast and pass the night there after all. Sara would likely be secluded with the other women, alone with them where he could not defend her. But making excuses to leave, when they obviously had come prepared to stay, might make things worse.

Even after Sir Edmund had announced their party and they rode through the gates of Harbeth's Keep, Richard still had not decided what to do.

The tangle of newly arrived guests and their animals crowded the courtyard. In the midst of the confusion, Richard assisted Sara from her mare. He sent Sir Edmund to get instructions as to the disposition of their baggage and the stabling of the mounts.

"Aha, if it isn't *little* Sara of Fernstowe!" shouted one portly gentleman who pushed through the milling throng. He bowed low when he reached them, bumping a fractious mule with his generously proportioned backside. With a guffaw at his own clumsiness, the man slapped Richard on the arm. "And her new lord, I trow! Strode, is it?"

"Richard Strode, at your service," Richard confirmed. He raised an eyebrow, waiting for the raucous man to introduce himself.

"Jem Harbeth! I am the *groom!*" the man shouted over the melee, beating a pudgy fist on his chest. Then he giggled, a singularly unattractive sound that matched his appearance. "Not the stable groom, y'understan', but the *bridegroom!*"

The man was so flown with drink he could scarcely balance himself. Richard nodded in acknowledgment. "Congratulations."

"Well then..." the man began, then seemed to forget what he was about. His unfocused gaze wavered and wandered away to settle on something else. "Aha, 'tis Dismoth over there. Ho, Dis, good fellow! Well come!" He staggered toward the man he had spied and disappeared into the swarm of people.

Sara laughed and nudged Richard with her elbow. "You see what I mean? I hope the bride has a sense of humor."

"And an impaired sense of smell," Richard added with a snort. Their host reeked of sweat and soured ale.

"Come," Sara advised, "I have a feeling we must find our own accommodations. Harbeth's mother is elderly and infirm and, as far as I know, he has no chatelaine as yet. Shall we simply make ourselves at home?"

"God forbid," Richard muttered, raking the unkempt keep with his gaze. He heard Sara laugh again. At least her mood was improving.

Thus far, no one except Harbeth had even noticed her. He eased his arm around her waist and kept her close by his side, as much to signal his possessiveness and protection as to afford her comfort.

The two men who had ridden with them in addition to

Sir Edmund, followed with Sara's clothes chest, Richard's leather saddle pack containing his own change of garments and the silver chalice he'd brought to gift the newlyweds.

As he looked around the hall, Richard commented, "I'd rather pull my own teeth than sleep in here."

Sara made a face. "I wonder if we could slip out unnoticed after the feast."

"And ride home in the dark?" Richard admitted privately that he was tempted, despite the danger involved, but he could not put Sara at risk. "We should stay."

"Very well then, but mind where you step, not to mention where you lie tonight," she advised, wrinkling her nose at the smell of animal droppings and rotting food. "I am for the solar now to freshen myself before the ceremony." She beckoned for the lad to bring their baggage along.

"I will await you by the outer door when you have done," he called out as she disappeared into a walled-off enclosure at the back of the hall.

He heard random chords of a lyre overlaying the cacophony of barking hounds, chattering guests who were now drifting inside, and the frantic grumble of servants rushing to make order out of pandemonium. Richard followed the faint, tuneful sound.

It emanated from a small alcove near the hall door. There sat a slender man holding the instrument and strumming, seemingly unaware of the discordant noise around him. The old minstrel dressed simply yet elegantly. He had well-trimmed hair and beard the color of new snow.

"Master Melior?" Richard asked as he approached and joined the man within the arched alcove.

"*Oui, m'sieur,* one and the same." He played two chords with a flourish of his long supple fingers.

"I am Richard Strode. Do you recall the name?"

Melior smiled, his eyes sharp and dark as night. "*Oui,*

I remember you well, though as a squalling infant. You have not the look of your brother, save for those eyes. Grass green and unmistakable. How does your lord father?''

"Right well, for his age," Richard answered. "Approaching eighty now."

The minstrel laughed and set his lyre aside on the stone bench and stood. "Give Lord Adam my regards when you see him next. Ask him does he recall our capture of Lord Hume. Ah, those were wild times, I do swear."

"He has recounted it often and with great glee." Richard offered his arm as he would to greet a friend. Indeed, he counted Melior as such even if he could not remember the man.

"I wish to thank you for rescuing us at Rowicsburg all those years ago. How many times have I heard the tale of our escape, I wonder? A hundred times, if once."

He did not wait for Melior to respond. "Now I have come to beg further aid of you."

Melior smiled knowingly. "You wish to meet with your brother."

"Yes. Could you arrange it?"

"*Done and done,* as Sir Alan would say. He has already heard of your marriage and that you are living nearby. He wants very much to see you. What place do you suggest for the meeting?" Melior asked.

"Will he come to Fernstowe? Assure him he will be safe there. My word on it."

Melior looked past Richard toward the opening of the alcove. "My lady, do you seek someone?"

Richard turned. "Sara! I thought—"

"That I would take longer in the solar?" she asked curtly. "Obviously."

She noted the lyre on the cushioned seat. "Master Melior.'' Then she turned a faintly accusing eye on Richard. "Friend to Alan the True."

"*Oui, madame,*" Melior answered, glancing from one to the other as if he expected mayhem.

Richard nodded to Sara. "You heard?"

"I did," she admitted with a chilling smile and returned her regard to the minstrel. "Add my own invitation to my lord husband's, Master Melior. I will gladly receive Sir Alan to my home in the same manner he would welcome my husband to his."

"As you wish, *madame,*" Melior answered.

Richard took Sara's arm and led her out to the hall door where many were exiting for the chapel. "What did you mean by that?" he asked as they walked together.

"Precisely what I said," Sara replied. "Make what you will of it."

Richard expelled a breath of frustration. How could he ever convince Sara that Alan had nothing to do with his abduction and demand for ransom? Or her father's death? Surely when his brother came to visit and she met him, she would realize that Alan was innocent of the deeds attributed to him.

Her enmity ran deep—with good cause, since her sire had been murdered—but soon she would see that the hatred was misdirected. At least, he fervently hoped it was.

Sara stood beside Richard in the courtyard, mulling over what had just taken place inside the hall. She would suffer Richard's brother coming to Fernstowe, if the man dared to show his face. She doubted that he would be so foolish. Nonetheless, she would prepare well for his treachery beforehand in the event that he did come.

Unless she took measures to protect Richard, he would see too late that he had placed trust in the wrong man, the very man who had played him foul.

She then put her planning aside to witness the wedding of Harbeth to the diminutive Lady Hildegard. The couple took their places to say vows before the priest at the chapel door so that all in attendance could see.

"They are an odd match," Richard whispered, his comment nearly lost in the hum of conversation around them.

She inclined her head toward him. "Any match with Harbeth as a party would seem odd. Yet Lady Hildegard seems resigned to it. I had visions of his having chosen some feckless girl to wed, but this woman will suit much better. Thank goodness she is a widow with experience."

"Even so, she does not smile on the venture," Richard observed. "I daresay she realizes her work is cut out for her. Harbeth obviously needs her, but bringing order to his place would daunt the hardiest of wives."

Sara scoffed. "The state of his keep is the least of her worries, I should think."

Richard rocked on his heels, his hands clasped behind him. "In your opinion, that would be the bedding."

"In *everyone's* opinion, that would be the bedding. The poor fellow's like a giant, grubby puppy. And drunk, to the bargain."

"Merely overserved this morn. It is his wedding day," Richard argued, feeling obliged to defend the poor fellow.

"No need to excuse him to me. This is the man at his most ordinary. Trouble is, Harbeth could clean himself, cease drinking and become as respectable as any man if he wished. Obnoxious as he can be, I still sympathize with him. If anyone bears more of our neighbors' taunts than I, it would be the luckless Harbeth. I should not add to them, even to you in private conversation."

Richard frowned severely. "I have heard no one ridicule you, Sara."

She took a deep breath, released it and forced a smile for him. "The day is young yet."

He took her arm as the ceremony ended and they made their way toward the chapel for the Mass.

"Felicitations on your recent marriage, Lady Sara," said a voice behind her.

Sara turned enough to see the wife of Sir John Horton wearing a smug smile. "You've done right well for yourself, I see." The woman inspected Richard with a lascivious eye.

"I certainly have," Sara replied. "Richard, Lady Emma Horton. Lady Emma, meet my husband, Sir Richard Strode."

Richard bowed as well as he could while pressed on all sides by the crowd. "Charmed."

"Or forced," came the laughing reply as the woman blended back into the horde of well-wishers.

*Everyone knew.* Somehow, the circumstances of her marriage to Richard had become known to all. Likely the king's men had talked of it all across England. Now her neighbors had yet another jest to bandy about amongst themselves, she thought with a grimace.

Guiltily Sara realized she'd been hoping that old Harbeth would be the brunt of all their barbs while she was here. After all, he would be too numbed by drink to notice or care.

No chance now that she would be spared. Sara of Fernstowe, the aged and battle-scarred tower of a woman, had waylaid a handsome knight hunting on her lands. Wed him by trickery while he was out of his head, the only way she could gain a husband of any kind. That tale would draw many more chortles than any of Harbeth's drunken antics might engender.

That she had—even unconsciously until this moment—wished mockery on another to spare herself, made Sara feel petty and small-minded. She must pray for forgiveness during this Mass. And while she was about it, she would also pray for the future happiness of Lord Harbeth and Lady Hildegard. Small matter that Harbeth had teased her for years, he was not a truly unkind man like some, even when in his cups.

Richard's fingers bit into Sara's elbow as he glared over everyone's heads at the Lady Emma. But he said nothing, for they had reached the doorway and entered the chapel.

Once they made obeisance, he quickly guided her to stand against the back wall and slipped his arm behind her, his hand clenched upon her waist, a protective gesture Sara appreciated.

She leaned into his side, so glad of his presence for her own sake, yet sorry for his. Her husband had just become a laughingstock whether he knew it or not. Sara suspected he did.

After the Mass, everyone returned to the hall for the wedding breakfast. It proved a hurried affair due to the traditional hunt that was to take place.

Richard brushed his hand down her arm and caught her hand as the men began to gather to ride out. "Will you be all right here alone?"

"Alone?" Sara scoffed, and swept the crowd with a gesture. "I shall scarcely suffer for company. The place is jammed to the rafters, as you can well see."

"Will you be all right, Sara?" he repeated, his eyes telling her of his reluctance to leave her.

"I shall be fine," she assured him. "Now go along and show them how one hunts while sober. You appear to be the only man who is."

He nodded and squeezed her fingers before he left.

Richard could be very gallant when he wished, Sara thought with a smile. Again she regretted drawing him into this farce. And that was exactly what their marriage seemed to everyone.

Even she could see how doomed it was. He had protested the dissolution only for form's sake. Or, more likely, he did not want to admit to one and all that he had been royally duped. Too late. Now that every soul in England probably had heard what had really happened, Richard would have no cause to stay with her and she did not blame him.

"*Madame?*"

Sara greeted the wandering minstrel with a nod. She had fully intended to seek him out and here he was. "Good Melior. I see you do not enjoy the hunt."

He shrugged in a typically Gallic way. "Lords and knights do not favor the company of a lowly jongleur, *madame*. I had no invitation."

"Their loss," Sara said lightly, "and my own gain. Will you play for the ladies?" She glanced around to see that most of the women had disappeared into the solar. Dread at joining them there prompted her to add, "Or we could stroll about the hall and get better acquainted."

He nodded his acceptance of that suggestion and they walked idly together. "I may have need of music in future," she told him. "My father did not have an ear for such, but I so enjoy it. Would you come to Fernstowe someday?"

"If you like," he said. His wrinkled, foxlike features produced an expression of pleasure just short of a smile.

"We shall look forward to it," Sara said carefully, feeling her way toward the discussion she really wanted to initiate.

"Do you play at Byelough Castle often?"

"I always winter there," he admitted. "Sir Alan has been most generous over the years."

"Ah, then you know him well, I see. Would you tell me something of my husband's brother? I would learn more of my new...family."

The wily minstrel's eyebrows slanted and his thin mouth drew to one side. "What would you know?"

Sara thought for a moment before she proceeded. "Sir Alan is near fifty years of age, so Richard tells me."

"That is so. He was a man grown when your husband was born."

"He has sons," Sara guessed. No one had actually mentioned any, but surely he must. Richard believed a young man responsible for the border problems. Who else could it be?

"Three fine sons," Melior confirmed. "Adam, the eldest, has his father's great size. Dairmid and Nigel are still growing. There are two daughters, as well. Christiana and Margareth, both wed with babes of their own."

"A goodly number of children!" Sara exclaimed politely. "How fortunate for them. But tell me of the older lad. What age is he?"

"Adam is four and twenty, I believe."

So that explained the border brigand's youth. Their problem might not be Richard's brother, after all, but the son of Alan. Sara wondered if she should tell Richard this, or simply arrange for him to capture and wrest a confession from his abductor. Better that he should see for himself, she supposed.

After a moment's silence, Sara asked, "Would young Adam join his father when he comes to Fernstowe?"

Melior considered. "Would you wish him to do so, *madame?* He might be persuaded."

"Yes," Sara said with emphasis. "I would wish it. However," she added, "you must make clear to my brother-by-marriage and the...our...nephew, that they will be welcome only if they are willing to enter Fernstowe unarmed. Just a precaution, you understand."

The old man smiled knowingly. "I understand very well. You harbor distrust of the Scots."

"As do all the English hereabout, and with good reason, you must admit."

Melior inclined his head toward her, neither in agreement or protest. "Rumor runs rampant, *madame,* while the truth is elusive. I shall put forth your request and relay the reasons for it. You did hear your husband give his pledge of a truce?"

"Will they comply and arrive sans weapons, do you think?"

"I cannot answer for either man, *madame.* As a rule, the Strodes do as they please and no one dares oppose."

*Not for much longer,* Sara decided. That nephew of Richard's would never terrorize the Middle March or murder an English lord again. She would make certain of that.

To be fair, she would first determine whether Richard's nephew worked his madness alone or on the orders of his father, Alan the True. It only made sense that he did so.

She felt a harsh pang of sympathy for Richard, who suffered such betrayal by his own kin. Yet there was no way to spare his feelings in this matter. He needed her protection until he could accept the truth.

# Chapter Thirteen

"The only thing edible is the turnips," Richard muttered as he poked one of the gray cubes with his knife. "I suppose we go to sleep hungry."

"Sleep? You mean to sleep?" she asked in a low voice. He could feel her tension even when they were not touching. "Not I! I plan to spend the night on rat watch."

She shuddered as he laughed.

"Oh, come, 'tis not that bad. Look, Melior comes to play now. We can stop pretending to eat." He motioned for the boy who served them to take away their shared trencher.

"More ale?" he asked Sara.

"I think not," she answered, glaring at the head table. Their host lay sidewise in his chair, dead to the world. The bride looked bored. "Coming here was a mistake, Richard. Let us go home. I care not if every brigand in the north of England is out there waiting."

"Well, I do care."

"Play for us, man! Are we to dance or no?" a loud voice boomed from the dais. "Truth, 'tis well past May, but we still have a maypole to dance around!" The bride's father beckoned to her. "Come, Lady Sara, lead us out!"

*"Maypole?"* Richard growled as he stood, ready to tear the man apart.

"Cease!" Sara hissed. "You will only make things worse."

"I'll make things *dead,* particularly *that* cur!" he assured her through gritted teeth.

Sara rose and moved gracefully toward the open area. Richard followed right behind her, his hand on her waist. Couples gathered until they had formed a circle of eight. Melior and several other musicians began to play.

Stiffly at first, Richard joined Sara in the stately steps of the dance. She smiled sweetly and gave no indication that anything untoward had been said. He admired her aplomb. It was certainly in greater shape than his own.

The dance ended, but they did not return to their seats. Richard thought to keep Sara engaged in dancing as long as the music went on. She seemed much happier doing that than anything else they had done since coming here. It would also afford less chance that another of these misbegotten neighbors of hers might say something else to hurt her feelings.

Bringing her to this cursed wedding had been such a mistake.

His ploy worked for a while. Until Lady Emma joined them between dances. In a high-pitched voice that carried all too well in the drafty hall, the woman bleated, "Lady Sara! I had no notion that you knew *how* to dance!"

She placed a clawlike hand on Richard's forearm and leaned close, speaking as loudly as ever. "You must pray they play nothing livelier, Sir Richard, or you might be obliged to lift her!" Her tittering laugh scraped along his nerves.

"I have not seen *you* dancing, Lady Emma. Envious of my lady's grace, mayhap?" Richard smiled evilly.

Nearby chuckles greeted his words. He had never felt such an urge to do bodily harm. En masse.

Sara pulled a wry face and then grinned. She appeared delighted, as if he'd made a jest. He knew she hurt. He drew her close to his side.

"Might I have the next dance, Lady Sara?" someone asked in a deep drawling voice.

Richard felt her stiffen, though her expression never changed. He had never met the man who asked her, nor had he seen him at the hunt or about the keep before now. Obviously Sara knew him, but was offering no introduction.

"No, you may not," she answered baldly and without explanation.

The fellow inclined his head, a gesture short of a bow, and stepped away. Richard noted that he was a right handsome fellow, finely dressed and well formed. He had regular features except for one dark eyebrow, puckered from some battle or other. That only lent him a haughty yet rakish look, as if the eyebrow were permanently raised in question. Though his skin must have been pitted by boils when he was younger, it had healed well enough and was cleanly shaven.

The newcomer stood only slightly shorter than Richard himself, certainly tall enough not to be intimidated by Sara's height. Nothing really objectionable about him that Richard could see.

Why had Sara refused to dance with him? Richard would have thought the man's invitation reassuring to Sara, coming as soon as it had on the heels of Lady Emma's gibe.

"It seems you have a champion other than myself," he said, so that only she could hear. He probed shamelessly, he knew, but he wanted to find out who the man was.

Jealousy pricked him, but not too sharply since Sara did not seem interested.

She made a slight, scoffing sound—distinctly at odds with her carefully placid expression—and then looked past him as she whispered, "Get me from this place, Richard. Please."

The music began again and Richard drew her into the circle. "Brave it out, love," he advised. "Trust me, 'tis best you do."

She did, and with fortitude. Richard watched the faces of those who observed them dancing. Every male, to a man, envied him Sara. He could see it clearly, even if she could not. Every female wore a look of either fear or disparagement.

Sara daunted them, he did not doubt. She was quite beautiful. But beyond that, Sara wore an aura of self-worth that had nothing to do with her appearance.

Here was a woman who behaved as though she needed no man to support, defend or define her. And that attitude—not her long-legged beauty, the scar or her aggressiveness—was what made her an oddity to these people.

A sudden revelation struck him like a mace: that was what had made her an oddity to him. He also realized that he liked her odd ways. She might have turned his idea of the perfect woman upside down and back to front, but he cared not a whit for that. Sara was Sara. Incomparable.

He clasped her hands and stepped close as the dance required. "You are like no other," he said next to her ear, his tone caressing. His gaze locked with hers as they drew apart, hands still joined, and came together again. "And I love you for it."

His own words shocked Richard, as they must have done her, but he meant them nonetheless. Her eyes closed and her lips tightened as she pulled her hands from his and turned about in the circle their dance required.

When she faced him again, her smile firmly in place, Richard saw one lone tear trickle down her left cheek. It was the very first he had seen Sara shed.

He would give his soul to know whether she shed it in happiness or despair.

Sara ached to be alone. Why had Richard said what he had? Pity for her plight, she supposed. Lord, how she despised pity, and especially his.

"I need to have a quick word with Lord Selwick about the meeting tonight," he said as soon as the dance was over. "He is just over there. I will be gone but a moment."

Aelwyn approached her right after Richard left her side. "Ah, Sara, deserted already? We cannot have that! Come." His hand had locked on her wrist and he pulled her forth so that they stood directly before the head table.

His voice rang out. "Attend me, good people! We have yet another wedding to drink to this eve. Huzzahs for our mighty Sara of Fernstowe, and her newest conquest! Where is that luckless husband of hers, eh?"

The hall filled with raucous laughter and bawdy calls.

Richard appeared like magic, wresting Aelwyn's hand from her arm. Beneath the shouts of encouragement, Sara heard his growl to Aelwyn. "Touch my wife again and I will kill you."

Before Aelwyn could answer his challenge, Richard raised both his hands while holding one of hers. "Quiet!" he boomed. The hall fell silent as a tomb. Sara held her breath.

He reached for the chalice sitting before the bride and lifted it toward Aelwyn. "I acknowledge your envy, sir. Come, all you who know her, and drink health to Lady Sara of Fernstowe, a gift of my king and my dearest treasure."

Aelwyn glared at Richard, then at her, but remained silent. A spate of nervous laughter filled the short silence, but most raised their cups as Richard bade them do. He saluted her with the borrowed chalice, sipped and set it down upon the head table. Then he continued in a deep, sonorous voice that commanded every ear, "On this happy occasion in honor of Lord Harbeth and his bride, I would tell you of my own good fortune."

Aelwyn rolled his eyes and chuckled. "Oh, do tell, for we have all heard how she—"

Richard's fist shot out so rapidly, she hardly saw it move. A bone cracked and Aelwyn crumpled to the floor, unconscious.

Sara ducked her head and pressed her lips together to hold in her laughter. Uncertain what he would do next, Sara cut her gaze to one side and watched this husband of hers.

"Now then, on to my story," Richard said, as though naught had happened to distract him. He smiled fondly at those gathered and then at her, as though he held her in greatest esteem. The hall fell quiet as a tomb as everyone waited.

"As you might have heard, I came north with the king not long ago. We crossed into Fernstowe lands a-hunting. Ere I knew what happened, I lay sorely wounded, an enemy's arrow deep in my chest." He touched the place and invited their sharing of his pain.

Richard sounded much as a bard might, regaling a rapt audience with a new tale of romance. Someone sighed.

"The dark angel hovered, my friends, all eager to bear me away," he intoned quietly. "And yet, despite my pain and longing for the peace death would bring, I clung to life, for the face above me…this countenance of such incredible beauty," he whispered, drawing one hand lightly along her cheek in a gesture of reverence, "held me enthralled. Our King Edward, my liege and lifelong friend, swore then that if I did live, he would grant me the wish of my heart.''

He raked the expectant, spellbound throng with those sharp green eyes and nodded slowly, meaningfully. ''Can you guess my demand, good people? Can you doubt whose love held me earthbound? Can you say the name of the woman I desired more than heaven itself?''

''Lady Sara!'' someone nearby breathed her name. ''Sara of Fernstowe!'' another called out. '''Tis our Sara he demanded to wed!'' came a shout. ''Sara was your choice!''

The cheering grew louder as everyone joined in, clinking cups and laughing merrily. Only this time their laughter was not mocking. They sounded truly happy for her.

Melior struck a chord and lively music roused some to dancing, not the refined and decorous dance they had performed earlier, but a raucous reel more worthy of a peasant revel.

People who had once spurned her company now surrounded her. They poured forth with sincere wishes for her happiness, lauds for her healing skills and delight that their king held one of their own in such high esteem. It was too much, too much.

Sara leaned into Richard's embrace. He lifted her chin and kissed her firmly to the delight of everyone, most of all, herself. She laughed when he released her. With relief, but more at the absurdity of his ploy.

Never in her life would she have expected such from the taciturn Richard, the reserved knight whom she had trapped into marriage.

''Are you certain you're not a Welsh bard?'' she asked him as he dragged her to the middle of the floor to join the rowdy frolic in progress.

He grasped her by the waist and lifted her high against

him so that she looked down on his grinning face. The love in her heart at that moment nearly overwhelmed her.

They whirled and hugged as they danced, bumped against the others, trod upon feet, and laughed recklessly all the while. At the rousing finish, Richard lifted her again and spun about as she held up her hands, threw back her head and gloried in it all.

He allowed her to slide down his body until they were eye to eye. She clutched the dark green velvet of his rich tunic. "I must have you," he whispered. "Now."

She giggled, a singularly childish sound she never employed. "Not here," she answered.

"In the garden, then," he growled impatiently, "or the buttery. The garderobe…I care not where, but I must."

Sara settled her mouth near his ear. "As soon as may be, but not in this place. Let us go home."

He groaned through a pained smile as he lowered her to her feet. "I regret we cannot. We should stay to make this work."

"What work?" she asked, her stomach roiling with apprehension. She knew what he would say before he said it.

"If we are to convince them our marriage was not your doing, then we should play the loving couple before them, don't you think?"

Sara's happiness melted into a sad little puddle that evaporated on the instant. She lowered her chin to her chest and nodded, for she could not say a word. What was there to say in any account?

Richard meant none of what he had said. He had not lied to everyone and treated her with affection in order to make these people accept her as something other than a curiosity to be mocked. He had done it to save face for himself.

She accepted that he did not really love her, but now he

did not even *want* her enough to abandon this farce of a celebration and ride three hours in the dark.

Her heart pained her so, she knew it must be breaking.

Richard led Sara back to their place at table. When he had seated her, he straddled the bench and wrapped his arms around her, drawing her close to him. She seemed to resist resting against him for a moment before she gave in.

Melior had begun singing a ballad and all had grown quiet again to listen. Two other musicians accompanied him upon the bodhran and the flute. His melodious voice and the notes of his small harp added a sweetness that stirred passion in the soul. Already well stirred by his own words and the dance, Richard wished for privacy to hold Sara even closer, but he knew that was not to be.

As dearly as he wished to hurry her back to Fernstowe and the seclusion of his bedchamber, he could not leave this place as yet. Soon now, after the newlyweds had been properly bedded for the night, he and several of the other border lords had planned to meet outside the hall to discuss the matter of the raids and Lord Simon's murder.

In his heart, he knew his brother was not the culprit they sought, but he still needed all the information he could gather from those who had been victims. Alan's name could never be cleared until he found the man responsible for the deeds and brought him to justice.

The song ended and the applause woke Harbeth from his drunken slumber at the dais. "I'm for bed," the man declared, and the guests took him at his word. Richard remained where he was, holding Sara fast, and watched as a gaggle of women surrounded and rushed Lady Emma to the stairs. A half-dozen men struggled to lift the bilious bridegroom to their shoulders to carry him to the bridal chamber.

"You want to go up with them?" Richard asked Sara, for the hall was nearly cleared of people now.

"No, I have no desire to see Harbeth naked. If he has faults uncovered as yet, his wife may have the pleasure of discovery." She pulled away from him and got up from the bench. "Good night, Richard."

He caught one of her hands as he stood with her. "Sara, are you angry that I will not take you home? There is the meeting tonight, remember?"

She smiled sadly. "Of course. Morning will be soon enough."

With that, she tugged her hand loose of his grip and headed for the solar built into the back of the hall.

Richard thought to follow for a kiss good-night, but saw how weary she looked and let her go. However, she left him with an uneasiness that would not go away. Something had diminished the joyfulness with which she had greeted his affection as they danced.

His knuckles ached from his blow to the man who had jeered at their marriage. Richard rubbed his fist and wondered belatedly at the meanness he had seen in the fellow's eyes. Jealous meanness, bordering on hatred, seemingly directed at Sara. Judging by her reaction, there was no love lost there. But *why?*

"Oh, dear God," Richard muttered, "could it be?" Could that man be the suitor who had scarred Sara, thinking to force her into accepting him as husband? There was that puckered brow to consider. Had Sara done that? Richard meant to find out.

He summoned one of the maids now clearing the tables. "Where is Melior, the minstrel?"

"Gone, milord," she said with a clumsy curtsy. "Gets his coin aforehand and ne'er stays the night when he comes here."

"I had a question for him, but mayhap you might tell

me. Who was the dark man before the dais, the lord in the crimson tunic? Did you see him?''

She grinned and ducked her head. "The one with the new broke nose?''

"That one, yes," Richard answered. "His name?''

"Lord Aelwyn o' Berthold." She hesitated before adding, "He'd be gone as well. Took hisself away soon as he come around.''

"Pity," Richard muttered to himself, rubbing his knuckles harder.

"Aye, m'lord, 'tis that," the maid said with a grin. She dared one timid pat to his fist. "We thanks ye.''

Richard merely nodded and the maid scurried away, his mind fully occupied with piecing together the facts he had and the suspicions he had just acquired.

Berthold was a border keep, one whose lord had applied for help from the king. Help in ridding Northumberland of the dreaded Scot, Alan the True. His scapegoat?

Sara had named Lord Aelwyn of Berthold only as one who had offered for her hand. The man loathed Sara, a fact made evident this very night by his behavior. The reason for that hatred had to be because she had spurned him.

Just how deep did Aelwyn's hatred run? Deep enough to set Sara's new husband against her with the lie about the ransom? Deep enough to beggar her through blackmail? And had that malice really begun the day Sara had marked him after he had marked her?

Richard would find out, he promised himself.

Shortly thereafter, the guests descended the stairs, still shouting and jesting toward the upper chamber where Harbeth and his bride would pass their wedding night.

Richard bided his time until most had settled down for the night. Four of the men wandered toward the hall door, each giving him a meaningful look as they passed the place where he sat.

He got up and joined them, lifting a torch from its stand and carrying it out to light their way. All remained silent until they reached the pleasuance, a small knot garden sadly overgrown with weeds poking up through dead grasses. He did not envy Lady Emma her future walks or gardening chores hereabout.

He cleared a place, stuck the slow-burning torch in a handy rabbit hole, and sat down on the ground. Smoke from the brand hovered around their heads as he waited for Lord Selwick, the older of the lords, to commence.

"We are not all here," the lord announced, searching each face. "Where is Lord Aelwyn?"

"I believe he is gone," Richard said evenly. "One of the maids said he left."

Lord Beringer laughed and shared a knowing look with Richard. "Nursing his nose, no doubt," he guessed. "Sound punch, and well deserved, by the way. Aelwyn can be rather tedious."

"He should be here. He's lost more than most," Selwick said, ignoring Beringer's words. "Should we call another meeting, do you think?"

Richard shrugged as though it mattered little. "I will send word to him by messenger if we decide anything important. We are all here now, and if he did not choose to attend…"

"Lord Bankwell's not here," Beringer noted. "His lands border mine, but are just over in the East March. He had some trouble there a while ago."

"Oh, that one never attends anything but his own business," Selwick said. "You can tell him what we decide, if you please, Beringer."

*Bankwell.* Richard recognized the name as Sara's other suitor, the one she'd not heard from in years. There was another he would investigate when he had opportunity. Did that man harbor as much ill will against Sara as Sir Aelwyn did?

"Quite right," one of the others said, nodding. "Let us get on with it then." He had addressed Richard, rather than Selwick. The older man and other two looked to him, as well.

Obviously they expected him to take charge. And since he was the king's answer to their cry for help, Richard did so. "I would have in writing the amounts you were required to pay the brigand and all property stolen or damaged. Can any of you identify the man you assume is Alan the True?"

"Nay," they answered in turn. Then Selwick added, "However, Lord Aelwyn did say they met once. The man slew Aelwyn's father."

"Recently?" Richard asked.

Selwick shook his head. "Nay, at Bannockburn, in the battle. That Scot took down a number of us, so I hear. Parmer of Berthold was one."

Richard scoffed. "That was over twenty years ago. How then did the son meet him?"

Sir Meckville spoke up. "Through a priest. Most of Berthold's beasts had died off. A goodly number of tenants, as well. Some kind of pox hit them hard. Place was going to ruin after that. Seems the cleric arrived one day and offered aid to the widow and the boy, Aelwyn. He explained to them that Alan the True sent the coin as tribute to the brave man he once slew."

Richard worried the stubble on his chin with his fingertips as he pondered Alan's gesture. "What then?" he asked.

Meckville laughed. "Aelwyn near killed the priest. Threw the coin in his face and hit him over the head with a fire tool. The widow sent out the gates for one of the priest's escort to come and get him. Alan himself marched in and hauled him off.''

"What did he do to the lad?'' Richard asked.

"Bade him keep the gold and mind his foul temper,'' Meckville said, "or he would do the dead father a favor and thrash sense into a bairn with more pride than wit.''

"One can imagine how the Scot's gloating affected the boy,'' Lord Selwick said, shaking his head.

"Gloating?'' Richard asked. "Seems strange to me that Sir Alan did not punish Aelwyn for his attack on a man of God. This Scot could very well have come without the gold or the priest and laughed at the state of Berthold. That is, if he only wished to gloat on Aelwyn's misfortune. Why do you suppose he came in peace with an offer of help to restore what the family had lost by the father's absence?''

Selwick sighed and spoke to Richard as though he were a lack-wit. "Because, the gold he brought likely came from the lad's father in the first place! The Scots stripped all the English after the battle. He used a portion of that wealth he gained there just to taunt Aelwyn.''

"I see,'' Richard said, though he did no such thing. "Still, the way any Scot hates to part with coin, I cannot envision one wasting any just to plague a small boy and a widow who mean nothing to him.''

"That is passing strange,'' agreed Tomlinson, the youngest of the lords present. "But Scots *are* a strange breed, as we all know.''

Richard had the answers he needed. Aelwyn had held grudges for years, obviously. And mayhap sought vengeance, against both Alan and Sara. And Alan had practiced compassion for a brave enemy's family. Asking anything further seemed pointless as far as the meeting was concerned.

Lord Bankwell was likely what Sara claimed he was, a suitor who had asked for her hand and accepted the refusal without rancor. Still in all, it would not hurt to know for certain.

"Fine, then. Make the lists I asked for tonight. Each of you, write down how the Scot contacted you, every word that passed between you and Sir Alan or whomever he sent to represent him. Be exact. When I have studied everything, we shall meet again."

"Where?" Meckville asked.

"At Fernstowe, if you like," Richard said. "Lady Sara and I have not yet held a feast to mark our marriage. Let us say a fortnight hence, on the Friday. If there is a change in the day, I shall send a messenger."

"What of Lord Aelwyn?" asked Tomlinson.

Richard smiled as a plan solidified in his mind. "Do not worry on it. I shall notify him myself."

# Chapter Fourteen

The early morning departure from Harbeth Castle seemed remarkably like their arrival. The same crowd of folk, though more subdued now than yesterday, milled about, chatting and taking farewell of one another.

More of her neighbors addressed Sara now and with warmer regard than they ever had. She knew this was due to Richard's unplanned and totally false tribute to her as a *treasured* wife at the feast last eve.

They viewed her through new eyes this day, and saw her as valued by their king and by this strong and handsome man they thought had chosen her above all others. If they only knew how deliberately he had played with their thinking, Sara thought, they would likely shoot a few arrows in places that would not heal.

She felt inclined to do that herself at the moment. Yet Sara felt even more anger at herself for holding such hopes that he would put her feelings before his own pride. As if any man would do such a thing. If only he had not uttered those love words as they danced, she might even forgive him. That byplay had been for show, as well, Sara felt certain.

A night spent lying awake among a score of snoring

women, breathing through her mouth to avoid the stench
of unwashed bodies and stale drink, had not improved an
already sour mood.

She felt less than fresh herself, craving a bath and weary
to her bones. The hairpins beneath her veil poked painfully
at her scalp while doing poor duty in confining her wild
curls beneath the silk. She shrugged uncomfortably in her
heavy, wrinkled woolen travel gown.

Richard appeared as he usually did, well turned out in
his rich blue velvet surcoat and costly mail with its shining
plates attached at arms, knees and shins. Ever the king's
knight. Aye, *all* for display, she thought with a scoff. He
did not even wear a helm as one would if truly expecting
attack on the road.

"A right showy piece of work," she muttered to herself,
staunchly refusing to take pride in the way he looked.

When he'd finished speaking to Sir Matthew, he turned
to her. After studying her for a moment, he spoke. "What
is amiss with you this morn? You look troubled." His
pretense of worry annoyed her further. "Did someone give
you insult?" he demanded.

She raised her gaze to his and nodded. "A man I
thought to trust. But I have learned my lesson."

"Who is he? I'll set the matter to rights," he promised,
glancing around the crowded courtyard.

"Then see to yourself!" Sara told him sharply. Grasping
her pommel and reins, she raised her foot to the stirrup
and mounted easily before he could come close enough to
assist. She looked down at him and waited to see what he
would say.

Instead of taking up the gauntlet she had flung before
him, he chose to ignore it. After a hasty check of her
mare's saddle girth and the length of the stirrups, he turned
away to mount his gelding.

Richard then issued a few words of instruction to Sir

Edmund and led their party out the open gates. They turned west and silently commenced the ride home.

When they came in sight of Fernstowe, Richard fell back beside her and motioned for the men to continue riding ahead. "Now will you tell me?" he asked in a more conciliatory tone than he had used at Harbeth's. "What have I done?"

"You lied to everyone last evening," Sara said, "so eloquently that I near believed you myself, though I was there when we wed and know differently."

He grunted, a small laugh. "I near believed it, too." His smile almost disarmed her, but then he added, "My words served our purpose, so why are you vexed?"

Sara shot him a mean-spirited look. "'Tis not what you said, or that you lied, but why you did it! And, beyond that, when we danced, you lied to *me!*" She kicked her mare to a gallop, passed the men and rode on to the keep alone. *Vexed,* indeed!

The children ran out the gates, waving to welcome her. She forced a smile, offered both a hasty word of greeting and left them there to greet their father.

Berta was pouring her bathwater when she reached her chamber. In no mood to discuss the visit or the wedding, she held up her hand to prevent Berta's speaking to her.

She would have her bath and then to go to bed. Neither food nor company appealed to her at the moment. In truth, nothing appealed. Sara wanted to be left alone.

"Leave me, Berta," she ordered in her most commanding voice. "Go and see to the little ones and order a meal for the men. If anyone asks for me, I am resting and do not wish to be disturbed."

Berta frowned, but complied without protest. Sara pulled off her clothing and veil and stepped into the warm water. She completely immersed her head, hairpins and all, and sputtered when she emerged. The sweet-scented water disturbed her. Everything did. She wanted to weep. To weep, wail aloud and throw things until she exhausted herself too much to move.

It troubled her sorely that Richard's consideration meant so much to her. Not his consideration, she amended, but his *love*. How had she ever let herself entertain any hope of that, all the while knowing...

She sat up straight and began to soap herself vigorously. "No more of this!" she muttered with vehemence. "He did what he did and it is done now. For all his self-serving reasons, he did do you some good. Let it go at that. Be *glad* that he did."

She ducked under the water again. "And *thank* him for it!" she added when she emerged. She yanked the stubborn pins from her hair, flung them toward the corner and raked her fingers through the wet tangles.

"You are welcome, whatever it was," Richard answered unexpectedly.

Sara rounded on him, grasping the edge of the tub with both hands. "What are you doing in here?" she demanded.

"About to repay you in kind for a lovely bath you once gave me, dear heart," he replied. Slowly he approached, hands on his hips and amusement on his face. He leaned down, dragged a wet curl off her brow and tucked it behind her ear.

She batted his hand away. "Get out!"

"Why, Sara, I thought to get in."

"I will not have it!"

"Remains to be seen."

Sara covered her face with her hands and drew in a steadying breath. She was just shy of screaming like a shrew. This would not do. Even if he had dented her pride, it was not entirely destroyed.

Slowly, calmly now, she spoke. "I beg you leave my chamber and let me be, Richard."

He laughed aloud, a rich ringing sound that whipped her anger to a froth. "You? *Beg?*" he said with an inelegant snort. "That event many would pay to witness! Come now, Sara, why this temper? Last eve you were ready to ride here in all haste and find our bed together. Is it that I refused to put you in harm's way on the road after dark? We are here now, after all."

"So we are," she replied, fully in control now. Well, almost in control. She *was* still sitting naked in a tub of cooling water with her bird's nest of hair tangled round her head. A dreadful sight, surely, and not one to stir a man's lust. What was he after?

Might as well be blunt. "What are you after?"

"You, of course," he said, as blunt as she.

"And if I refuse?" she asked, not coyly, but honestly wanting to find out what he would do.

He smiled knowingly. "I would honor your wish, if I thought you meant it."

"I do mean it," she assured him.

He reached down, grasped her beneath her arms and lifted her out of the tub as though she weighed nothing. "Show me," he dared. Then he kissed her.

His large hands tunneled through her hair, his palms covering her ears. The feel of his mouth on hers, the abrasion of his clothing against her body and the whip of chilly air against her wet backside confused her senses. She longed to sink into the warmth he offered, and she longed to push away and run. For the moment, she clung.

His tongue sought entrance and found it as his hands brushed down her neck. One remained there, holding her steady in the deepening kiss while the other moved to her hips, drawing her fast against him. One great palm flattened at the base of her spine, his fingers flexed, kneaded, impatient and eager.

Against her breasts and belly she could feel the very

pattern of his chain mail beneath the fabric of his surcoat. Hard steel encased in soft velvet. Ah, saints, that brought another thing of his to mind that had naught to do with clothes. Sara groaned, unable to move away, most parts of her not truly wanting to.

"I need you, Sara," he whispered against her lips. "All the night long I could think of nothing but this." His hands moved over her, setting her skin to tingling and craving more of his touch. "All the way home...this." He kissed her again.

She responded, helpless to battle the desire he kindled within her. When his mouth left hers, she sighed with defeat. Or need. What did it matter?

He trailed his hands to her shoulders and moved her a little apart from him, gazing down into her face, his eyes hooded with passion, his mouth wearing a lazy, promising smile. "Play squire and help divest me?"

Sara nodded, her fingers already seeking the tail of his surcoat. Together they removed it and then the heavy chain-link tunic beneath.

"Untie your gambeson while I see to these," she said, kneeling before him to unbuckle the straps of his silvered leg guards.

"Kneeling naked at my feet. As near to subservience as I shall ever see from you, I think," he said, laughing softly. "And how beautiful you do look." He tossed the padded gambeson on the floor beside her and began unfastening the points at his waist.

Sara's hands stilled at their task for a moment as she remained on her knees before him and digested what he had said. Teasing words he'd uttered, but underneath them lay his real meaning. Richard did not know how to deal with a woman who revealed her feelings, who was honest about her desires.

She looked up at him as he yanked impatiently at his

waist ties. If he truly wanted a submissive wife, then why not try to give him that? Mayhap she had played this matter wrongly to begin with. Richard obviously desired her. He said he did not find her terribly ugly. The only problem was that he did not love her.

How many times and in how many ways had he told her why he did not? Not straight out, but clearly enough with his frustration and gentle chastising. And she, stubborn as usual, had not listened.

Sara finished removing the protective armor plates and sat back on her heels while he took off his chausses. She had vowed she would never change herself. Not for Richard or for anyone else. However, if he could play the part of willing husband to save his pride—and hers, if she were honest—then so could she pretend. If she held herself aloof from passion as he seemed to think she should, he might at least think better of her. She resigned herself to doing that much to please him.

He angered her, yes. He puzzled her and worried her and made her weak with wanting when she wished to remain strong. But she did love him. More than anything, she loved him, wanted him to stay with her, and feared above everything that he would not. Subduing, or at least concealing, her own needs was surely a small price to pay.

His disrobing accomplished, Richard offered her his hands. She placed hers in them and rose to her feet. Instead of throwing her arms around him and kissing him madly, as she wished to do, Sara remained still. The next move—and all moves hereafter, she reminded herself firmly—would be Richard's.

For his sake, for his children's and for her own, she had just become the most demure wife in all of England. Mayhap in all the known world. Sara prided herself on her determination, and she was fully committed to this change.

For a moment, Richard stood there, caressing her with

his eyes. His hands tightened on hers and he drew her close. Sara squeezed her own eyes shut and struggled inwardly to dismiss the heat he sent winging through her when his body touched hers.

This might be more difficult than she thought. She drew in a deep breath and held still. He enfolded her in his arms and kissed her again, moving her slowly toward the bed. Her mind scrambled for something to occupy it other than Richard's taste, his scent, and the smooth glide of his skin against her own.

*The bed.* She would think of that. Sara tried to calculate how long it was compared to Richard's height and how far his feet might hang over the end. The picture that brought to mind amused her, almost distracting her from the tongue that played against her ear and the hands that were driving her mad.

She trembled with the effort to accept and not give. Lord, how she longed to touch him, just the slide of one hand over his muscled back, to feel the flexing of it. *No. Not this time. Not ever again.*

"Sara?" he whispered, almost desperately. Just her name, sweet upon his lips, sent a shudder through her. She could not stop that, but she must refrain from responding.

He laid her down gently upon the covers and braced one knee beside her hips to lever himself over her.

The bed collapsed. Sara screeched. Richard cursed.

Before they could catch breath, the door flew open. "Sweet Mary!" Berta cried out, wide-eyed at the sight of them sprawled naked on the collapsed bedstead.

The tray Berta carried hit the floor with a crash. Her hands flew to reddened cheeks. "I...I only came to..." She quickly shut her eyes and turned her back on them. "Are...are you hurt?"

Sara's laughter bubbled up and spilled out in great gusts. She pushed at Richard's chest until he moved off her, still growling curses most foul. She covered her face and laughed until she could hardly breathe.

By the time she recovered, Richard was up and half dressed. He had donned his surcoat, which hung too loose upon him without the padding and mail beneath. His great, hairy legs and large feet were still bare. With tousled hair, peevish frown and outsize garb, he looked an overgrown child denied a sweet. The sight and thought sent her off in fresh peals of laughter.

Berta's shoulders were shaking, too. Richard was not amused. Hands on his hips, he glared at her and next at Berta. Then without a word, he stalked out of the chamber and slammed the door behind him. Sara rolled over and buried her face in the pillows, trying to muffle the sounds of her mirth.

In truth, it was great relief she felt, more than glee. Thank heavens the blessed bed had broken just when it did. Her resolution not to enjoy their loving had been blowing away like smoke in a fierce wind.

Today she'd been exhausted, confused and in great need of comforting. And Richard had surprised her. Next time the occasion arose, she would be better prepared to withstand him.

Richard marched into his chamber and straight to his clothes chest. Throwing garments hither and yon, he chose a somber tunic and dark hose to match his mood.

Once dressed, however, he began to regain his humor. His lips quivered and he bit back a chuckle, lest he laugh outright at the memory of Sara, oblivious to her nudity, her long, graceful limbs at awkward angles, pointing at him and giggling like a lack-wit. He must have looked even more ridiculous to her.

He straightened his belt, brushed back his hair and headed for the door. Now that he'd conquered his embarrassment, he would go to Sara. He would ask her pardon, offer his stouter bed for sharing, and they could laugh about this together. It would be a tale they would recall into their old age. *The day the bed broke.*

Sharp blasts of the guard's signaling horn on the outer bailey wall interrupted his thoughts. With a regretful glance at her chamber door, Richard immediately changed his direction and headed down the stairs. Riders approached and none were expected. Surely it was too soon for Alan to come. One could only hope it was not the king again.

Moments later, he watched the arriving party from the roof of the gatehouse. Not the king, but a stately procession, nonetheless. No pennons flew, no colors. The leader of the party, a big man garbed in mail and green surcoat with no device, rode a large gray charger. A length behind came another, near as large, dressed much the same and similarly mounted. Six others, common soldiers in padded jacks and half helms, rode in pairs, flanking a lady upon a dainty mare.

"Who goes?" shouted Terrell, who had gate duty this day. Richard noted that he and every other man along the wall walk and within the bailey stood alert and with weapons ready.

The leader drew up just outside the gates and removed his helm, resting it in the curve of his arm. In a deep, commanding voice, he announced, "I am brother to Sir Richard Strode, come in answer to his invitation."

*Alan.* Richard moved closer to the crenelated wall and leaned out for a better view. The man had the look of their father right enough. Surely this could be none other than who he declared he was. If not, Fernstowe's archers stood ready to deal with him.

"Have the gates opened," he ordered Terrell, and then

turned back to the visitors. "Enter in peace," he called down.

The gates creaked and he heard the portcullis grind upward as he made his way down the steps. For dignity's sake, he hid his eagerness. At last he would meet the brother he could not remember but felt he knew so well. If, indeed, this was the man. Another had claimed that name falsely. Judging by the timbre of the voice, the two claimants could not be one in the same.

Once Richard reached the open inner gates, he looked past them through the outer ones to see the older knight hand off his sword and dirk to the younger. Then he beckoned and the woman in their train rode up beside him. The two entered together while the others remained without, watching intently as though expecting trouble.

Once clear of the tunnel created by the two gates and portcullis, the two halted. Richard marched forth. "You can prove who you are, sir?"

The knight laughed, his green eyes alight. "If 'tis Wee Dickon who asks it, then aye, I will."

*Wee Dickon.* He hated that. No one but Alan had ever used the name for him. Father had laughed over it for years when reading Alan's letters to them. "Your address of me is proof enough," Richard declared with a wry grin, "though I do not prefer it."

With agility that belied his age, Alan dismounted and rushed forward, grabbing Richard around the shoulders in a bone-crushing hug. "God's truth, lad, I ne'er thought to see ye again!" He turned, keeping a hand Richard's shoulder. "Come, meet your sister-by-law. Here is my guid lady, Honor."

Richard bowed and reached up for the hand of his most unexpected guest. She regarded him with huge gray eyes and a sweet smile, a beautiful woman, still, despite her years.

"I am happy to meet you at last, sister," Richard said, "though Alan's letters have told us of you for years."

"And I am glad to see you again, Richard, though I am certain you do not remember me. Are your parents well? We have been in France this past half year and returned home only a few days ago. We've not had letters from your father for some time."

"They were hale last I heard," Richard assured her.

He released her and invited them to the keep. "Come, let us to the hall for warmth and wine."

Richard wondered what reception they would get there from Sara. She might either play the pleasant hostess or go for Alan's throat with her eating knife. One thing for certain, she never did as he expected her to do.

He and Alan walked together and beside Lady Honor, who remained seated upon her mare.

"You unarmed yourself before you came in," Richard said, gesturing toward Alan's empty scabbard. "Your trust in me is appreciated, but that was unnecessary."

Alan shrugged. "Yer lady wife told Melior 'twas a condition, so I did abide by it."

Richard frowned at that. He would never ask another knight to lay down his sword except in surrender. Nor would he have put his own aside had he visited Alan's keep.

He assisted Honor in dismounting when they reached the steps leading up to the hall.

"I hope I am not imposing," Honor said softly. "Alan insisted that I come. Truth told, I wanted very much to see you again, and to meet your new wife."

"Yes, well…we are most pleased to have you here," he said politely. In fact, her presence could prove a blessing. Sara might feel more obliged to act agreeably with another noblewoman present.

They entered the hall together and Richard ushered them

to the comfortable chairs set beside the fire. "Sit, rest. I will go and fetch Sara. We only arrived home from Harbeth's wedding a while ago and she was, um...at her bath when we heard the horn."

He knew they must wonder that he did not send a servant for Sara instead of going himself. But Richard needed to gauge her mood before she came downstairs, and see what he might be obliged to deal with.

"No cause for that," Sara announced. "I am already come."

She emerged from the shadowed corner of the hall and approached them. Her closed expression told him as much about what she was feeling as a glare of animosity would have done. She was livid, seething with hatred for his brother. He hoped Alan and Honor would not guess as much.

"Sara, meet Lady Honor and my brother, Alan. My wife, Lady Sara of Fernstowe." He prayed she would not opt for an open confrontation at the outset of the acquaintance.

"Sir, my lady," she said stiffly, dropping a half curtsy.

Alan bowed, straightened and met Sara's eyes. "Melior the Minstrel has apprised me of what's gone on of late. Word's about that I killed yer father, lass. I'm thinking ye believe it."

"I do," she admitted with a lift of her chin.

"I swear before God Almighty, I did not do that deed."

Sara said nothing, but her silence told all. She did not believe him. His brother could swear on the heads of his children, fall prostrate before her, remind her all he liked of his legendary reputation for truth, and still Sara would judge him guilty.

Richard tried to smooth over the breach until he could get Sara alone and think of some way to convince her.

"Lady Honor says they have been in France most of the year. They returned but a few days ago."

"A goodly alibi," Sara said smoothly. She and Alan had squared off like two opponents about to draw swords, though, thankfully, neither was armed.

"I do not lie," Alan declared, quietly but with vehemence.

Honor stepped in. "Do you think we might have a cup of wine, Lady Sara? That mare of mine has the gait of a warhorse and I ache to the marrow of my bones."

She sat down and stretched her feet toward the fire, calmly ignoring the tension between Sara and her husband.

Sara gave Alan one more assessing look and then turned to beckon a maid. "Wine for the guests, Darcy. And inform the kitchens that supper is to be served as early as may be. Send Grace to prepare the guest chamber."

Darcy nodded and scurried away while Sara returned her attention to Alan. "For my husband's sake, I shall say no more." With that, she left them and marched gracefully to the stairs.

Richard felt the heat of embarrassment glow red on his face. "I do apologize. I fear Sara is..."

"Rightly troubled," Alan finished for him. "If I believed someone killed my da, I would not welcome him with a smile, either. Would you?"

"Well, no," Richard admitted. "We must prove to her that you are innocent. But first, allow me to tell you everything. Melior would not have heard some of it, especially my encounter with the miscreant." He proceeded to lay out all that had taken place.

Alan sighed and sat down in the armchair farthest from the fire. "It grates upon my temper that your wife will not credit me with honesty, but she does not know me yet." He squinted up at Richard. "How is it that ye acquit me so readily, knowing me scarcely any better than she does?''

"I know you have killed before in battle, but I do not believe you would do murder." He hesitated a moment before adding, "Besides that, you are not the one who took me for ransom and called himself by your name. While I never saw the face, your voice is not the same as his. I believe he was English."

"Ah," Alan said, accepting the cup of wine Darcy now offered him. He quaffed it and returned the cup to the tray she held. "This fellow who seized you spoke without the brogue that taints my own? Is this so?"

Richard almost gasped at the change in Alan's voice. Gone was the lilt of the Highlands. Not a trace of Scots remained. He sounded as English as King Edward at his most formal.

"Or did he perchance use the more courtly language your nobles borrow from France?" Alan asked in perfect French.

"Saints!" Richard whispered, shaking his head in wonder. For a moment he considered that mayhap...no, he knew Alan was not the one. "Higher in tone than yours," he declared, "not the same. Not at all." Yet for the first time, Richard realized that he could not trust his sense of hearing to identify the one who had taken him prisoner. A man could change his voice drastically, in tone, timbre and cadence, as his brother just proved. No one Richard knew had ever had reason to do such as that, so he had not accounted for it in this instance.

Alan chuckled. "Not certain, are you? Well, Dickon, you must draw your own conclusion. Ask yourself if I would have come here if I were guilty. Would I have left my sword and all protection outside your gates? Would I have risked the safety of the person dearest to my heart by bringing her with me?" He cut his narrowed green gaze to Richard, deliberately looking sly. "Or is that, too, but a trick to disarm you? To gain your trust?"

"No! No, of course not," Richard said. "Someone has set out to lay this blame on your shoulders, Alan. I was but pondering the possibility that the man I heard, yet did not see, may have fooled me. I would have sworn he was English. However, now—"

Alan shook his head. "For what it's worth, I believe you are right in this. Any Scots entering England near the Meadow of Dispute would need pass through either my lands or those of Ian Gray. I swear on my soul Gray is as blameless as I am in this and ask you to take my word on it. Our patrols along our boundaries would have marked anyone passing through. I checked. No one has."

Richard pounded his fist in one hand. "For some devilish cause, whoever it is takes your name and spreads it like a plague along the borders. He has set our king's and the barons' minds against you and yours. He intended to make me blame you. I asked you here so that we might right that wrong and bring the knave to justice."

"There's a guid lad," Alan said quietly, falling back into his more natural patterns of speech. "And I am come to help ye." He uttered a sad little chuckle. "But I'm guessing the first order of business should be changing the mind of that wife of yers afore she poisons my food or runs me through wi' some pointy wee blade."

Richard could do naught but agree. He had the same worry himself.

# Chapter Fifteen

Sara paced in her chamber while Eustiss and Tam repaired her broken bed. She shot a dark look at the offending item. At least that embarrassing topic of jest had quickly lost potential with the arrival of the Scot. No one was laughing now. Not about anything.

She could not abide the man in her home. Something had to be done about him. As the man vowed, he might not have killed her father himself, but he surely was responsible for spawning the one who did so. Who else but a son would have used his name?

Eustiss had told her all he had observed during the arrival of the Scots. Sara decided that it must be Alan's son, the one Melior had described to her, who remained outside the walls with the men-at-arms who rode with them.

At this very moment, they were camped within sight, likely preparing to gain entrance to Fernstowe by treachery. After all, their lord was inside her gates now and had the absolute trust of her husband. 'Twould be a small matter for the Scot to sneak out in the night, kill the guard, open the sally port for his men and take possession of her home.

She could order her men to take Richard's brother hostage, bind him and lock him in the cell at the back of the storage floor. Then the king could come and deal with him. But the men of Fernstowe took their orders from Richard now, and he would never countenance such a plan.

She sensed Richard's arrival at the open door of her chamber, even though she now faced the window and did not see him. She turned and crossed her arms over her chest.

"Eustiss, Tam, leave us and finish that later," he ordered.

"'Tis fixed," Eustiss said with a final whack of his mallet to one of the new pegs. He grabbed one of the posts and shook it, testing the bed's give. "Sturdy enough now," he muttered.

Together the two hefted the mattress in place, picked up their tools and took their leave.

Sara watched them go with trepidation. What would happen now? Had he come to punish her or would he continue what the breaking bedstead had interrupted? A beating might be preferable at this point, she thought wryly.

Richard wasted no time with small talk. Nor did he approach her as she'd feared he might. This was obviously to be a hurried bid for cessation of her hostility against old Alan the True.

Sara felt a moment's compassion for her husband, caught betwixt an angry wife and a newly met brother. His faith in the blood tie might be the death of him and all under his care.

She was not to blame for this coil, however. Richard should have known better than to ask the man to come here to the home of the man's own victim, of all places.

"You must hear him out, Sara. Alan did swear he had naught to do with Lord Simon's death and knows nothing about the new threats to the border lords. Why are you so set on his guilt?''

She clicked her tongue with impatience. "Why are you so set on his innocence? Just because you share a father? Does that make him all that is honorable and good? I think not!''

"I believe him. This is not the man who held me for ransom. Alan was in France all that time, visiting Lady Honor's family and seeing to her properties there.''

"What of his son?'' she asked, trying to sound reasonable so that he would listen to her. "He could have wielded the sword that killed Father. And you have not heard that one claiming his innocence. I doubt this son would dare act without his father's leave in these matters. Can you not see that it is one or the other of them causing this trouble? Or most likely, both.''

Richard raked a hand through his hair and huffed with frustration. "There is no proof of Alan's involvement. I tell you, Sara, someone is throwing guilt upon him to conceal their own perfidy. And a man such as Alan could never raise a son so dishonorable as to blacken his own sire's name. True, I do not know my nephew, but I wager he is as guiltless as Alan in this.''

Sara could understand why Richard needed so desperately to believe this. According to King Edward, his loyalty was legend, and family *was* family. That loyalty of his was dangerously misplaced, however, and might be the death of him.

What would the king think if he learned that Richard had befriended this brother and allowed the violence along the border to continue? She could not bear to see her husband charged with treason.

She saw how torn he was by the whole matter. Grudgingly she promised, "I shall attempt to be civil to him.'' After all, she thought, outright hostility would accomplish nothing. If the Scot could use the subterfuge of good manners to accomplish his deceit, so could she in order to prevent it.

On that thought, a plan began to form—one not without risk—for she alone must carry it out. The hardest part would be keeping it secret from everyone until the king could come. But even that could be done if she was careful.

"I would appreciate the effort, Sara," Richard said. "You will see I am right in this." He moved into the chamber and held out his hand to her. "Come down to sup with us? And listen to what he has to say?"

Sara looked at Richard's hand, but did not offer her own. "Oh, I would not miss it," she answered calmly. "But go now without me. Give me a while to collect my wits. This *has* been a trying day and it is not over yet."

He glanced at the newly repaired bed and issued a wry hum of agreement.

"Richard?" she said in afterthought, tracing a finger over her scar as though doing so unconsciously. "Do they know yet why you wed a woman such as I? Mayhap you should tell the tale before I join you. I'd not like them to ask me...questions."

In the corner of her vision, Sara noted that he watched her. Surely he would tell Alan the story of her scar. That was her intent, to encourage the telling. It would help her mission considerably if he did so.

"I had not intended explaining, for it's none of their concern. However, if you wish it, I will tell them," Richard agreed. She hated the soft quality of sympathy in his voice.

The instant the sound of his footsteps on the stairs receded, Sara sat down at her writing table and composed the letter that would summon royal help. Then she penned another, shorter message for Richard's brother. That done, she sealed both and carefully tucked them inside her sleeve, a place where no one would find them.

First of all, she must gather what she needed to make the cell livable for at least a fortnight. Then she would deliver the instructions to her infamous brother-by-law.

If he took the bait and if she was successful, she would send the other missive to King Edward immediately afterward. When the king arrived, Richard would be clear of blame, the border would be safe, and she would have avenged her father's death.

Richard might never forgive her for it, but better she suffer that than his execution. Then again, he might see reason in what she'd done once he was forced to admit his brother's guilt. Whatever the outcome, she had little choice but to proceed.

Sara fully understood that King Edward had possessed a far greater reason for seeing her and Richard wed than to reward her healing skills. He must have learned of Richard's filial relationship to Alan. This was a test of Richard's loyalty to the crown and she meant to see that he did not fail due to his goodness of heart.

For the nonce, however, she must play gracious hostess and disguise her obvious hatred for the Scot. She took a deep, steadying breath, set her face in a pleasant expression and went down to see to the evening meal.

While she was about that duty, no one would miss her when she slipped down to the storerooms and saw to the more pressing matter of stocking the cell.

The Scot ate as if he expected famine on the morrow, Sara thought. Though his manners were better than she'd expected, he did consume an enormous amount of food. That could be a problem, since she had not had time to put by a gracious lot to sustain him in his captivity. Hopefully the wretch wouldn't starve while awaiting just punishment.

She turned her regard to the Lady Honor and pretended not to watch. "Melior told me of your children when we met him at Harbeth's," she said politely.

After the glowing description of Adam, the eldest son, Sara paid little attention to the woman's words. The dainty Honor fascinated her. Here was no downtrodden hag of a Scotswoman, but a lovely French heiress dressed to perfection and seemingly delighted with her lot in life. Her ready smile and sweet disposition were distinctly at odds with what Sara would have expected of a wife of Alan the True.

Sara wondered what must it be like to possess Lady Honor's ageless beauty? Her hair gleamed dark as night against a fair, smooth skin, and her clear gray eyes sparkled beneath perfectly shaped eyebrows. She gestured expressively with small, delicate hands as she talked about her brood. Kindness and gentility radiated from the woman, and Sara found herself struck with admiration. A shame the lady would be hurt by all of this. And there was yet another sin Sara placed upon the Scot.

In all truth, she had to admit the two made a handsome couple. Alan stood as tall as Richard and remained near as solidly built. He would look English to the core if he had not pinned that length of plaid fabric across his shoulder. He had not worn that hated Highland symbol earlier when they arrived, but she supposed he was now reminding everyone here that he was not, and never would be, English. As if she needed any reminder.

His long hair appeared almost blond rather than the silver it should be at his age. She knew the golden cast to it was common, however, to those with ruddy hair in their youth. Richard's would likely be the same when he grew older.

The green eyes were the same color as her husband's, yet the laugh lines around them spoke of a merrier nature. He must greatly enjoy the thieving and murdering life he led.

"We met your children earlier," the lady said, pulling Sara's attention back to the conversation. "Christopher is the image of Richard. And Nan puts me in mind of our Kit when she was a child. The bright red hair, of course, but something more…ah, that lift of the chin, I think."

Sara looked down at the lower table and nodded. "Strode arrogance, no doubt."

Lady Honor laughed. "Assuredly so! With them it is an attribute acquired in infancy."

"Do not be telling wild tales, wife!" Alan warned as he motioned for an additional serving of greens. "There's not an arrogant bone in my body! Or in my Kit's."

The two laughed heartily and continued their cheerful banter, often including Richard with questions about the family in Gloucestershire. Sara tried to ignore them. She smiled, inclined her head and toyed with her food. Waiting.

Not until after they had finished eating and were leaving table, did Alan address her directly. "Sara, lass, how are we to resolve this, eh? What must I do?"

Sara glanced toward her husband. Lady Honor now engaged him in a discussion of some cousin who had come north to live. The distraction was obviously planned so that Alan could speak privately with her and lull her into believing him. Nothing could have suited Sara more. "To resolve my suspicion of you?"

"Aye, that. There ye sat throughout supper, proper as a saint on a cloud, despising me. How can I prove to ye I did not kill yer da? Tell me and I will do it." He spoke very gently in a tone Sara suspected he might use with a troublesome horse or hound.

"My insistence on your guilt is but a ruse, a distraction for my husband," she whispered, reaching into her sleeve and withdrawing the lesser of the two hidden messages, a scrap of parchment folded small enough to fit in the hand. She slipped it into his and said, "Meet me in this place and tell no one. I need your help, but Richard must not know the name of the man I truly suspect. Not yet."

"Why so?" he asked, squinting down at her.

She covered her scar with one hand, bringing his attention to it. "Because he would kill him. Outright, he would slay him for another reason, and we would never know whether this man is the one we seek!"

Alan nodded once, his eyes full of sympathy. As she'd intended, Richard obviously had told him about the nameless man who had scarred her. Alan had taken her bait.

Choosing Aelwyn as the object of her pretended suspicion gave her not a moment's pause. Next to the Scot, he was the man she most despised, so it was natural that she thought of him. No one would hear his name. She had merely needed a reason of some kind for enlisting Alan's help, and a sound and believable excuse for Richard's not knowing of it. This was working perfectly.

"Tell no one you are to meet me. Let no one see you come. Swear?" she demanded.

He hesitated only a moment before answering. "I so swear."

"Good. You will see I know what I'm about. 'Til midnight," she reaffirmed.

Sara quickly skirted around him then, bade a hasty good-night to Lady Honor and left before he could ask any more questions. All she had to do now was be there at the appointed hour and believe that this would work.

Richard followed her when she would have quit the hall, stopping her with a hand on her arm. "Where are you going? You promised to be cordial to him."

She stretched her mouth into a smile. "And so I have been. Berta has taken Christopher and Nan up to bed, and I would help to settle them for the night. I have not seen much of them these past few days. I do want them to like me."

"Very well." He smiled his approval and squeezed her arm affectionately. "Come to my chamber afterward."

She very nearly rolled her eyes in frustration. This was all she needed. How could she fight on all fronts? Dragging reluctant regard from the children, resisting Richard's seduction of her senses, capturing the Scot for the king? But she would manage, she told herself firmly. Everything in its turn.

"If you wish," she said, lowering her lashes demurely. Above all, she must remember to remain demure.

She had until midnight to handle the children and Richard. Plenty of time.

"I want the tale of the wizard and the cave," Christopher demanded the moment prayers were finished. He was a perfect echo of Richard at his most demanding.

"The lady in the lake," Nan argued, cuffing Chris's shoulder with her fist.

"The coney and the fox," Sara declared, wedging herself between them where they sat upon the edge of the bed.

"That one's too quick," Nan said, scooting over. "You have missed telling tales these past two nights. So, we shall have three now."

At least Nan had found a practical use for learning her numbers, Sara thought with a sigh. "Two," she bargained.

"Done," Christopher agreed. He and Nan shared a wily, satisfied look. Sara told the tales, willing to be outmaneuvered this once.

She must overcome their reluctance to accept her if they

were to be truly hers. Even if Richard did leave—which he likely would after this night's work and its results—Sara wanted very much for Chris and Nan to stay. He probably would allow it since his parents were rather old and he would be away much of the time in service to King Edward. The children needed her badly, even if Richard did not. Somehow she would convince him to let them stay.

When she had finished the stories, Christopher crawled beneath his covers. Sara tucked them snugly around him and leaned down to kiss his forehead. He did not resist, but he did close his eyes and pretend sudden sleep. The boy was unused to open affection. She smiled down at him, determined he should have it anyway.

Nan stood by the door and kept her back to them, her little shoulders held stiffly as though she could not bear to watch.

Sara joined her there and reached down to take the girl's small hand in hers for the walk down the corridor to Nan's chamber.

How well she recalled wishing for her own mother to take her hand, just once, but she never had. Though her father had offered occasional endearments and truly loved her, Sara had had to demand every scrap of attention she received from Lady Eula. She wondered then if that habit was what had caused her unseemly forwardness with Richard.

"Is Uncle Alan really my papa's brother?" Nan asked as she hopped into her own bed.

Sara sat down beside her and arranged her covers as she had done for Chris. "He certainly is, though he's much older. Is this uncle of yours much like your grandfather?"

"He's nicer," Nan confided. "He patted me on my head today and smiled. Lord Adam was very old. He always looked past me unless I bothered him."

Sara smiled, sad for the child who had to misbehave to be noticed. They had that fault in common. She brushed the red curls off Nan's brow just to touch the softness of it. "And did you bother him often?"

Nan returned the smile generously and moved her head into Sara's palm much as a kitten seeking comfort might do. "I was not very good there. I am better here."

Unable not to, Sara enfolded Nan in her arms and hugged her close, touched to the heart by memories of her own bids for attention. "You are home now, my girl. I *want* you here."

"I'm a bastard," Nan whispered, a lonely almost aggrieved sound.

Sara sat back and took Nan's face between her hands. "Not any longer," she said with feeling. "You are mine now, do you hear? Just as surely as is your brother. No matter what you do or where you go or what folk say, you are *my* child for good and all. Your father is wed to me, so that makes you as legitimate as...as a royal princess."

Nan sniffed, but she grinned, her green eyes shining. "Will you *make* me call you Mother?"

Sara laughed with joy. "I shall take a stick to you if you do not!"

Nan giggled. "Good night...Mother," she said, as though tasting the new word on her tongue.

"Good night to you, daughter," Sara answered. She ruffled Nan's hair, smoothed her palm down the soft cheek and tapped the small nose with one finger. "Sleep well, my dear."

When Sara pulled the door closed behind her, she leaned against it and hugged herself.

If she succeeded in nothing else, she had at least triumphed with Nan. So easily, she thought. Just a few words of reassurance and kind touches. Her heart swelled with determination to make that child feel truly loved.

Christopher, as Richard's heir, already knew he was valued by everyone. He needed her love, of course, and a
mother to teach him the things he must know that only a
female could impart to a child. But Nan had spent nearly
eight years of her life thinking herself a mistake, one to
be hidden or ignored. That must be remedied.

Richard loved his daughter well, as anyone could see,
but he had left her care to others for too long while he was
away with the king. Things would be vastly different now.
If Richard must be away, Nan would have a mother to
love her in his stead.

Encouraged by the victory, she marched toward her
chamber to make ready for her next trial—Richard.

"Welcome, wife," Richard said, handing her a cup of
wine the moment she entered the room. "I wondered
whether you would change your mind."

"I came as soon as I could," she replied, taking the cup
from him and sipping. She strolled about the room, well
aware that he watched her every move.

The royal blue bed gown flattered her, she knew, and
she had chosen it for that reason. The velvet appeared soft
and draped her frame in graceful folds.

If she was not allowed to incite him with her touches
and frank appeals as she had done previously, then she
would use whatever she might. Their loving would induce
his sleeping soundly. Above everything, she wanted Richard to sleep very soundly through this night.

She shifted her shoulder slightly so that the front of the
gown gaped, affording him a glimpse of the valley between her breasts. His eyes narrowed with desire.

"Come to me," he entreated.

Sara moved slowly, eyes down. *Be modest*, she thought
to herself. *Act reserved. Shy. Be what he wants*.

Richard's clean, warm scent enveloped her as surely as

did his arms. The sensual softness of his lips upon her cheek and neck sent a ripple of longing through her that nearly destroyed her firm resolve. His eager hands molded her body as though reshaping, even as he whispered how he treasured every part he caressed.

How on earth would she remain unaffected by him? She could not. But she did manage, hands fisted at her sides, to refrain from touching him back.

His thumbs grazed her breasts as he parted the velvet and moved it away. The garment slid off her shoulders and pooled about her feet.

"How lovely you are," he murmured, "and how I have missed seeing you thus." He clasped her wrists and placed her hands on his bare chest beneath the loose woolen robe he wore.

All unthinking, her fists uncurled and she spread her fingers over the hard, hot muscles. The dark, springy hair teased her palms, urging her to explore, to enjoy, to revel in the feel of him.

*No.* She would not. He thought he wanted that now, but later he would remember if she threw herself into this with all eagerness. Sara did allow herself a sigh of disappointment.

"What's amiss?" he asked gently.

"Nothing," she assured him breathlessly. "Nothing at all."

Again he gathered her close and moved toward the bed. Unhurried, he encouraged her to lie down, and joined her on the down-filled comfort, stretching out full-length beside her.

With a lazy slide of his hand, he measured her from breast to thigh. Sara shivered with anticipation, heat shooting through her veins. "Do you not want me, Sara?" he asked with an enticing smile.

"Yes, of course," she said breathlessly. Almost gasped the words.

She must think on other things. She must divorce her mind from what he did to her, from what he made her crave. But what? What subject under heaven would dismiss his touch, which seemed heaven itself?

Sara focused on the crewelwork of the bed hangings and set herself to counting stitches. They were too tiny to see individually, but she pretended she could. She imagined the tedium of setting each one, even though she had not done these herself.

Richard's hand swept slowly down her midsection and, despite herself, she had to catch a moan before it escaped. Saints, was the man a sorcerer? Was there no respite from this heady pleasure? How would she bear it?

Just as her will to hold herself apart from desire deserted her, Richard moved over her and entered her swiftly. Sara's breath caught in her throat. She froze beneath him, mindful of how close she had come to surrendering her wits completely and clasping him to her.

He moved slowly at first within her, coaxing her with his body to move, to aid in the quest for the sweet, wild flight they had shared before. She clenched her eyes shut and bit her lips together. And counted.

Richard suddenly abandoned his control and took his pleasure quickly.

Here was no joy, Sara thought. Little for him and none for her. She *hated* this. Not him, for he had done all he could to please her. But she hated the feeling of loneliness this kind of loving engendered.

He must feel it, too, for he rolled to her side and expelled a deep breath that sounded much like resignation. For a long while, he regarded her, a deep frown marring his brow.

Sara thought he would say something then, either to

chastise or to praise her. She truly knew not which. While she had done as she believed he wished her to do this time, he seemed to like it less than he had when they had loved before. As it happened, he said nothing at all.

Confused and unhappy, her body still afire with need, she closed her eyes and breathed in and out, evenly, deliberately, until he turned away from her and snuffed out the candles beside the bed.

"So be it," she thought she heard him mutter, but the words were indistinct and she did *not* want it to be so.

Sara remained still as death for what seemed hours until she was certain he slept. Then she rose as carefully as she could, pulled on her discarded bed gown and left his chamber.

Leaving his side provided some relief at last. The urge to embrace Richard, to give and seek comfort of him had grown more and more difficult to resist with each passing moment.

Sleep would not come to her in any event and, even if she were inclined to it, she did not dare succumb. She had one other important matter to see done this night. That would likely give her as little good feeling as the feat just accomplished, but at least she was certain that this thing she was about to do was right.

Sara returned quickly to her chamber to dress for her midnight rendezvous with Alan the True.

Richard gave no sign that he heard Sara leave his bed. He had wanted her to go even before she did so. The whole episode dredged up memories of Evaline and his bedding of her.

He had not endured much of that, to be sure. No loving words or learned skills had ever softened that first wife of his, yet she'd demanded he do his duty as husband and give her a son.

Three times in as many months, and thrice cursed, he had gone to her. Then she had quickened with Christopher and Richard had not troubled her more. The relief had proved so great, he had thanked God daily he did not have to rise to the occasion again.

What guilt he had felt at seeing her revulsion and the way she struggled to conceal it from him. He had tried so hard to love her, knowing that his inability to do so might be at least half their problem. Not so with Sara. He *did* love her.

Was Sara that much like Evaline, after all? Had her earlier enthusiasm been a pretense that she no longer thought necessary to keep up, an enticement to hold him here? Well, she *was* noble.

Before his first marriage, his father had warned him to expect coldness from women of that station. It was bred into them and reinforced by their learning piety, he'd said.

The church taught them that there should be no other cause for coupling than that of getting a child. His father had said as much, and Evaline had reminded him of it time and again. Even when he had no thought of bedding her, she reminded him, lest he should forget it.

He no more believed that teaching than he did the idea that women were the root of all evil. Some things worked out by the minds of celibate men should be questioned a bit more closely, he thought. Richard had questioned, and he'd decided they simply were not true. But a woman gently born and reared to obedience in all things would never question her priest.

That's why Sara had surprised him so with her openness at first. He had not expected that. Truth be known, she had shocked him more than a little with her ardor. However, tonight's disaster left him cold inside and wishing she had not changed at all. He could not bear going through this again, and neither should she.

But he could not lose all hope yet. Mayhap she was merely wrung out from the day's events and too tired for loving. Small wonder. Tomorrow or the next day, when she felt more rested and he had figured out what to say, he would speak with her about it.

But he could not leave all hope that Margaret should someday return to him that deep chasm still lay open for hope to fill. So all was lost. He might as well be dead, even.........................................................................

# Chapter Sixteen

Sara pulled on her darkest gown and hurried silently down the stairs, keeping to the shadows until she reached the deserted storage floor beneath the hall. She had left it unlocked in the event that he arrived before her. Only when she had entered and closed the well-oiled door behind her did she risk lighting the fat candle she carried.

Indeed, the Scot was already there. He waited, lounging amongst the sacks of grain and barrels of salted meat. The night candle he had set upon one of the barrels near him shed a sparse light, eerily illuminating only half his features. When she neared him, he stood, cradling one of the tabby mousers that had free run of the place.

"Good of you to come," Sara said, almost breathless with apprehension. Could she trick him, or was he too wily? "You did not tell anyone that I asked to meet you here, did you?"

"I promised I would not, and I always keep my word."

Sara could almost believe he meant that. At the moment she had to believe so. She breathed a sigh of relief. "Did you not confide in your wife?"

He shrugged one shoulder and continued stroking the

cat he held. "A promise is a promise. I make no exceptions."

For all the casual attitude he assumed, Richard's brother looked somehow larger and more menacing down here in the storage chamber than he had in the hall. Sara drew herself up to full height and still he towered over her by a good handbreadth.

"Ye think the one who injured you so long ago might be responsible for these problems of ours?" Alan asked. "Richard suspects him also, but said ye refused to consider it. Or to give him the man's name."

Sara looked away, unable to lie while looking him in the eye. "There's reason for that, as I told you. Richard would kill him."

"Likely he would, and so might I, but I promise, I'd have his confession first. What is his name, lass?"

"I cannot tell you that as yet. First I would show you something," she explained hesitantly. "Tell me what you think it means before we decide on this man's guilt."

He pursed his lips and nodded. "Let's see it then and not linger down here. I doubt my brother knows me well enough to ignore it should he discover me hanging about this deserted place with his wife."

Sara nodded. "Leave your candle here to light our way out." She turned toward the cell she had prepared. "This way." Carrying her meager light, she led him to the very back of the storage, down several steps and through the heavy door that she had left half-open. Alan followed and entered behind her.

"Just over there," she said, pointing. "Take my light and look hidden underneath those sacks."

He looked at her curiously, but he set down the cat he held and accepted the beeswax taper she offered him. Then he turned his attention to the objects stacked in the corner.

When he had affixed the candle to the floor and began

lifting the blankets and food sacks to one side, Sara slowly backed out the door. Soundlessly she pushed it shut. The huge iron key already inside the lock turned easily, its click hardly noticeable. She risked one quick peek through the small, barred opening. He was still occupied with the futile search.

Without waiting for him to discover that she was gone and he was securely locked in, Sara rushed back through the storage chamber, snatched up his candle and ran to the door that led to the stairs. She quickly locked that one from the outside.

There would be no cause for anyone other than her to open it again until the king came. Sara had the only key.

Another of the mousers brushed against her skirts and meowed, reminding Sara that this huntress and the others like her had their own entrance and exit, the small hole cut in the bottom of the door. That allowed them to perform their necessary task of ridding the storage area of vermin. Sara gave a rueful huff. Mayhap the other cat would keep the larger, captive vermin company in the days ahead.

This floor of the keep would not be used again until harvest, two months hence, when Fernstowe needed to restock for the winter. The supply of victuals in it now were solely for provision against a siege or a famine. No one touched this store upon pain of death unless that became necessary for survival. Fernstowe subsisted on what was readily available from the gardens and fields now that it was summer.

Her prisoner would be securely concealed. The thick walls should easily contain his shouts for help. His absence would cause questions, but she would be asking those herself, along with the others. And if this place were to be searched, she would do it.

Sara's feet flew as she ran up the steps. Slowing at the

top, she picked her way along the edge of the cavernous hall, careful not to wake those sleeping on pallets within the hall itself. She stopped at the recess in the wall where Sir Matthew slept. Thank heavens, he hated sleeping in the barracks.

"Wake up," she whispered, shaking his shoulder. He mumbled a protest and buried his head in the pillow. "Wake up, I say! Sir Richard would have you carry an urgent message to the king."

"Wh-what's amiss?" he mumbled sleepily.

"Find your cloak, hood your head and make certain the guard does not recognize you when you leave by the back gate. Take the gelding Sir Richard usually rides, for that is our strongest mount. Ride as quickly as you may to Morpeth and give this to the king." She grabbed his arm and shoved the message into his hand. "Make haste! Lives depend upon you and utmost secrecy. Lie if you are asked. None must discover what you are about. Do you hear?"

"But Sir Richard said nothing earlier—"

"'Tis obvious he could not, for we have guests. He has declared that my word is as his own. Go now!"

Sara left the young knight and waited in a dark corner of the hall to see if he would obey her command. Sir Edmund, older and wiser, would have required the order directly of the man he served, but young Matthew probably would not dare waken Richard this late in the night just to confirm her directions.

Within moments, she watched him leave, cloaked and hooded, his steps as swift and furtive as her own. Relieved, she hurried up the stairs and slipped down the corridor to her own chamber.

Feeling her way, careful not to make any noise, she made it to the bed without mishap, slipped off her clothes and crawled beneath the covers. Only then did she take a proper breath.

She had captured Alan the True.

Sara pulled the coverlet around her ears to ward off the chill that would not leave her, despite the mildness of the weather. Richard would hate her for this, but she'd had to do it, both for his sake and her own.

If the son, Adam, was the culprit, he would soon reveal his true nature when he heard his father was missing. She hoped he would, so that Richard could no longer deny the guilt of his kinsmen. The son might have done the deeds himself, but not without orders from his father. The king would arrive within a fortnight or less, punish Alan, have the son captured and all would be well. So she hoped.

Sara allowed herself another moment's pity for the Lady Honor. One could not help but like her. It would grieve the woman to lose both her firstborn son and her husband to the king's justice, but there was no help for it. When wed to a dreaded Scot and producing sons like him, what else could the woman expect?

Sleep eluded Sara, but that did not surprise her. She used the time concocting what she would say when morning came and the disappearance of Alan became apparent. Richard would eventually miss Sir Matthew, as well, but she could not think how to explain that, or even if she should attempt to do so. All would be clear when the king came.

"Where could he have gone?" Lady Honor demanded. "He would never have left Fernstowe without me!"

"I cannot imagine that he would," Richard agreed, as troubled as his sister-by-law.

They had gathered in the hall to break their fast and discovered Alan missing. A hasty search turned up no clue as to his whereabouts.

"Not without reason," Honor stated. "And not without telling me first." She wrung her small white hands and paced before the low-burning fire that warded off the chill of early morn. "Something is wrong here. Terribly wrong."

Richard looked from one to the other of the women. Sara appeared unworried, but she still had a low opinion of Alan.

Lady Honor spoke the truth. His brother obviously held his wife dearer than anyone. That was plain for all to see, even to those who did not know them well. To abandon her here in a strange keep with people they had only just met—even if they were family—made no sense at all.

He, Sara and the others had already searched the keep, top to bottom, in the event Alan had simply taken a walk and fallen ill somewhere. Sara had even opened the storage rooms and looked there. They found no trace, and no one they had questioned thus far had seen him since he and Honor had gone above for the night. Honor had awakened to find him missing.

"Why don't we ride out to your son and see if Alan is with him?"

"Not you!" Sara objected. "Let someone else go!"

"Why?" Richard countered.

Sara's face reddened and she now appeared as upset as Lady Honor. "Be-because if...if your brother is not there with him, and if Adam thinks there is foul play, he might...hurt you!" She drew in a deep breath and expelled it harshly.

"Nonsense!" said Lady Honor.

"Do you think there has been foul play, Sara?" Richard asked, suspicious of the reasons for her objection.

She stared at him, all innocence. "Foul play? What sort could there be? We all retired, did we not? And whilst everyone else slept soundly, your brother must have taken it in his head to quit Fernstowe. Surely he will return whenever he's done whatever he set out to do."

"I shall go to my son," Honor declared. "If Alan set foot outside these walls, that is where he would have gone, to Adam. Although I cannot think why he would need to do that."

"The big gelding is missing, m'lord," said Eustiss as he approached. Richard had sent him to organize the search outside. "Stable lad said he slept sound all night. Heard no one take the beast." He made a face. "Nor did I, sorry t'say, and I sleep there, too. My hearin' ain't what it once was."

"The guards?" Richard asked.

"Tam's on the sally port. Says a man left on the gelding around midnight. Since you always ride it, he thought 'twas you and asked no questions. Just opened the gate and let 'im through."

Richard pounded his hand with a fist, wondering what might have induced his brother to leave without word to anyone. He looked long at Sara, wondering if she had said anything untoward to Alan.

Even so, his brother would not have left Lady Honor behind. He turned to that lady. "We will go out and speak with your son."

"*No!*" Sara shouted, grabbing his arm. "Do not, Richard! I beg you! Let her go. Send an escort if you must, but please do not go yourself!"

Richard sighed. Sara's fright for his safety did warm his heart. She must care for him more than she let on last night.

"She might have a point about your going out there," Sir Edmund said. The knight had listened to the exchange, but had remained silent until now. "You do not know how impetuous this nephew of yours might be if his father's not there with him. Allow me to go," he offered.

"And let you suffer his wrath, eh?"

"My son is not wrathful!" Lady Honor exclaimed indignantly.

Edmund laughed ruefully. "I have served his grandfather since I was fourteen. I can deal with the grandson."

"Have at it, then," Richard said with a smile of thanks. "But bear in mind the old Adam's temper. Could be inherited."

Lady Honor, still protesting their reservations, accompanied Sir Edmund and Eustiss to the hall door and out to the stables.

Richard addressed Sara. "You spoke to Alan alone after we supped. What did you say to him?"

She gave a small shrug, her gaze locked on her fingers, which toyed with the ends of her belt. "He asked what he might do to convince me of his innocence. I said mayhap he could help us discover the real culprit."

"Do you believe he might be at that task even now?"

"Anything is possible," she replied, not meeting his eyes.

He shook his head, thoroughly puzzled. "Well, I am going to the gatehouse to await Lady Honor's return. Would you come?"

"No. I will stay and see to the children when they arise."

Not for the first time, Richard wondered at Sara's paleness this morning. Dark shadows beneath her eyes told him she had not slept well after she left him. He should not have asked her to come to him last night. Harbeth's wedding celebration had been such a trial for her. Also, Alan's sudden visit troubled her, and now this mystery of his leaving must be added to that.

Richard reached out and cupped her shoulder with one hand. "Nan and Chris are not babes. Besides, Berta can do whatever needs doing. Why not go and rest? You look tired."

She smiled, but it looked forced. "I am fine. Go along now."

He did as she said, anxious to solve the mystery of his brother's departure. But he wished he had time for a private visit with Sara. They needed to speak of what had happened between them last night.

That could wait, however. He and Sara had years in which to work out their differences. For now he must see to Alan's whereabouts. He needed him to help set up the plan that would trap the murdering thief preventing peace along their border. They must do that right soon. Otherwise, in five days Richard must answer the demands of that wretch, or those living in the outlying reaches of Fernstowe would suffer the promised consequences.

Fernstowe itself could easily withstand a direct attack, even with few to defend it. Siege was nothing to worry about, not with all the stores put by already, and two working wells within the walls. It was those outside these walls' protection that concerned Richard. Somehow he must get rid of the threat for once and all. He did have a plan, but he would need Alan's help.

The matter weighed heavily on his mind as he climbed the stair to the gatehouse tower. When he looked out toward the camp of Alan's men-at-arms, he saw that Lady Honor and Sir Edmund had already arrived and dismounted. The men gathered around them.

Richard watched as the distant voices grew louder and several of the men began to gesture angrily. One was Sir Edmund himself.

At a curt order from the man Richard supposed was the nephew Adam, two of the larger men seized Sir Edmund and carried him struggling to one of the tents.

Once they disappeared inside, the nephew helped Honor to mount and then leaped upon the large horse Sir Edmund had ridden. The two rode hell-bent back toward Fernstowe.

So Alan had not gone to his son, after all, Richard deduced.

He motioned for the gates to remain closed, not about to let in that hotspur who had just taken his knight hostage. Not armed, at any rate.

"Throw down," he ordered as they halted out front.

"My father did so," Adam shouted up to him. "Do you think I would repeat his mistake?"

"Alan is gone from here, as your mother has told you. Again I say, throw down your sword and you are welcome to come and see that this is true. You have my man as proof against treachery."

Adam glared up at him, a near reflection of his own form and features, Richard thought. The son had his mother's ebony hair, but the rest was pure Strode.

Suddenly Adam reached behind his neck, drew his broadsword from its sling and held it high. With one mighty throw, he buried half the blade in the earth. "There! Now, open your gates!" he thundered.

Lady Honor inclined her head and shrugged as though to say, what could a mother do?

Richard did not mind. He would have reacted much the same as Adam had just done, given a like circumstance. At his order, the gates opened slowly. By the time they permitted entrance, Richard had descended and was waiting.

"Welcome, nephew," he greeted Adam. "Dismount and come inside. We need to figure out where Alan might have gone. Do you have a notion?"

"He is in there and I mean to find him," Adam said, frowning toward the keep. "If I do not, you are forfeit one knight." He nodded at the wall, in the direction of his camp where they held Sir Edmund. "I'll have his entrails delivered on a trencher for your hounds."

Richard grimaced. He imagined Adam saying such to

Sir Edmund, who was not noted for his tolerance of a young knight's boasting. Small wonder they'd had a struggle with him.

"Well, if your father were here, and I meant him harm, do you think I would have let Lady Honor ride out to you?"

Adam said nothing. He merely stalked ahead, one hand on his mother's arm while she fairly ran to keep up.

"We believe he rode out at midnight through the back gate," Richard informed him as they mounted the steps to the hall.

"That was not my father."

Richard stopped him with a tug on his sleeve. "You saw the man?"

Adam smirked as he shook off Richard's hold on him. "Aye. You think us lack-wits that we would not mark your comings and goings?"

"Well, who was he if not your father?"

"One of your knights. A young lackey. Near wet himself when we ran him down."

"Adam, you did not harm that boy, did you?" Lady Honor demanded to know.

"Nay, Mother. Only frightened the lad a wee bit."

"Sir Matthew. Had to be him." Richard ran a hand through his hair as he shook his head. "Where the devil was he going?"

"Off to see some woman, so he said. We followed. He did stop at a hovel twixt here and Harbeth's Keep where he'd told us she was to meet him. We left him to her."

Most peculiar. Matthew had said nothing of any woman. But Richard merely nodded and opened the door for them to enter. "Please, come in now. We shall have some wine, break our fast and decide what we must do next."

"We search here," Adam declared. "My father did not leave or we would have seen him go. Even whilst we chased your boy-knight, three of my men kept the watch on your gates. Da's here, I tell you, and I mean to find him.''

He smiled but his eyes were cold as a green sea in winter. "And if I do not find him *well,* Uncle, you should know this. I need no blade to rend a man limb from limb.''

Richard smiled back in kind, weary of the fool's bragging. "Rest assured, nephew. If anyone here has harmed my brother, I shall save you the trouble.''

"Will you two cease this squabble?" Lady Honor shouted, stamping her foot. "It is not helping to find him.'' She shook her small fist and her gray eyes snapped with anger. "I shall take a stick to you both if you do not behave!''

The urge to laugh at the dainty shrew welled up. She looked such a saint when she was calm. Adam shot him a look of warning, but Richard thought it had more to do with crossing the mother than any continued threat of his own.

"I am content to desist,'' Richard said evenly.

"As you wish,'' Adam agreed, sounding rather resigned. He held out an arm to Richard in reluctant truce.

They clasped and shook.

"Drink on it quickly then, and let us get down to business,'' Honor suggested as she stalked toward the table laden with the morning's bread, cheeses and wine. Without waiting for a maid to serve her, she grabbed up the flagon and splashed a bit of wine into three cups. "Here!''

Richard took one and rapped it against the one Adam held. "Pax?''

"Aye, peace,'' Adam repeated grudgingly. He downed the contents and slammed down the cup. "I shall take the dungeons.''

Richard laughed ruefully. "There *are* no dungeons.''

"Where do you keep your prisoners?" Adam asked, as if truly astounded at the lack of proper facilities.

"We have had no prisoners since I came here," Richard admitted. "I suppose if we had any, we would keep them in the tower chambers. We have searched there already."

Without pause, Adam strode toward the spiral stairs that led to the upper floors. Richard followed.

They found nothing. The tower rooms stood open and were empty save for musty pallets where the wall guards took turns sleeping on the nights they had duty.

Adam pushed past Richard on the stairs that led down to the next lower level.

Nothing would satisfy him but a thorough search. He checked under beds and in every chest large enough to hold a man. Richard watched, arms folded, to insure nothing was damaged in Adam's determined exploration. Lady Honor stood by, ostensibly to keep her two *charges* from each other's throats.

Richard supposed she regarded him as a charge, since he was near the same age as her oldest daughter. If he remembered rightly, Adam was barely four years younger than himself.

The three of them had just entered Sara's chamber to search it when she came upon them there.

"What in God's holy name are you doing?" Sara demanded.

Adam jerked around, dropping the bed hanging he'd just lifted to look under. "Who's this?"

Richard unfolded one arm and gestured toward her. "Your auntie Sara. Sara, meet young Adam."

She shrieked and leaped toward Adam like a demented fury. Richard caught her about the waist before she made contact. Lord's mercy, she was a handful! *Strong!* He held her tightly with one arm and clamped his other hand over her mouth. Her legs flailed and fingernails dug at his hand.

"Leave! Now!" he warned Honor and Adam.

They wasted no time. Richard threw Sara on the bed, landing on top of her and fearing the frame would collapse under their weight again. It held. She struggled until both of them were exhausted.

When she finally lie still, he removed his hand.

"Why did you let that wretch inside my gates?" she said between clenched teeth.

"Wretch? Such name-calling! I'll wager he's asking Honor, at this very moment, why I would take such a madwoman to wife. Whatever possessed you?"

She said nothing, merely sucked in and released deep breaths. He must be crushing her with his weight, but he dared not let her go until he was certain she was fully subdued.

"Look, he is not armed. I saw to that. I let him in to look for Alan. Otherwise he would not be satisfied his father is not here. We have searched the towers and were working our way down. No harm in that, is there?"

She renewed her writhing. "Please, Richard, let me go. I promise to keep my head."

He did so, easing off her and sitting up on the bed. He caught her arm when she started to get up. "Do not test me, Sara."

"No, no, I promise I will not. But we must go downstairs. I...I would explain...if I can explain. It's just that—"

Richard got up and pulled her to her feet. "Come then, I would hear this."

No amount of explanation would nullify the fact that Sara still believed both Alan and his son guilty of the foul deeds committed along the border. Richard was interested in hearing how she would gloss over this attack of hers.

She had calmed herself and pretended to be civil after

her harsh accusations of his brother. Because of that, and her present willingness to appease Adam, Richard suspected Sara knew more about Alan's disappearance than she admitted.

## Chapter Seventeen

Moments later in the hall, Sara and Richard found Adam and Lady Honor engaged in conversation with the children. Nan and Chris had obviously just discovered their new cousin. Sara suppressed the urge to order the little ones to run.

Christopher stood near him, holding one of the mousers that roamed at will. Nan had latched onto the man's hand and was chattering as though she had known him forever. True, he smiled on the children gently enough, but she wondered how many like Nan and Chris this Scot had left homeless after his burning raids.

Sara cleared her throat and wondered what she might say that would excuse her behavior in the bedchamber. Her wits had flown at the very sight of the man who must have slain her father.

Had Richard not restrained her, she'd have scratched out his eyes, stabbed him with her eating knife or choked him with her bare hands. She wanted to even now, but knew she must stay calm.

Somehow, she would find the strength to pretend, to make him feel welcome enough to stay nearby until the king came north.

Her main concern at the moment was that he might discover his father hidden away in the lone cell at the back of the storage floor. God only knows what he would do then.

Adam pulled his attention from Nan and stared at Sara when she and Richard approached the group. His look was wary, as though he observed a madwoman. Richard had the right of it then. Adam did think her mad. She must have been, for a moment.

Determined to keep them all here until the king arrived, Sara wet her lips and forced a smile. "Greetings."

"Aunt," the man acknowledged. Nothing more. His watchful expression did not alter, his face so like Richard's, the sight unnerved her. They might have been twins, the good and the evil.

"I must apologize," she said simply. "Seeing my chamber invaded disturbed me."

He gave one nod, then looked to Richard for a better explanation. And got none.

"You have met your cousins, I see," Richard said to Adam, as though nothing out of the ordinary had happened. He left her side and laid his hands on Nan's and Christopher's shoulders.

"He looks like you, Papa," Nan said, smiling at her father.

Christopher turned a little to one side and glanced over his shoulder at Sara.

That was when she saw it: a scrap of plaid tied around the cat's neck. A remnant of the very fabric worn by the Scot when she had locked him in the cell.

Sara's breath rushed out. Terror shot through her. *Please God, they will not notice the plaid.* But they had heard her gasp. Adam was now looking at what had shocked her so.

"What is the matter, Sara?" Richard asked her, his brow furrowed with concern. He whirled and caught her just as her knees buckled, then lowered her to a nearby bench.

"This, I believe," Adam announced, snatching the cat from Christopher's arms and shaking it in Richard's face. "This is what the matter is!"

"A cat?" Richard muttered, paying little attention as he continued to hold Sara's shoulders steady.

Adam stuck one long finger beneath the woolen necklet and slipped it over the mouser's head. He dangled the circle with its firmly tied knot and raised one eyebrow. "Where is he?"

Richard's expression of worry immediately changed to one of fury. "Sara!" he thundered, standing away from her, fists clenched in anger. "Tell me what you have done!"

The game was up. She sighed wearily and buried her face in her hands. All was lost and there would be no justice.

They were already inside Fernstowe. First they would take everything, the gold chest, the valuables and the weapons. Then they would slay every soul within because all had seen them. Faces were known now, as well as names. *No hope.*

Richard tore her hands away, his fingers biting into her wrists. "Sara?"

"Tell us, or I'll *beat* it out of you!" Adam shouted, shaking the fist that clutched the telling scrap.

Richard released her and squared off with his nephew. "Beat me first, if you dare. This is my wife, Adam Strode, and you are in my home. Remember yourself!"

Lady Honor came between them, a hand on each chest. "*Hold!* Both of you, listen to me!" She looked from one to the other. "Move away and put down those fists."

When they complied, she came to Sara's side and knelt by the chair. "You know where my husband is."

Unable to lie anymore or even to speak, Sara nodded. "Is he hurt?"

Sara shook her head.

"Lead me to him, child, before there's harm done here."

Slowly Sara rose from the bench, stepping well away from the menfolk. There was no point in trying to keep the Scot imprisoned. His son would take Fernstowe apart stone by stone to find him. More likely they would guess immediately since the cats spent most of their time amongst the stored supplies.

"Downstairs," Sara muttered, so distraught she could hardly speak. She watched Richard grab a wall torch out of its sconce and ignite it in the hall fire to light their way.

He lit another and handed it to Adam. Sara winced at the sight, wondering if that very flame Richard gave his nephew would be the instrument of Fernstowe's destruction.

Would Lady Honor be able to save them? Or when she got what she wanted, would she encourage retribution for Alan's capture? For such a small person, she seemed to wield much power over men. Sara prayed she could command some mercy.

The shock wore off on the way to the lower floor and her wits began to function as they should. Sara realized that Adam was not armed. But then, neither was Richard. Once Adam released his father, there would be the two of them against her husband.

Would the castle folk help? They were not trained to do so.

Sir Matthew was gone with the message for the king, Sir Edmund held captive, and Eustiss was out at the stables or the smithy. The other men were on duty at the gate or the wall. What could she do, alone, to save her husband and the children?

She stopped outside the door to storage and took the ring of keys from her belt. Before she fitted it to the lock, she faced Lady Honor, Adam and Richard.

"This is all my doing," she confessed. "Only mine. Richard knew nothing of it, I swear." She appealed to Adam, "Please, I beg you, do not visit your rage on anyone else."

"Unlock that door," he ordered in a low, dangerous growl.

Richard snatched the keys from her hand and performed the task himself. In moments, they were inside. He grasped her elbow. "Where is he? Show me."

She led the way, winding between the sacks and barrels until they reached the cell. Richard turned the huge key and threw open the door.

There stood Alan in all his thunderous wrath. His green eyes glinted with fire in the torchlight. He looked ready to do murder. Sara sucked in a deep breath and held it.

"Alan, I do regret—" Richard began, stepping forward.

"I'll wager ye will." The Scot shouldered past them and out of the cell. He cradled his wife's face, examining it in the flickering light. "Are ye well, hinny?"

"Yes, of course," Honor replied, covering his large hands with her dainty ones.

He turned his attention to his son. "Adam?"

"Well enough. Shall I lock them in, Da?" he asked with a cursory glance at Richard and Sara.

"No need. We'll be takin' our leave now. Come." He released Honor's face and took her hand. Pulling her along behind him, he led the way out.

Only the scuff of their shoes upon the stones broke the silence until they reached the hall. Sara dreaded what would happen once the Scots left the keep, rearmed and sent for reinforcements. Even so, she thanked God they would delay their revenge for the time being.

Richard stopped his brother when he would have gone straight for the hall door. "Alan, heed me. Sara made a mistake, one I can explain. All her life she's been warned of Scot treachery, steeped in fear of all who bear the name. Her men swore it was you who slew Lord Simon."

Alan rounded on him, slinging off his grip. "And I swore to her I did *not!* She pretended to believe me and then she lied, Richard. She tricked—"

Richard calmly interrupted, "Sara did what she felt she must. I do not condone it, but I can understand. Can you not? Consider, Alan. Every man this side of Scotland, save myself, thinks you are guilty. Sara knows nothing of what your word means. But I do. Stay, we must settle this once and for all."

*Go!* Sara thought silently. *Go, and be damned.*

Alan fumed. His nostrils flared and his eyes narrowed. When he spoke, he was no less angry. "What am I to do then? Stay and risk a blade in my back?" He jerked a thumb toward Honor and Adam. "She might harm them if she cannot kill me!"

"She's hurt no one thus far," Richard reminded him. "But if it will rest your mind, I will confine her."

"No!" Sara shouted, backing away, preparing to run. She knew not where she'd go, but they were all against her, even Richard. "You trusting fool! Can you not see the danger?"

Adam grabbed her left wrist to halt her flight and Sara swung. Her right fist connected solidly with his jaw. Suddenly freed, she dashed blindly toward the hall door.

Richard caught her. One arm locked around her waist and the other pinned her arms. He hefted her against him and headed upstairs. Over her curses of outrage, he shouted down to his brother, "Wait there."

He half carried, half dragged her to his chamber. "Let

me go!'' she screeched again. Richard dumped her face-down on his bed.

''Do not move,'' he warned her, one hand splayed in the center of her back, forcing her to stay. ''Do not!''

She turned her head to one side to watch him. He backed away from her and grabbed up his sword and dagger from the top of the chest where he had left them.

''Richard, please listen—''

He silenced her with a look. ''Do not try me further this day, Sara. Not…one…more…*word!*''

Nothing she could say would ever change his mind about the Scots anyway. Richard would suffer doubly when he discovered the truth— first a betrayal by his own brother, and then whatever vile deeds those wretched Scots would devise for him.

Sara turned her face from him and lay there in defeat. She could not spare him that. She could not save Richard, Fernstowe, or even herself. Surely here was cause to weep, but no tears came. What would be the use?

For the first time in her life, she felt there was nothing left that she could do to right things. Even her father's death had not left her so hopeless and without a plan.

The sound of the key turning in the lock made little difference.

Richard hoped he could mend the breach Sara had caused. His brother might never trust him now. By rights, he should punish Sara severely for breaking the truce he had promised Alan.

He could just imagine his own bitterness if the situation were reversed and Lady Honor had locked him in some hellhole beneath Alan's keep.

The three stood right where he had left them, their gazes fastened on him as he descended. ''Come with me,'' he said, motioning them toward the solar.

By chance, he noticed Nan and Christopher huddled together in the alcove nearest the stairs and looking frightened out of their wits. Better they should hear what he had to say than to worry and wonder over it.

"You two, come out of there and join us," he ordered.

Adam protested. "Surely the bairns need not—"

Richard had had enough high-handedness for one day. He stopped at the door and addressed Adam. "Hear me well. We may be of an age, you and I, but I *am* your uncle. When I need the advice of a nephew, I shall ask it. Alan and I have important matters to discuss. You and the other *children* are here by my leave to *listen*. Do we understand each other?"

Alan laughed unexpectedly and grasped Adam around his shoulders, probably to prevent an attack. Richard almost wished for one. His muscles screamed for action, any kind.

He envied Sara her punch to Adam's jaw. The mark remained on that stubborn chin and would likely bruise. That thought brought some satisfaction.

They drew up chairs and benches around the fireplace and Richard added a few logs to the low-burning flames. Rain now beat against the windows and the damp chill had increased. Another coolness filled the chamber, as well, one not susceptible to the physical warming of a fire.

"Did you hurt my mother?" Nan asked timidly, still clinging to Christopher's hand.

The belated question and his daughter's unusual shyness diverted Richard from what he was about to say. "What? Why do you ask after her now, Nan? You know what happened. The fever took her, remember?"

Nan grew bolder and met his gaze with one of defiance. "Not Annie. My *new* mother. Did you harm her, Papa?"

He had to smile, and not only to reassure Nan. Angry as he was with Sara at the moment, he was pleased that she had won Nan's regard. "No, daughter, I did her no hurt at all. She was overset and I put her to bed."

"She did not appear sleepy," Christopher said, one eyebrow raised in a wry expression Richard recognized as his own.

Lady Honor smiled and reached out to them. "Come, sit by me and let us hear what your father has to say."

He waited until everyone was settled and then spoke to Alan. "As we know, someone has been using your name to strike terror along our border. Our first task is to discover who the man is."

"Yer Sara mentioned a suspect to me, but it was only part of her ruse. It's me she blames, that's clear enough."

"Who did she say?" Richard asked.

Alan tapped his cheek. "Wouldna give me a name. Had something to do with her scar. She wanted me to think that anyway. Kept fiddling with it when she spoke of him."

Richard leaned forward, propping his elbows on his knees. "I believe I know who he is. This man does have reason to hate Sara. Good cause to kill her father, as well. Lord Simon denied him the match he sought. Sara stabbed him."

Adam barked a laugh. "That, I can believe! What will you do with that wife of yours? She's a danger to man."

"Worried?" Richard smirked. "I do promise I'll not let her strike you again."

Adam lowered his head as a chuckle escaped. He rubbed his face. "My hearty thanks. I think she loosened a tooth. This man gave her that scar, you say?"

Richard nodded. "When she was little more than a child. She took after him with her knife. Sara's no faint heart."

"Ye're preachin' to the converted, I think," Alan observed. "Sara's a braw lass for all her wrongheadedness. Built like a warrior, that one."

"She is *not!*" Richard argued heatedly. "Tall and strong, yes, but all grace and lithe beauty. Are you blind with old age?"

"You love her then?" Honor asked.

He sat back in his chair, gripping the arms of it, wanting to deny that he did. But even his current fury at Sara would not permit that lie.

"Do you, Papa?" Nan asked.

"Aye, do you, *Uncle?*" Adam queried with a sneer. "Do you love the woman who broke your vow of truce?"

"Hold your tongue, lad!" Alan ordered sharply. "Richard will see to his own."

And how would he do that? Richard wondered. How would he see to Sara? Must he keep her locked away to have her? She would surely insist on the annulment when this was over. Her hatred of his brother and nephew would extend to him now because he had taken their side against her. Rightly so, but even if he proved them innocent of killing Lord Simon, Sara would always view this day's rough handling as a betrayal.

It might be wise to part from her, deny their intimacy and accept the dissolution the king offered. Sara did not really want him, other than for making her lands and people safe again. That, he would do, and soon. Afterward, he knew that he would find no welcome here of any kind.

He loved the Sara who had come to him with eagerness and smiles, the teasing temptress who embraced passion and gave back full measure and more. That woman no longer existed, and mayhap never had in truth.

"Who is the man?" Alan asked.

"Aelwyn of Berthold. His lands border these," he explained to Alan. "They lie not far from the Meadow of

Dispute. Also, he bears ill will toward you as well as Sara.''

''Ah, I remember him now,'' Alan said sadly. ''Puir laddie. I did kill *his* da, but 'twas in battle.''

''I heard you tried to help him and how he acted. He still holds a grudge, it's said. I'd like to think it is Aelwyn who is behind the murder, but in fact, Sara had two suitors. The other is Lord Bankwell. He's twice Sara's age and wanted to wed her mother before the lady wed Lord Simon. Years later, when Bankwell became a widower, he applied for Sara's hand. Lord Simon said no, of course. There was likely bad blood between them. He could be the one we seek, but I think not.''

''Aelwyn's the most likely,'' Alan agreed, nodding.

''Yes. Whoever captured me—using your name, Alan— did all he could to turn my wrath on Sara. Said she paid only half the ransom, which proved untrue. I asked myself why the man would want her punished. He seemed almost as eager for that as for the added gold. Bankwell has no call to hate Sara that I know.''

He looked from Adam to Alan and back again. ''I think Aelwyn of Berthold saw a chance to exact vengeance on all of us. He devised the kidnappings and extortion to raise the king's wrath against you. He killed Lord Simon so that Sara would have no protection against him.''

''Then why did he not come and take her?'' Adam asked, sounding as though he wished the man had.

Richard shot him a dark look of warning. ''Without a word to Sara about it, Aelwyn applied for the king's permission to do just that. Had Edward given him leave, Sara could have done nothing to deny him.''

''I'd not wager on that!'' Adam commented dryly.

Alan shushed him and continued their discussion of Aelwyn. ''Question is, which is his true motive, revenge or greed?''

Adam threw up his hands. "Both! 'Tis clear enough to me. He sets you against Sara, uses you as his instrument of revenge on her. Then he collects all the English lords' gold with no risk of getting caught. Everyone is certain Da is the culprit."

"Why did he not simply kill you when he had you? Then he could have taken Sara and her lands for his own," Lady Honor said.

"Because King Edward knows Richard is my brother and that Strodes do not kill their own. Da always refused to fight against the Scots, nor would he pay scutage for any other to do so in his stead."

Richard stood and raked a hand through his hair. "You're certain the king knows?"

"Aye. Da wrote me that he told him."

"I figured as much, and that is surely why I'm here and wed to Sara. Edward is testing my loyalty. Sara should be hearing all of this. It might change her thinking."

"Wait, Richard," Lady Honor objected. "Give her the day to rest. She could not have slept last night, and this morn certainly upset her more." She placed a hand on his arm. "Leave Sara be for now. Go to her tonight and soothe her. There is no great hurry. We will stay the night here and longer if need be."

"Honor has the right of it," Alan added. "In the meantime, we can form some sort of plan to flush out this fox of Berthold."

Richard agreed. After languishing in that musty cell, Alan must be starving and was certainly in need of a bath. The rest could entertain themselves as best they might.

He needed seclusion. There was much more for him to think through than the capture of Aelwyn of Berthold. There was the possible end of his marriage, the future of his children and how to prevent Sara taking arms against his kinsmen if he set her free.

# Chapter Eighteen

A few hours of sleep cured Sara's hopelessness. She chastised herself soundly for allowing it in the first place. Proper wits restored, she set about reviewing the conundrum to see what might be done about it.

She carefully recalled every word, every look that had passed, since they had come here. On closer examination of those memories, Sara decided that she might have overestimated the danger to Richard, the children and the castle folk.

At the moment, *she* was the only one hereabout who believed the Scots guilty. Clearly Richard had declared against her by locking her away.

She did wonder why Alan kept insisting on his innocence. Did he mean for Richard to plead his part to the king? Anyone with sense could see that would be lethal for all concerned. King Edward hated all Scots, even the Balliol king he had set on the throne after Bruce. The current peace was a jest, though certainly no one laughed about it.

Try as she might, she could not understand what her brother-by-law was trying to accomplish. Had he come to determine Fernstowe's defenses from the inside? Unlikely, since Richard had asked him to come here. Alan had not applied to do so.

She sat up on the bed and rested her elbows on her updrawn knees. Could she be wrong about Alan and Adam?

"No, it has to be them," Sara muttered to herself. "It has to be." Even if it was Adam doing the black deeds, Alan would be the one giving orders for them. Faith, Adam would not even go against his mother's wishes, much less Alan himself. If those two were not responsible, then who else could it be?

Just then she heard the key rattle and looked up to see Richard enter. He seemed weary and disheartened as he put aside his weapons and drew off his tunic. Ignoring her, he went to the basin, splashed water on his face and washed his hands and arms.

"Berta is coming up with food for you," he finally said, his words muffled as he dried off with the linen. "After you eat, we will talk."

Sara got up and went to the smaller chair beside the fireplace and sat down. "It is cold in here," she muttered, rubbing her arms and staring at the ashes in the hearth.

He sniffed impatiently, then came to lay a fire. Sara watched how efficiently he did so, marking the stretch of his muscular back and shoulders. A comely man was this husband of hers, one to stir a woman's blood. But he had a head like a cursed rock.

"You are ever right, are you not?" she said. "No one else may have a thought."

"You may have one, just do not recount it aloud."

"Even should it be a doubt about your brother's guilt?"

"Save the breath. I would not believe you." He blew on the blaze he'd made and added splinters to the flames.

Berta came in and laid a cloth-covered wooden tray upon the table next to the window. Sara smelled the fresh bread and roast pork from across the room. Even that did little to spark her appetite though she had not eaten all day.

"Tell Nan and Chris that I said good-night to them," she said to the woman. "Do not forget you must hear their prayers."

"I did that," Richard informed her. "They are asleep."

While she resented missing the nightly ritual, she felt glad that Richard had remembered.

It seemed to her that she often had these ambivalent feelings where he was concerned. She loved him more than life itself, yet she could cheerfully choke him. Sara wanted him to be wrong, but she feared he might be right in this matter that divided them.

"Richard, tell me who you blame for my father's death and the border troubles."

He gave the fire one final poke and then got up, brushing his hands together. "Why? You have made up your mind."

Sara sighed. "Before today, I will admit that I had. Yet, once I took time to consider all that has happened—Alan's coming here, bringing his wife, laying aside his weapons— I have to ask why he would. He'd be a fool to identify himself to you when you were his prisoner, and then turn up as your guest, claiming innocence."

He watched her closely, attending every word she said as though to judge it for truth or lie.

She continued, "And if Adam was the man who held you for ransom, it is strange that he would leave his blade and venture inside our gates. You might have taken *him* as he took you, if you recognized his voice. True, his men hold Sir Edmund hostage, but how could Adam know whether you value that knight's life?"

"You might have employed all this reason of yours a bit sooner," he muttered.

"I agree," she admitted, and leaned forward to address the mystery that troubled her most. "The man who took you captive blindfolded you, yet he gave you a name. Neither Alan nor Adam care whether you see them. This seems of more import now than I first thought. Either you knew that man who captured you, or he thought you might meet him later and recognize him. That had to be his reason."

Richard nodded. "I told you as much, if you recall."

"Do you know very many Scots besides these, Richard?"

"A few messengers who came to the king from Balliol's court, but they are not suspect."

"You still think the culprit's English," she stated. He had said as much before, but she had not credited that it could be true. "Now I see how you might."

"Well, at long last, the light dawns," he replied sarcastically. He got up from his chair and went to the tray of food. When he had returned and set it on her lap, he ordered, "Eat something. Then I have some questions."

Suddenly she did feel hungry. And hopeful. The more she considered Alan's behavior—and even that of the contentious Adam—the possibility of believing them innocent increased.

She broke off a portion of the warm bread and relished its flavor as she handed half to Richard. He accepted it and smiled at her, a real smile this time that signaled his approval of her new right-thinking.

Doubt remained, of course. She could be dreaming excuses for his brother and nephew out of her desperation, because she so dreaded what would happen if they were indeed guilty.

Sara knew what was coming when she finished her meal. He would want to know all about the man who had given her the scar. Alan would have told Richard what she had implied. He would insist on the name. To show her good faith, she would give it.

He wasted no time when she finally set the tray aside. "First, let us speak of the two who wanted to wed you," he said.

"I have told you of them."

"Tell me again. All you know."

"There is Bankwell, the old fellow who once wanted Mother. His keep is in the East March, on the border, and is a goodly distance from Fernstowe. I only met him once when he came for my father's answer to the proposed betrothal. That was a resounding no, of course. Upon seeing me, I believe he counted himself fortunate in the refusal. You see, he expected me to look like my mother had at seventeen." She laughed at the memory now, though the occurrence had hurt her then.

She added, "The man who took you was young, you said. Due to Bankwell's age and lack of any further interest in me or Fernstowe, I think you may eliminate him from your list."

"We shall see. And the other suitor?"

"Aelwyn of Berthold," she answered. "You've certainly met him. He might well be wicked enough to murder and extort money from his neighbors, but the wretch hasn't sense enough to concoct a scheme of this magnitude. He's but a nithing, a bully who preys on those he thinks weaker than himself."

"I agree he acted a lack-wit." Richard then looked away from her and into the fire. "Now I must ask you the name you would not give me before, Sara. The man who marked you."

She sighed and stretched, affecting an attitude of nonchalance. "Oh, well, 'tis one in the same. Aelwyn."

"I see," he said, not in the least surprised. "So, the one is too old, the other to stupid, you think?"

"I do," she agreed. "Could it be someone unknown to us? What about a Scot other than your brother or nephew?"

He shook his head. "I posed that question to Alan. We discussed and have eliminated that possibility. We agree that the one we seek must be English."

Sara shrugged. "If you are right, it could be anyone, not necessarily a nobleman. Was he well-spoken?"

"Yes, he was," Richard declared. He thought for a moment longer and then rose from his chair. "Tomorrow we will begin our plan to flush him out. Instead of the added ransom he demanded, our man will leave him an empty coffer with news of my untimely death by dropsy."

She laughed aloud. "*Dropsy?* Do not be ridiculous!"

His sheepish smile tickled her even more. "Well, whatever the reason for my death, it must be of natural cause so he will not fear implication."

She shrugged. "He had no compunction when it came to killing my father, one of the king's barons. How do you explain that?"

"The king knows that Alan is my brother and would not kill me. Edward would naturally cast about for someone who *would* want me dead. Aelwyn might come to mind since he wanted you."

Sara shook her head. "What do you hope to gain by *dying?*"

Richard rubbed his chin, thinking. "I believe his reaction to my demise will be immediate. The moment he learns of it, I think he will rush here to fill the void I leave. He will use his offer of protection from the Scots as his reason."

"Why would you think so? He did not arrive in force after Father died. And you saw his contempt for me at Harbeth's," she reminded him.

"He would wed you still," Richard explained. "How

better to deal out vengeance? And the king would not object if the deed were done before he knew of it. Edward halfway planned for Aelwyn to have you anyway." Then he grinned. "But we will be ready to give your suitor the welcome he deserves when he comes for the *widow!*"

Richard's excitement increased as she watched him. The gleam in those green eyes bespoke his eagerness. She longed for him to hold her, to feel the tenderness beneath that ferocity. More than anything, she needed Richard as her ally. Even if—against all she had been taught—she had to change sides in the conflict. She prayed doing so was not the worst mistake of her life.

"For good or ill, I am with you, Richard," she said softly.

He smiled and embraced her fiercely. The sweet feel of his body against hers nearly made Sara forget that she must remain submissive.

She almost forgot, but not quite.

The next morning Richard did not speak to Sara. He nodded at her from across the hall when she arrived downstairs. Then he left immediately. His anger at her shamed him into avoidance. What right had he to be angry with her, he asked himself for the hundredth time? It was not as though she had refused him last night. Oh, no, he thought with a furious huff, but she *had* kept him hoping for and attempting to gain more than mere compliance on her part. She would respond. And then she would not.

He muttered curses all the way to the stables, now deserted by the lads and Eustiss, who had gone to break fast. Only when his brother spoke, did Richard realize Alan had followed him.

"I'd not curry any horses in that mood were I you. You're like to skin the hide right off 'em."

Richard threw down the brush he had just picked up. "Do not ask me."

"What the matter is?" Alan grinned and leaned against the wall, arms crossed. "Verra well, I won't."

Richard propped against one of the beams and shook his head. "I swear, women are wont to drive a man mad. Why is that?"

"They canna help it?"

"Oh, yes, she could!" Richard exclaimed. "First she's hot as coals 'neath a forge, next she's cold as a winter loch." Richard snapped his fingers. "Like that, her mood shifts!"

"Forge fires need stoking or they go out," Alan suggested.

Richard glared. "Make a jest, then. 'Tis naught to you."

"Right enough. Did Sara take ye ta task for lockin' her away all day?"

"No!" he said, so overset he had to begin pacing. "That had nothing to do with it. She was that way the night before and again when I went to her last eve."

"Mayhap she's breeding."

Richard stopped in his tracks and turned, suddenly bereft of breath. Joy leaped in his heart. *"Breeding?"* He stared at Alan, then shook his head. "No, it is too soon for that to affect her, even if she is with child. With my first wife, it made little difference."

"Da wrote me about her. Said she was a saint."

Richard shrugged. "I suppose she was. A noble lady to the bone." He glanced over at Alan. "She was taught that duty is all there is to a marriage. I know that's genteel, and the way they should be, but Sara most assuredly is not…well, not usually."

Alan's delighted laughter filled the stable. "My Honor must ha' missed her duty lessons, too, thanks be!"

Richard stilled. "She is not cold to you?"

"Nay!" Alan walked over and laid a hand on Richard's shoulder. "Who fed you that tainted pap about women? Da?"

"Yes." Richard winced, understanding that he'd been roundly duped. "Our priest. My *saint*, Evaline. They all said the same."

"Ach, there you have it!" Alan said, holding out his hands like a supplicant. "An auld man, a jealous cleric and a spoiled young lass. Who better to give you daft advice?"

Richard laughed with him, "A wise older brother, I suppose?"

"Damned right. Tell me, Dickon, have you mentioned this to Sara? The business about what's *genteel*, as ye call it?"

Richard winced. "I may have done. Yes, I did." He pinched the bridge of his nose and clenched his eyes shut. "Damn me for a fool!"

Alan clapped him on the back and offered a grin of sympathy. "Were I you, Dickon, I'd be admittin' that fact to the one who counts."

"Count on that," Richard said. He had no idea how he would explain the grin on his face if anyone asked about it, but he could not suppress it.

From now on, he would do all in his power to encourage Sara to show him what she felt and to act on it. He had learned much today, or rather had verified his true beliefs in the matter which he had been fighting all along.

How he wished he could go to Sara now, to reassure her that he would always love her. He definitely owed her apologies. However, it would be best if he waited until the night.

Sara pretended not to notice when Richard and his brother returned to the hall. She and Lady Honor were deep in discussion on the use of herbs and their effectiveness as cures.

The woman had a wealth of knowledge and Sara had determined to make use of it while Honor was here. To that end, she had just sent Darcy to fetch a quill and parchment so that she could write down some new mixtures mentioned.

The two men interrupted them. Richard smiled ear to ear and drew up a bench to sit beside her. Alan stood behind Honor, his hands on her shoulders. It was he who spoke. "Where is that son of ours this morn?"

"He was making a nuisance of himself," Honor answered, nodding toward the solar. "I prevailed upon him to entertain his new cousins with a history lesson while Sara and I become better acquainted."

"What sort of history?" Richard asked with a chuckle, though Sara saw nothing amusing about it. She had not objected since it was Honor's idea.

"Who can say what kind? Adam is well-versed in history, however, so do not worry on it. Sara and I were just comparing—"

A loud clatter arose as Eustiss hurried in, half-dragging a man Sara did not know. She and Richard stood immediately and hurried forth.

"Who is this?" Richard demanded as Eustiss released his hold on the newcomer.

"Sim Carterson," the smithy announced. "Comes from Sir Meckville. Says tell you he refused to pay yesterday when gold was due, and the Scots wasted no time. They attacked last night. Some cots was burned, and a brace o' villagers is dead."

"I'll go straight away," Richard promised.

"No need, m'lord," Carterson said, catching his breath. "Sir Meckville sent me to advise you what had happened. Lord Beringer's already there, and he'll give the help we need. My master said you'd need to know, you being the king's man.''

Richard and Alan exchanged meaningful looks.

Sara addressed the stranger, "Master Carterson, we thank you for this warning. Eustiss, see our friend fed and rested. I'm certain he will want to return home anon. Supply him a fresh horse whenever he wishes.''

Richard said, "I prefer you to stay a few days, Carterson.''

"Why, my lord?'' the man asked.

"Later, we will speak of it. First, go and refresh yourself. I have a goodly number of questions for you.''

The man nodded and Eustiss guided him toward the kitchens.

Sara smiled ruefully at Alan, "The most important question has just been answered. At least, for me. A man cannot be two places at once, even a fool such as I cannot deny that truth. Alan, I must ask your forgiveness and that of Adam, as well.''

"A woman who admits she was mistaken?'' Alan retorted, laughing. "Here is a wonder in itself!''

Honor struck him playfully on the arm. "Cease jesting. As it happens, Sara had already begun rethinking your guilt. Last night's attack but confirms your innocence for good and all. Now we must center our thinking on the one who incriminates you.''

"I've set a plan in motion to do that,'' Richard informed them. "Before Alan and I came in just now, I sent a messenger with word of my sudden death to all the border lords. So here will be Fernstowe, bereft of protection, and my poor widow disconsolate in her grief. Ripe for a new lord's rule, in other words.''

Sara rolled her eyes. "Richard, all that will do is bring the entire countryside to your funeral, curious to see if all that is so.''

"In three days time, they will come for that," he said. "The one who arrives far too early for that occasion, and with an armed retinue in tow, will be the one we seek."

"Aelwyn of Berthold," Sara said, nodding. "It might work."

Richard shrugged. "I hope it is him, but it could be Bankwell. And never rule out the fact that it may be some man we have not yet considered."

Sara decided to throw herself wholeheartedly into this plan of Richard's. And she'd not make any more assumptions based on the all too obvious as she had done with his brother and nephew.

"You are right, of course," she agreed as she marched across the hall toward the solar. Over her shoulder, she said. "I will send Adam to bring his men and Sir Edmund within the walls. If there's a fight, they should be well fed and rested. I'll see to the food. You two, see to the weapons."

"We'd best find that lass of yours a sword, Dickon, and show her how to use it," she heard Alan tease.

Sara turned, walking backward a few steps, and grinned wickedly. "Oh, I *have* a sword, brother. And I need no instruction."

# Chapter Nineteen

That day, everyone at Fernstowe worked, preparing for guests. The first to come would require only ready weapons and a large enough place to lock away the ones who were not killed. But in three days, the entire noble population of the Middle March was like to arrive, expecting a funeral and a feast.

Richard decided there should be a grand celebration then. He had promised the neighboring lords he'd met with at Harbeth's that he would have one here. It was earlier than they would expect, and the reason for it would surprise them when they arrived. But this would provide everyone opportunity to rejoice at the reestablished peace along the border.

Sometime before that celebration, he must get Sara alone and mend matters between the two of them. Once she understood why he had rebuked her for unseemliness, and how dreadfully wrong he had been to do so, she would be herself again. How sweet their life together would be then. She would see another foe had been conquered and cast out, his own narrow-minded attitude. He would do it now if she were not so distracted.

Sara's taking command of their preparations amused

him. One would think the whole of the plan was her idea. She worked harder than anyone, and offered him no special consideration, either. However, he had not liked it that she'd fallen asleep at table last evening, exhausted and rather pale.

After putting her to bed, he'd threatened anyone who might think to disturb her rest the next morn. As it happened, she was the one who stormed his chamber before dawn and woke him, setting down her candle and urging him to dress quickly.

"He will come today. I just know it," Sara declared, ignoring his nudity when he arose from the bed. She tossed him underclothing and hose from his clothing chest, then went back to it and dug around for a sark until she found one suitable.

"Whoever *he* might be," she continued, as she took up his gambeson and swiftly examined it before handing it to him. "I do believe it's Aelwyn."

"As do I," he replied. No sooner had he donned the quilted jack than she approached with his heavy mail.

"Give me that!" he ordered. "It is too heavy for you."

"We can argue later. Hop to, Richard."

He leaned over and worked his way into the mail shirt, then stood, settling its weight on his frame. Her hands were already at the buckles, fastening them as expertly as any well-trained squire. "There! Strap on your sword and you are ready," she declared, and spun to leave the room.

Richard caught the back of her gown. "Come back here, whirlwind!"

"What?" she asked, eyes wide with frustration at the delay.

He framed her face with his hands. "A kiss if you please. Or even if you do *not* please." He settled his mouth on hers and enjoyed her surprise that quickly melted into sweet compliance. When he broke the kiss, Richard smiled at her confusion. At least for the moment, he had stilled all that wild energy. "All will be well, Sara. Trust that I will protect you and defend our home."

"I do," she said in a small voice, one of her hands covering his where it lay against her cheek. "Oh, Richard, you will take care? You promise?"

"I vow it, but there'll be no great danger. The archers will be ready. Have I not explained all this time and again? The moment the enemy enters our gates, all unaware, we shall take him and whatever men he brings with him. If he elects to fight, he will die before his sword leaves its scabbard."

"Nothing can go amiss," she affirmed with a nod.

"Nothing," he assured her, and offered his arm. "So come, let us break fast. For a corpse, I am dreadfully hungry."

An air of anticipation permeated the keep. Even the children could not be still. She sent them to the solar and set them to measuring and cutting leather strips with which to bind the prisoners that might be taken. Anything to keep the small hands busy and out of the way. Berta supervised and was sworn to keep Nan and Christopher contained within that chamber.

When Sara exited the hall at mid-morn she saw that those in the bailey, even as they went about their assigned tasks, kept eyes and ears trained upon those who patrolled the wall walk.

There were few up there walking, only two to each of the four walls. Several of those were women. Sara had chosen the folk with the keenest eyes. The bowman sat against the wall on the upper walkway, facing the bailey, waiting. Richard stood beside the gates, his back toward her, speaking with Adam and Alan.

She liked that Richard had listened to all of her suggestions. Even Alan seemed to approve her participation, and asked her opinion now and again on matters of the defense.

It would not come to fighting, Richard had assured her repeatedly. Sara was not so certain he was right. A cornered animal fought furiously, even against all hope of success.

"Milady, you should remain within," Sir Edmund said as he walked up behind her.

She turned to argue, but the urgent, mournful sound of the horn on the battlements interrupted.

"They come!" she shouted, and took flight for the stairs to the parapet.

The knight grabbed her from behind and pointed her toward the keep. "Get you inside or Sir Richard will have my head!"

Sara jerked out of his grasp. "I will witness this, sir! Now go and aid my husband. I shall watch from the wall."

Before Sir Edmund could catch her again, she lifted her skirts and ran. Soon as she reached the wall walk, she heard the arrival outside the gates and rushed to peek between the merlons.

"Bankwell!" she gasped, shocked and disappointed that it was not the man she had expected. And this gray-haired old wretch had not even worn his armor! Only a half-dozen men rode with him. How did the fool expect to gain an entire keep and the lady of it with only six at his back? His confidence in doing so insulted Sara nearly as much as his reason for coming.

One of Bankwell's number announced him. So the fine lord had come to "pay his respects and speak with the Lady Sara," had he? She smiled to herself when she heard Richard's order to open the gates. Bankwell was about to get the surprise of his life.

Chains creaked rhythmically as the portcullis rose, its deadly spikes leaping a measure each time the gears were turned. Two of her men pulled down on the lever that lifted the enormous bar and the thick oaken gates swung wide. A hush had fallen over the place. The open bailey would appear deserted to those about to invade it.

The soft clop of hooves, the squeak of leather, and faint jingle of harnesses broke the ominous silence as the stately Bankwell entered first. Sara saw that he was not much changed these past few years, still of stately bearing, rather handsome for his age and obviously aware of it. Haughty, she thought, but not for long.

As he rode, he looked around curiously at the number of armed men, archers on the wall, bows aimed. Sword and pikemen stood in positions to attack on command. Even then he did not appear very concerned.

"Throw down or die!" boomed Richard in so deep and loud a voice, Sara thought it might have shaken the rafters back in the hall.

Bankwell's mouth dropped open and his eyes widened. *Now* he understood, Sara thought with satisfaction.

Metal scraped and clattered as Bankwell and his men discarded their weaponry. Not one objected or even hesitated. The archers sitting high on the wall walk had chosen their targets and there was no mistaking their eagerness to let fly.

"Now dismount, well away from your blades!" Richard ordered.

"We come in peace!" Bankwell declared in a high, frightened voice. He nearly fell off his horse as he left his saddle. "Do not harm us!" With hands raised, he circled, imploring, "Lady Sara? Where is she? *Please,* may I have a word with her?"

Sara descended the steps as rapidly as she'd gone up. She stalked across the bailey until she stood within speaking distance, though not near enough for any to take her hostage.

"So, my Lord Bankwell!" she greeted him. "Pray, talk to me, if that is what you came here for. What have you to say for yourself before we truss you up like the great goose you are?"

Greatly agitated, he lowered his hands, supplicating. "Tell your men I come in peace, will you? I hurried here to offer my protection!"

She laughed. "I'll wager you did! Take him," she ordered the men who now surrounded the captives, swords drawn. "King Edward will be mightily pleased with this day's work."

Everyone's attention was focused on the capture. While Bankwell sputtered his protests, Richard, Alan, Adam and Sir Edmund herded the whole troop toward the hall steps.

Sara waited in the bailey to thank the keen-eyed women and her guardsmen for standing careful watch. Most were headed down from the wall now. The archers were busy laughing and congratulating each other. Jubilant cheers echoed throughout the bailey. She glanced up at the parapet to see who remained there.

"Ware! Drop the 'cullis!" the lone wall guard shouted over the merrymaking. Had she not been looking directly at him, she might not have heard. Sara whirled around and saw the gatekeepers had not.

"Ware, m'lady! Run!" came the cry.

The words were cut off when horses thundered through the open portals. Bowmen scrambled to nock arrows. Her guards leaped, some weaponless, at the intruders. Mounts reared and screamed. Swords swung and war cries rang out.

"Aelwyn!" Sara gasped as she marked the colors. Knowing she had no time to flee, Sara ran for the pile of Bankwell's discarded weapons. The largest was his broadsword. Sara grasped it in desperation.

He rode straight for her. Sara sprang to the right, swung

the heavy sword and nicked his mount with the tip of it. The horse reared and Aelwyn lost his seat.

Sara risked a quick glance toward the hall door. Richard, his knights and kinsmen must have heard the commotion. They ran down the steps, even now engaging with Aelwyn's men, most of whom were still astride. Those mounted were between her and any help.

"Oh, God!" she cried, and swerved back to Aelwyn. Why hadn't she struck a fatal blow when he was down? She cursed her panic. He'd recovered from his spill and now approached her cautiously, frowning beneath his half helm.

Sara hefted the sword aloft, daring him to come closer.

"You'll wed me now, damn you!" he taunted. "Or you will die!"

"I have a husband," she said, grinding out the words from between clenched teeth. "He will cut you down like the mad dog you are!"

For an instant, he froze. "Strode's not dead?"

"He whittles your vermin down to naught even now. Look, if you do not believe it!" She steadied her blade, watching for a chance to strike if he should glance away from her.

Instead, he circled her as he spoke, opening and closing his fingers on the hilt of his sword. Taunting her. His eyes glinted evilly through the helm's eyeholes. "Then he *will* die, along with all here. You, as well, but not until I've done with you."

He chuckled as he edged around her, causing her to turn and nearly lose her balance. "You'll not have Fernstowe," she declared, playing for time until Richard could come to her aid. Assuming he survived his own battle. The weight of the sword strained her muscles to screaming, but she held it steady.

"This place?" Aelwyn scoffed. "'Twas you I craved,

you foolish wench, from the time you sprouted. I shall have you, too. But then you must pay." He waved his sword in a menacing arc. "Give up now, Sara, so I won't have to kill you too soon."

He closed in. Sara swung with all her might. Aelwyn easily met the blow and the clang near deafened her. Her very bones vibrated. "Y-you knew they were brothers? How?" she demanded as she moved out of reach. All she needed was a moment to reclaim her breath. If only she could keep him talking.

He snarled. "I made it my business to know all about the heathen who slew my father *and* stole our wealth! The king will hunt him down for this day's work. He'll kill them *all!*" Aelwyn lunged.

Sara deflected the blow, but barely. Sweat stung her eyes and she blinked. "All this for war? You *want* a war?"

"Aye, and I'll have it! I'll have you, too. Alive or dead!" he cried, face reddened with rage.

She tightened her grip and positioned her blade. "Do your worst, *traitor!*"

He ran at her, his blade hefted for the death blow.

Sara waited for his down swing, then ducked and thrust. He howled, but she saw his mail had caught her point. She'd drawn blood but not impaled him.

Shocked at her success, he stared dumbly down at his wound. She rose, swung in a complete circle to add momentum and caught his helm with the flat of her blade. A resounding blow. It rang like a bell.

When Aelwyn came to, Richard's foot rested on his neck. Sara thought he might crush it. Indeed, hoped that he would.

"He wanted the king to declare war on the Scots," she said, still unable to believe anyone, even Aelwyn, could wish such as that. "I think he's mad!"

Richard looked down at the man. "Mad or no, you'll

die as a traitor. Much as I would love to deal you death myself, the king shall have his due."

Aelwyn glared but said nothing. Likely he had no spit to speak, since he could scarcely breathe.

Then Richard addressed her wryly, "Have someone close those gates, will you? I'd not like to have another of your suitors come calling today."

Sara laughed, dropped the sword and dusted her hands together. "Weary, Richard? I was just warming up." With that, she strutted over to the gates and released the portcullis herself.

Her levity proved short-lived when she reentered the hall and noted the damage Aelwyn had wrought. His men had killed two of hers, wounded Sir Edmund's arm and dealt Adam a deep cut on his thigh. Eustiss suffered a broken leg, the result of a trampling by a mount he'd tried to overset.

By the time Sara got there, Lady Honor and several others were bustling back and forth among the casualties who lay stretched out upon the tables. The dead men lay on pallets in one corner, their women mourning loudly as they attended the bodies.

"Mother, Mother!" Nan cried, running headlong into her and clutching her around the waist. "Berta wouldn't let us out there to help you!"

Sara patted the red curls and cradled Nan's head. She met Christopher's somber gaze as he stood by watching, awaiting instruction, no doubt, like the steadfast little soldier he was.

"All is well now. Go back to the solar, both of you, and stay until we sort this out. Mind me!" she insisted when Nan began to object.

To Sara's relief, Chris took Nan's hand and forcefully led her away, talking to her all the while in the same soothing way his father did betimes. That child, bless his heart, would make a grand knight one day, just like Richard.

Now came the onerous task of apologizing to Lord Bankwell. At present, he sat at a table in the corner of the hall, surrounded by his men. They were nursing tankards of ale and grumbling amongst themselves.

She might as well get this over with, Sara thought. Richard joined her before she reached Bankwell and his cohorts.

"We have wronged you," Sara said without pause. "But you must admit, ours was a natural mistake. We were expecting attack and here you came. Why *did* you come, by the way?"

Bankwell huffed and took another swig of his drink. When he thunked the cup on the table, he gave answer. "I received word you were widowed and traveled all this way—at breakneck pace, I might add—just to offer you help with the funeral. And also my protection. I tried to tell you."

"And why should *you* be the one to offer that?" Richard asked, still sounding suspicious of the man.

Could it be that both Bankwell and Aelwyn had come to claim her, Sara wondered?

Bankwell sighed. "Your mother and I were wed five months ago," he stated. "As your stepfather, I considered it my duty—"

"*Wed?*" Sara demanded, aghast at the thought. "To Mother? How is this so? She entered a convent!"

"And I took her out of it," he declared. "She sent word to me soon after she got there, and I retrieved her forthwith. That was no place for my Eula!"

"*Your* Eula," Sara repeated, stunned by the news.

He frowned, his features still ruddy with anger. "We will be gone from here within the hour. If you have any word for your mother, write it down for me. I won't wait long.''

Richard wasn't finished. "You once wanted Sara for your wife, my lord. We thought you had come to take her."

Bankwell dismissed his men with a pointed look and waited until they left the table and moved out of earshot. Then he replied. "I have always loved Lady Eula, even when we were children. But her parents preferred Lord Simon."

He looked up at Sara apologetically, and then to Richard. "I only thought to have a part of Eula to console me when I asked for Sara's hand. But when we finally met, I saw she was nothing at all like her mother, in either looks or temperament. Lord Simon was right to refuse my suit. I thank God every day that he did say no, else I could never have wed Eula after he died."

"You waited long to tell me of this marriage," Sara said.

"Eula put it off for fear you would hate us. But we decided that you might need the help of family, and so I came."

Sara had trouble adapting to the news, but she supposed there would be plenty of time for that. She had to admit that it had been good of Bankwell to come, given that he believed she would need his assistance.

"Will you not stay here and send for Mother? We have a feast planned day after the morrow," she offered.

Bankwell's laugh was dry. "No, thank you. I'm for home as soon as may be, and Eula would not wish to travel here now."

Sara bit her lips together, disappointed that her mother did not care to see her again. But she ought to reassure this man who had come to offer her aid and received such poor welcome.

"I will not write her," she told him. "Only tell my mother that I wish you both happiness and pray that she is now content."

Bankwell stood and took her hand. He kissed the back of it and smiled up at her. "Eula worried for you, Sara. She loves you dearly. She would have come with me if she were not with child."

Sara's knees buckled. She would have fallen right to the floor in a heap if Richard had not embraced her quickly. She stammered, "But...but Mother is near nine and thirty! This cannot bode well at all!"

"Nonsense!" he replied proudly. "She is blooming with good health. Come and see for yourself whenever you like."

Bankwell moved past her and nodded to Richard. "I bid you both farewell. My regards to the king when next you see him." With that, he marched away, gathered his men and left.

"God love us!" Sara gasped, clasping her brow. She pushed away from Richard and plopped on a bench. "What next?"

"You go above stairs and lie down," Richard ordered.

"Surely you jest! Look around you at this chaos. There are the wounded—"

"Whom Honor is tending. Berta has the children in hand and Alan is in charge of the prisoners. There's nothing more for you to do. As it is, I would say you have done quite enough for one day," he said, frowning at her.

"The dead should be—"

"Their women will care for them. It is their right and duty."

"What of the feast?" she protested.

"The food's prepared, and we have all day tomorrow to ready the hall. Now do as I say and *go!*"

She simply nodded, too spent to do aught else. Her muscles ached from the sword fight and her hands were still numb. Richard raked her with disparaging glance.

She imagined what he saw: dirty clothes, sweaty face, her wild mane tangling about her shoulders. She must look a fright.

Richard's frown did not abate. He looked angry with her and she supposed he must be. No man wanted a woman who wielded a sword like a man. He must hate that it was her, instead of him, who had subdued Aelwyn. The king would have a grand laugh over that when he was told of it. Richard would suffer yet another humiliation because of her.

She trudged slowly toward the stairs, wondering whether she could manage them on her own. Tired and dispirited, she climbed toward the solitude of her chamber.

The horn sounded again, faintly through the cacophony in the hall, but distinct in its warning. Sara sat down on the top step, head in her hands, and waited to see who came now.

"The king!" someone shouted a few moments later. "'Tis the king's colors! Sir Richard!"

Sara pushed herself up and hurried to her room, entered, kicked off her shoes and collapsed on the bed. Richard wanted her to rest? By God, she would. She might have sent for the king to come here, but she had entertained quite enough guests for one day.

She lay there for the longest time, staring at her blistered palms, feeling begrimed and too weary to move. But she wondered in spite of herself what was going on below.

The king had come because of the message she'd sent, fully expecting to arrest Alan the True or find him dead. Would he believe Richard when he declared his kinsmen innocent of wrongdoing? He might not. Sara herself had not believed him. It would be Aelwyn's word against Richard's.

Sara dragged herself upright, trudged over to the ewer and basin and poured out water to wash her face and hands. She must go and speak to the king whether she felt like doing so or not.

As she pulled a comb through her hair, cursing the snarls, Sara admitted the real reason she did not want join the others. The fact of Aelwyn's guilt would be easy enough to establish. There were witnesses aplenty other than her, and they would vouch for Alan and Adam. What she really hated to face was the king's offer to dissolve her marriage to Richard.

The last time King Edward came here, he had said Richard might have an annulment. Sara feared her husband would accept it now, and she'd not blame him if he did. All Richard had to do was deny sharing her bed. Technically, that was true. They had shared only his. Hers had broken before they could make use of it.

Richard had been kind to her, but he had not liked how forward she was. Even when she had ceased being so, he was still not content. Sara had no doubt he would want rid of her, especially after today.

This morn she had proved beyond doubt that she was no lady, except by accident of birth. In truth, she had behaved more like one of the men-at-arms.

She could well imagine his embarrassment. Everyone had seen her hike skirts to knees and dash up to the battlements and down again. Then she had faced both Bankwell and Aelwyn as a man might do, and with the latter plied a broadsword in combat. And won. Judging by word and expression, Richard had not been best pleased by her actions.

She could not regret what she'd done. Had she not behaved so, she would be dead now. But she was sorry that he would always view her as crude and graceless when compared to his first wife. *The perfect wife,* he had once said in describing Lady Evaline to the king.

Sara twisted her hair into a coil, wrapped it around her head and secured it with pins. She might not appear lady-like, but at least she wouldn't look quite so wild as she had earlier.

Could she conduct herself with grace when she had to let Richard go? Probably not, but she vowed then and there to try her very best. She did not wish him to remember her only as a rough-and-tumble sort of woman with no dignity at all.

By thunder, she would not leave him with that impression of her. Quickly she plowed through her clothes chest and pulled out a pristine chemise, her best blue camlet gown and matching slippers.

"I am Sara of Fernstowe," she muttered to herself as she wriggled into her clothes. "Lady here, and I shall look the part!"

Snatching up a chased bronze circlet, she set it on her head so that it rested just above her brow. With angry, yanking movements, she fastened on a matching belt so that it draped around her hips, its extra length dangling to her knees. "There!"

Sara straightened her skirts, pinched her cheeks and bit her lips together to redden them. Then she strode determinedly toward the door. "If the wretch wants so desperately to leave me, then let him!"

# Chapter Twenty

"**N**o! Leave him be!" Richard shouted. He drew his sword and leaped forward. Yet even as blade left scabbard, he realized what he had done. His unthinking response to protect, as ingrained as self-defense, doomed him. Now he would share Alan's fate.

Richard lowered his weapon and bowed his head. He had threatened his king, a treasonous crime if ever there was one. His gaze locked on Alan's and he saw understanding. And a brother's grief.

The instant Richard had introduced Alan, the king's men had fallen upon him. Alan offered no protest, obviously assuming Richard would clear the matter in a reasonable way. Not so.

Two other knights—two Richard knew so well—disarmed him immediately while he stood stock-still, silently cursing his impulse.

His temper had betrayed him. After all these years holding it in check, his rage had broken loose at the worst possible time.

Even as he calmed in the aftermath, he knew there would be no taking back what he had done. The result would be fatal unless Edward felt merciful. At the moment he did not appear to feel so. "My brother has done nothing unlawful, sire," Richard said, by way of explaining his act. "I feared you would slay him without a hearing."

The king frowned, but not at Richard.

"Ah. Here is the lady of the house come to join us," the king growled. "Shall you make us more welcome than your husband has done?"

Sara stared wide-eyed at Edward and dropped into a deep curtsy. "By your leave, sire, what has happened here?" she asked softly. With a glance she seemed to take it all in. "My liege, you have the wrong man there. Sir Alan came here in peace and aided us in capturing the one you want for the crimes."

The king took a deep breath and propped his foot upon the bench where Bankwell had sat earlier. "You no longer need fear these Strodes, Lady Sara. You may speak freely to me."

"I always speak so, Your Majesty," Sara said with a wry smile. "And I fear no man, save your worthy self."

"Whether you fear me or not, at least you have learned to employ discretion. Unlike *some* we know," Edward commented with a dark look at Richard.

Sara wisely left that alone and got on to the business at hand. "My message to you was precipitate and faulty in its content, but I am happy you came. Less than an hour past did we capture the man who murdered my father. He is the very one who wreaked such tragedy along our border and would blame Alan the True for it all. Why, he even took Richard and held him to ransom, extorting other lords as well with promise of peace for pay. Aelwyn of Berthold sought to begin an outright war in our time of peace, and near succeeded."

The king sniffed thoughtfully and stood again, resting his hands on his hips. He scanned the hall. "So, where is he? And how do you know he is the one?"

Sara motioned for two of her guards. "Go and fetch Lord Aelwyn from the cell. Only him."

When they departed in a hurry to obey, she again addressed the king. "He admitted it to me at the end of a sword, Your Majesty. He taunted me and threatened to kill me after he had done his worst on my person."

"And that great lout saved you, I suppose," Edward nodded Richard's way, his eyebrow raised in disgust.

"In truth, no, he did not, sire." Sara cleared her throat and looked chagrined. "I saved myself." She quickly added, "But he would have done, had he not been beset by all the others Aelwyn brought with him. But for the help of my brother-by-law and his son, who lies wounded by the effort, all might have died here and you none the wiser. The Strodes are not your enemies, even the Scots among them. My husband reveres you, sire."

"Is that a fact?" the king mused. "Or could it be you think to save Sir Richard yet again so that you may keep him?"

"I say only the truth in this, I swear. He tells me you offered him his freedom when last you were here. I give it him now most sincerely. He is his own man—and yours, of course—not mine to keep. Richard wed me all unknowing."

"At your behest," the king reminded her.

"True, but I believe now that I did wrong on his account. Yet, despite that, he has done all he could to bring peace to my lands and that of our neighbors, including the Scots. I pray you listen to me, your loyal servant in all things. Serve up the justice you are famed for and do it upon the true villain."

"You plead this case well, lady. We shall see how matters go when I have questioned the one you hold to blame."

Everyone faced the stair where there came a scuffling.

The guards, one gripping each of his arms, brought forth Aelwyn and threw him down before the king.

Richard watched the man struggle to his knees and bow until his head touched the floor.

"Aelwyn of Berthold, this woman accuses you of murder, of holding her husband for ransom, and of extorting and plundering. What say you?"

"I avow the Scot did it all, my liege. My men and I came only to assist Lady Sara when we heard her husband was dead."

Sara stalked forward and stood over him. "Then mayhap you will tell the king just why you rode in upon my husband's warhorse, stolen when you took him prisoner? And why is it that same mount—one certainly recognizable to the king and his men—wears your colors, even as we speak?"

"Go and see," the king ordered one of squires. Then he turned to Alan, who wore the look of a mere interested bystander. "You, what business have you at Fernstowe?"

"My brother sent me an invitation," Alan said, sounding—thanks be to God—as English as the king. "I have been in France on a six-month visiting family and have only just returned."

He inclined his head toward Honor, who stood transfixed beside the table where Adam lay immobile. "May I make known to you the Lady Honor, my good wife, and my son, Sir Adam."

"Loyal subjects of the crown, I presume," the king said with a nod in their direction.

"Of Balliol's crown, and through it, your own, no doubt," Alan said conversationally and without a shred of contempt.

"Just so," Edward verified.

The squire came in at a run and halted breathless. "The lady speaks truth, my liege. Sir Richard's charger does

wear silks to match this man's tabard.'' He pointed to Aelwyn.

"Proof enough. Haul him away then and retrieve his
minions from whatever hole Lady Sara has stashed them.
We'll call this matter quit and be off to York with the
prisoners.'' He made a flicking motion to the men holding
Alan. "Release this one.''

Richard did not fare so well. Edward was not yet finished with him. The king ambled over to where the knights
held him and shook a finger in his face. "No man who
rides in my wake draws steel against me or any in my
train. You know this better than most, for you have ridden
with me for years. No more will you do so. Your punishment for this day's lapse, sir, is to remain where you are.
Is this understood?''

Richard bowed his head to hide a grin. "I am yours to
command, sire. As always.''

When he dared look up, Edward winked. "That offer I
made you before? The one to free you? I hereby rescind
it.''

"Your will is mine, sire.'' Richard replied, his voice
humble, his head bowed. He wanted to shout his thanks.

"We have what we came here for,'' the king announced.
"And so, *adieu!*'' He turned smartly and marched toward
the door. His men rounded up the prisoners and followed.

Richard picked up his sword and replaced it in the scabbard. He and Alan exchanged a look of profound relief.

"Farewell, my liege,'' Sara called out sweetly.

The instant the door closed behind the royal company,
Sara rounded on Richard, all sweetness forgotten. "You
fool! You almost got yourself killed! Are you mad?''

"Apparently so. But you saved me. Alan, as well,'' he
said, smiling on her fury. "My beautiful warrior queen,
my Boadicea.''

"Call me that again and *I* shall have to kill you!'' she

exclaimed. Her long arms crossed her breasts and she shook her head. "You've only yourself to blame for this punishment. Now you must stay wed to me, when I would have gladly let you go."

"Gladly, Sara?" he asked, knowing the answer. She loved him. He knew she did. It shone in her eyes, sparkling through her fury so brightly even he could not miss it.

"Gracefully, if not gladly," she qualified with a dramatic roll of her eyes. "I had made up my mind to it."

Richard threw back his head and laughed, even as he stepped closer and drew her into his arms. "Sara, Sara, can you not see I am well content to stay? Edward could not have dragged me away from here."

"Oh, yes. Yes, he could," she reminded him angrily, grasping him tightly around his waist. "In chains, and on your way to a scaffold. What were you thinking to draw steel upon the king?"

He shook his head ruefully. "In truth, I did not think at all. You were the only one showing good sense." He kissed her soundly, feasting on surprise and looking forward to response.

Alan tapped him on the back. "Let me have a say, will you?"

"You'd best speak quickly then," Richard announced, and scooped Sara up in his arms, ignoring her sputtering protests. "For I am going to thank her privately. Meanwhile, make yourself at home. We'll see you at the feast tomorrow."

*"Tomorrow!"* Sara gasped. "Richard! There are things to see to, things I must do!"

"Oh, and I shall let you," he promised with an eager grin.

Sara gave in and rested her head on Richard's shoulder, her body aflame with desire from that kiss of his.

She knew what would happen next. Not for the life of

her could she deny she wanted it to happen. Soon he would see how desperately so, for she would not be able to hide it now.

All her good plans to play passionless would fly right out the window as soon as they entered his chamber. He would kiss her again and she would be lost to all thought of propriety.

"I did try," she murmured. "I truly did try."

"What's this?" he asked tenderly as he booted his chamber door closed behind him and lowered her to her feet.

She grimaced and shrugged. "To be what you wish."

He framed her face with his hands and kissed her forehead just below her circlet. "But you *are*, Sara. All that I wish."

She pulled away, trying to distance herself and quiet the rapid beating of her heart. The thing felt as though it would burst right from her chest. She trembled with need, deeper than a physical joining would assuage. Yet how else could she express the way she adored him? And he would not want that expression.

"You think I am what you want at the moment, but I will never maintain the guise, Richard. Not this day of all days, and likely, not ever. You might as well know the truth."

He moved up behind her, clutched her arm and then brushed his lips against her ear. "Tell me later."

She laughed, a mirthless sound indeed. "Later, I'll not need to. You will know it."

"Know what?" he asked, distracted by the task of removing the pins from her hair.

"That I can never be to you what Lady Evaline was."

His hands stilled and Richard attended her then with all seriousness. "And just what do you imagine she was to me, Sara?"

"The perfect wife, of course. A truly noble woman without all these…" She made a futile gesture with her hands. "Faults!"

"Dearest, we all have faults. Evaline had many. What gave you the notion she was perfect?"

"You, yourself!" she exclaimed, exasperated with him for denying what he'd said just because he had not said it to her. "You told the king she was! That you would have none to replace her. Ever!"

"I never loved her, Sara. Guilt over that plagues me. Had I been able to love her, she might have loved me in return. In truth, the two of us never really knew each other. We were but sad strangers caught together in a trap not of our making. After she died, I hid my relief that I was free of her."

Sara turned to face him, disbelieving. "Oh, Richard…"

"Yes, even from myself, I tried to hide it by glorifying traits she probably did not even possess. Had Evaline and I spoken frankly together—as you and I do—we might have made a better match. She would never have done that, however, for candor was not one of her gifts. Nor one of mine."

Sara reached up and brushed her hand over his chest. "I *do* regret the king gave you no choice in remaining my husband, Richard. You had no desire to wed again. I know this is true."

"At times fate takes a hand, I think. You are valiant, steadfast, strong and beautiful. All I could ever ask for in a wife." His eyes darkened as she stared into them, seeking truth. He offered it, adding, "But for one thing."

Sara nodded, understanding perfectly. "I know." She looked toward the bed, her eyes sad. "Therein lies our difficulty."

"It need not be," he suggested softly, his lips hovering

over hers. "Did we not find the sweet accord there before? Give me the truth of you, Sara. Be who you are."

She closed her eyes to block out his entreaty and found that plea not altogether visual. His body pressed against hers, loudly proclaiming what he wanted. The urgency in his words echoed in her head.

"I cannot be who you want," she admitted. "I am who I am, Richard, and can be no other, no matter how I try. My best efforts at pretending proved dismal and I cannot bear doing it again. Not that way."

"Oh, love, I never want you to pretend with me. Nor will I, with you," he said with true concern. "Be yourself, for that is the woman I want. Give me all of you, your wit—your temper and your passion. I would have it all."

Sara's smile grew. She ducked her head to hide it. So, his reference to their *sweet accord* did not mean the time she lay still beneath him. How had she so misjudged matters?

"So, are you saying you'd like me to act *unseemly,* Richard? You chastised me for that," Sara reminded him, tracing a path down the front of his tabard to his sword belt. She played with the buckle.

"You unsettled me." His hands caressed her arms, soothing and yet suggesting more than comfort. "Not just there in our bed, but in *all* things. Sara, you never hedged in any way, never even thought to guard yourself against me. Can you understand how rare is that quality of openness?" His half laugh sounded of dismay. "I suppose I was one who took great comfort in the masques most people wear. You wore none and ripped mine away completely. There I was, with naught to hide behind."

"And now?" she asked, biting her lip.

He smiled. "I want my children to be as you are. *I* want to be as you are. Too long have I labored to conceal my nature, to be who others thought I should be. If you would have me as I am and help me discover who that man is, then I could ask no more. The only thing I am certain of at this moment is that I love you beyond all rhyme or reason. There is no doubt of that.''

Sara lay her head upon his chest and sighed against his heart. Tears burned her eyes, tears she had held within for so long they would not be stopped.

Richard *loved* her.

He lifted her away from him, gazed down at her and touched her face. "I know you love me, Sara, so why do you weep?''

She could not help but laugh even as she sobbed. ''Be-because you are the only man alive worth weeping for.''

Richard hugged her hard and let her cry. Never in her life had Sara felt such joy.

After a while, when she grew quiet in his arms, Richard loosened his hold. "What may I do, love? What will make you happy? You have but to tell me.''

Sara looked up at him, her amber eyes still teary, but shining with deviltry. He felt her hands at his waist. "This sword must go,'' she said as the buckle gave way. It slid off and dropped on the floor. "You are entirely too *aggressive* with that thing. Whatever will people say of your *boldness?*''

Speechless, he watched as she lifted the tails of his tabard and hauberk. He leaned over as she tugged both off over his head. The chain mail clinked softly as the garments pooled beside his weapon.

Then she clicked her tongue disparagingly. "Should a nobleman wear such *unbecoming* clothes, my lord? Mind you, wear better garb henceforth so you do not offend me!'' She helped him off with his sark. "There now. Much more *appropriate.*''

A self-deprecating grin hovered on his lips. "You are

going to make me pay for every word, are you not? Every
critical word I ever said to you.''

Sara smiled with pure anticipation. ''Oh, trust me, I
shall make you pay for the nice ones, as well. And *pay,*
and *pay,* and *pay* ...'' she continued, as she untied his
points one by one.

Richard chuckled, picked off her circlet and tousled her
hair with his hand. ''Willful minx.''

''Shameless coney,'' she replied in kind, dropping her
voice to a wicked growl.

Richard reached for her skirts and began gathering them
up slowly. ''I never should have called you those things,
Sara, even if I didn't mean them.''

''Yes, you did,'' she said, still smiling, almost taunting
him.

He continued drawing her gown and chemise up. She
held up her arms and he whisked them off. Then his heated
gaze caressed her, lingering on her breasts.

''You drove me mad that night,'' he whispered. ''You
were so foreign to me in your boldness and freedom, you
stole my very wits and all rational thought. Though I loved
that, I was not certain I *liked* it.''

She stood on tiptoe and kissed him softly while brushing
her body against his. ''Do let me know as soon as you are
certain? Not that it will make much difference.''

He embraced her fully, laughing, as he backed them
both toward the bed. They tumbled on it together and he
lay half-atop her, looking down into her eyes and smiling.
''You chose me, Sara, and I am wildly glad of it. My heart
is yours for all time.''

''I never thought to have your heart,'' Sara admitted
breathlessly. ''And so, was eager for the rest.''

Richard teased her lips with his when he knew she
wished for more. ''Are you eager now, my love?''

''Now and forever,'' she said, her voice compelling

even in its softness. "Heart, body, soul. I would have all of you."

And so she would, Richard thought as he surrendered himself gladly. Sara welcomed him with a generous sigh of pleasure as he slowly made them one for all time.

# Epilogue

*Five years later*

"You're certain the king's still in London?" Sara asked Richard as the guests filed in for supper. She smiled through her worry, nodding at Lord Adam and Lady Janet, the highest ranking, who already sat in the high-backed chairs where she and Richard usually presided. "God help us if he gets wind of this affair."

Richard reached down and grasped her hands to prevent her wringing them together. "No one outside Fernstowe knows Alan is here. How could we celebrate Christopher's ascent to squire without his only uncle and aunt?" He glanced down the table, a look of pride upon his face. "Renewed hostility between our countries has naught to do with this. Family loyalty is foremost over politics. That aside, Alan has not seen Father for years."

The men had greatly enjoyed their reunion, she admitted. The entire keep had rung with laughter all the day long. Sara seemed to be the only one concerned about Alan's risk in crossing the border. Scotland, allied with France, was at war with England.

Richard had fought in France for nearly a year, but these

past few months, due to winter, a lull had fallen over the unrest. Sara prayed for peace. For the moment, they had it and she hoped it would last. If the king ordered Richard to fight again, Christopher would accompany him as his squire. For now, she would not think of that, for this should be a happy time.

"They have spoiled Nicholas, all of them," Sara whispered as Richard seated her. Even now, their dark-haired two year old held his own court, flanked by Berta and Nan at the head of the lower table. Everyone loved the wee scamp, as Alan called him.

Sara brushed a palm over her abdomen. Before spring there would be another babe for the family to coddle.

A roar of approval arose as Christopher arrived last, garbed in blue-and-silver splendor. What a fine son he was, large for his age and strong, the very image of his father. He was twelve years of age now, young to make squire, but Richard had taught him well and he was ready.

"Lord Hepping presses for a betrothal," Richard informed her quietly. "What think you? Would his little Constance suit Chris?"

Sara turned and stared at him as though he were mad. "He is two years shy of the age of consent, Richard! And you, above anyone, should know he must choose for himself!"

Richard inclined his head, one dark eyebrow raised. "Yet if we claim her now, you may bring her here and train her up. I would that Christopher has a woman like you when the time comes to wed." He looked at his son, who already carried himself like a knight full vested. "Anything less will never do."

The compliment swelled her heart with happiness, though she would still oppose the early betrothal for Chris. "Would you also choose a mate for Nan?" she asked, daring him with a grin.

"Methinks she has already done so," he remarked dryly, cutting his eyes toward one of the young squires he was training. "Though the popinjay is still blissfully unaware. She is a girl after your own heart, that one."

Sara laughed gaily. "Are you so dismayed?"

"Not at all dismayed, love, only supremely contented with my fate." He leaned for a brief kiss, his lips stretched into a wide smile as he did so. "A man could do far worse than to be chosen by one such as you, my lady. But he could never hope for better, for you are the best."

Sara tucked her arm through his. "When we are next alone, I will make certain to pay you for that remark," she vowed, loving his answering growl of anticipation. "Best prepare yourself."

"I am entirely too well prepared as it is," he assured her. "So, let us get on with this squiring and have it done. Then we still have a feast to get through."

"And I shall deliver your just desserts, sir," she promised with a smile that was in no way demure.

\* \* \* \* \*

Return to the charm of the Regency era with

# GEORGETTE HEYER,

*creator of the modern Regency genre.*

Enjoy six romantic collector's editions with forewords by some of today's bestselling romance authors,

**Nora Roberts, Mary Jo Putney,
Jo Beverley, Mary Balogh,
Theresa Medeiros and Kasey Michaels.**

*Frederica*
On sale February 2000

*The Nonesuch*
On sale March 2000

*The Convenient Marriage*
On sale April 2000

*Cousin Kate*
On sale May 2000

*The Talisman Ring*
On sale June 2000

*The Corinthian*
On sale July 2000

*Available at your favorite retail outlet.*

**HARLEQUIN®**
*Makes any time special* ™

# MAD ABOUT ENGLISHMEN?

Meet four of our dashing and intriguing heroes from Harlequin Historical

In May 2000, look for

SIR RICHARD STRODE, loyal knight to the king
**MY LADY'S CHOICE** by Lyn Stone

LORD BENEDICT AINSWORTH, trusted royal adviser
**THE BRIDE OF SPRING** by Catherine Archer

In June 2000, look for

AGRAVAR THE VIKING, fierce warrior
**THE VIKING'S HEART** by Jacqueline Navin

LORD VALENTINE SINCLAIR, dangerous English spy
**MY LADY'S DARE** by Gayle Wilson

**Harlequin Historicals**
**The way the past *should* have been!**

*Available at your favorite retail outlet.*

Explore the American frontier
with these rugged Westerns from

## On sale May 2000

### THE CAPTIVE HEART
by **Cheryl Reavis**
(North Carolina frontier, 1750s)

### TANNER STAKES HIS CLAIM
by **Carolyn Davidson**
(Texas, 1800s)

## On sale June 2000

### BANDERA'S BRIDE
by **Mary McBride**
(Texas, 1870s)

### MOLLY'S HERO
by **Susan Amarillas**
(Wyoming, 1870s)

## Harlequin Historicals
## The way the past *should* have been.

Available at your favorite retail outlet.